Cornered Rats

Slocum drew his six-shooter and started walking at a steady pace toward Childress and Pine. He didn't know if Pine was packing, but Childress had his pistol out and was ready to use it. Slocum focused on the rustler to the exclusion of the lawyer. He got within fifty feet of them before some tiny sound betrayed him. Pine glanced in his direction and warned his hired gun with a loud shout.

Growling like a mountain lion, Childress spun around and began firing. Slocum returned fire and kept advancing. There wasn't anywhere for him to hide. He had to trust that Childress wasn't too good a shot in the dark. One bullet sang past his ear. Another kicked up dirt at his feet. Slocum kept walking. When he got to thirty feet away, he opened fire . . .

JAKE LOGAN

SLOCUM ALONG ROTTEN ROW

JOVE BOOKS, NEW YORK

THE BERKLEY PUBLISHING GROUP
Published by the Penguin Group
Penguin Group (USA) Inc.
375 Hudson Street, New York, New York 10014, USA

Penguin Group (Canada), 90 Eglinton Avenue East, Suite 700, Toronto, Ontario M4P 2Y3, Canada
(a division of Pearson Penguin Canada Inc.)
Penguin Books Ltd., 80 Strand, London WC2R 0RL, England
Penguin Group Ireland, 25 St. Stephen's Green, Dublin 2, Ireland (a division of Penguin Books Ltd.)
Penguin Group (Australia), 250 Camberwell Road, Camberwell, Victoria 3124, Australia
(a division of Pearson Australia Group Pty. Ltd.)
Penguin Books India Pvt. Ltd., 11 Community Centre, Panchsheel Park, New Delhi—110 017, India
Penguin Group (NZ), 67 Apollo Drive, Rosedale, North Shore 0632, New Zealand
(a division of Pearson New Zealand Ltd.)
Penguin Books (South Africa) (Pty.) Ltd., 24 Sturdee Avenue, Rosebank, Johannesburg 2196,
South Africa

Penguin Books Ltd., Registered Offices: 80 Strand, London WC2R 0RL, England

This is a work of fiction. Names, characters, places, and incidents either are the product of the author's imagination or are used fictitiously, and any resemblance to actual persons, living or dead, business establishments, events, or locales is entirely coincidental.

SLOCUM ALONG ROTTEN ROW

A Jove Book / published by arrangement with the author

PRINTING HISTORY
Jove edition / December 2010

Copyright © 2010 by Penguin Group (USA) Inc.
Cover illustration by Sergio Giovine.

ISBN: 978-0-515-14869-5

JOVE®
Jove Books are published by The Berkley Publishing Group,
a division of Penguin Group (USA) Inc.
375 Hudson Street, New York, New York 10014.
JOVE® is a registered trademark of Penguin Group (USA) Inc.
The "J" design is a trademark of Penguin Group (USA) Inc.

PRINTED IN THE UNITED STATES OF AMERICA

10 9 8 7 6 5 4 3 2 1

1

"Rustlers!"

The shout shattering the silence of the desert night brought John Slocum upright, hand reaching for his six-gun. He looked around the drovers' camp and tried to find who had given the alert. He counted four other lumps in their bedrolls, none stirring. For a moment he thought he had awakened from a nightmare. Then the cry came again.

Slocum knocked out the scorpion that had taken up residence in his right boot and then pulled it on. The cold leather around his foot brought him fully awake. By the time he had his gun belt strapped down, the outrider had finally reached camp.

"There's a whole passel of 'em," Long Drink Lonigan cried. He dismounted before his horse had come to a halt and staggered a few feet, forcing Slocum to catch him. The tall, thin man didn't weigh much more than a dried-out soda cracker.

"Quit your yammering and tell me what happened," Slocum said.

"You two gonna shout at each other all night?" The Circle Bar K foreman grumbled, throwing back his blanket.

"I'm tellin' you, Kennard, there's rustlers out there!"

"Slow down, catch your breath, and then tell us what happened." Slocum's grip tightened on Lonigan's shoulder. This pressure more than the advice calmed the man. He swallowed, his big Adam's apple bobbing in his goose-scrawny neck.

"It's like this. I was checkin' on them strays, the ones what got away a couple days ago, and found a wash 'bout a mile to the south. Then's when I seen 'em."

"The strays?" asked Kennard. The foreman obviously wasn't awake yet and rubbed sleep from his eyes before yawning.

"The rustlers! Ain't you listenin' to me? Four of them varmints. We didn't lose them strays. They was cut out of the herd and stolen! Right from under our noses!"

Slocum and Kennard looked at each other. They had talked privately about this the day before, but the identity of the rustlers had been a little different. Kennard had suspected two others riding with the Circle Bar K cowboys of the dirty deed. Even if Lonigan was right, that didn't rule out the two surly cowboys glaring at them from the other side of the mostly dead fire from being involved.

"Jones, you and Franklin go on back to sleep. We need somebody watching the camp," Kennard said, singling out the men he suspected. They grumbled and went back to their bedrolls. Slocum wondered if it might not be better to have the suspected cattle thieves riding where he and the foreman could keep an eye on them.

"What about the rest of us?" another cowboy asked.

"You guard the main herd. Me and Lonigan and Slocum'll track down the rustlers."

"You don't believe me," Lonigan said. He scowled hard. "I seen what I seen."

"Wouldn't be the first time you had a nip too many, Long Drink," Kennard said. "It gets mighty lonely ridin' night herd and the desert's enough to drive any man to drink."

"I haven't been drinkin'. Ain't got so much as a drop of whiskey. Dammit."

"Then you might be havin' hallucinations like you did the time they locked you up in Benson. Remember? You went dry for damned near a week and was seein' things crawlin' in and out of the cell."

"Wouldn't have happened if you'd bailed me out. And there *was* things, bigger 'n centipedes, all comin' fer me. I tell you—"

Kennard and Lonigan continued their long-standing argument as Slocum went to saddle his gelding. The horse protested being pressed into service again so soon. He had ridden herd until sundown when Lonigan had taken over the chores of keeping the cattle bedded down for the night. A quick glance up at the stars in the clear spring Arizona sky told him it wasn't even midnight yet. If there were rustlers plying their trade on the Circle Bar K cattle, they weren't even inclined to wait until closer to sunrise when a cowboy might be nodding off in the saddle. That made the cattle thieves either stupid or mighty bold. This close to the Mexican border, Slocum put his money on bold. Cut out a dozen or two head and they could have them sold in Mexico before sundown the next day.

"How do you want to handle this, Kennard?" Slocum asked when they were on the trail, heading due south. The bulk of the herd lay to the west, nearer the Whitestone Mountains. Any beeves wandering away in the direction they rode might be missed entirely as they moved the herd back toward the railhead at Benson.

"Depends," the foreman said. He nervously rubbed his fingers on his six-shooter slung butt forward on his right hip in the fashion of a cavalry trooper.

"We don't want it to end up like before," Lonigan said as he visibly swallowed. In the bright starlight he looked like a crane astride his horse. His long nose bobbed back and forth and he was hardly thick enough to cast a shadow.

"What happened before?" Slocum asked.

"Me and Kennard, we run into a bunch of rustlers when we worked for the Rolling J over by Tucson a couple years back. They shot us up somethin' fierce and Kennard, there, he got one in his—"

"Shut up," the foreman said. The pure venom in those two words caused Slocum to look at him closely. The foreman had turned as stiff as a board in the saddle. His eyes were fixed ahead, and Slocum wondered what it was the man actually saw. It probably wasn't the rolling desert, the clumps of ocotillo, greasewood, and prickly pear cactus. More likely he saw road agents ready to ambush him at every turn. The way he jumped when a soft breeze caused the leaves of a nearby mesquite to sway told Slocum he couldn't depend on the foreman if shooting started. He had probably been shot up good and proper and was gun-shy now. Sending Jones and Franklin out and staying in the camp himself would have better suited the Circle Bar K foreman. Slocum at least gave him credit for doing his job as foreman and not depending on others.

Still, in a shoot-out, the foreman was likely to be a liability rather than a help.

"They won't just give us back the cows," Slocum said.

"I know that," Kennard snapped. "I know that." He settled down in the saddle. His shoulders slumped, and his gaze fixed on his saddle pommel, not the desert ahead.

"Lonigan and I can handle it," Slocum said.

"Not your job. It's mine."

"I can handle it myself," Slocum said, unwilling to have a reluctant man with a drawn gun anywhere around him. Not only was Kennard likely to hesitate shooting if it came to that, but he might shoot the wrong one.

"We stand a better chance together. I know you got the look, Slocum, but this is company business."

Slocum said nothing. He knew what the foreman meant. When the owner of the Circle Bar K had hired Slocum, he'd commented on how Slocum looked like a gun slick. He had done his share of killing in his day—far more than his fair share—but he was no gunfighter. Anyone he killed needed killing and this had gotten him gut shot during the war when he had complained to William Quantrill about how their guerrilla band had blasted away at anything that moved in Lawrence, Kansas. Quantrill had a score to settle and had ordered his men to kill any male over the age of eight. That hadn't much mattered to some of the men riding with Quantrill.

Slocum had refused and Quantrill's second-in-command, Bloody Bill Anderson, had drawn and fired three times into Slocum's belly, then left him to bleed to death. Slocum was tougher than that, but it had taken long months for him to recuperate. When he did, he returned to his family farm in Georgia and found a different kettle of fish waiting for him.

A carpetbagger judge and his hired gunman had tried to steal the farm. Slocum had left them in shallow graves out by the springhouse and had ridden west, never looking back.

He had done his share of killing, during the war and after, but he was no gunfighter killing for money or the pure entertainment of watching a man die.

He wasn't the kind to let rustlers ride off with valuable cattle either.

"Where'd you see 'em now, Lonigan?"

"There. See where the arroyo bank sorta collapses? I rode down there and about fifty yards farther to the south I seen 'em."

Slocum held up his hand for silence. He dismounted and walked over the ground Lonigan claimed he had ridden before. The dry, sun-baked ground might have seen a horse ride over it, but Slocum couldn't tell in the dark. He slipped down the embankment into the sandy-bottomed wash. A couple steps in the direction Lonigan had said was all it took for him to retreat and step back into the saddle.

"Still men ahead. Didn't see them but I heard them laughing and joshing one another."

"Four, you said, Lonigan?" Kennard was visibly nervous now.

"We can get the rest of our boys," Slocum suggested. "That would even the score."

"Take too long. I'm surprised the bastards stuck around this long." Kennard licked his lips and looked around, as if he intended to bolt and run at any sound. "They must not care if they get found out."

Slocum nodded. It had to be twenty minutes riding to and back from the camp. What the rustlers were doing was something of a mystery since he didn't smell a fire burning. They might have slaughtered a cow for a late dinner or worked a running iron on the hindquarters to establish a more legitimate claim. If they intended driving the stolen beeves into Mexico, that didn't make much sense, though. The Mexicans who bought stolen cattle didn't much care what brand rode on the rump.

"They're just cocky," Slocum decided. He slid the Colt Navy from his cross-draw holster and made sure it carried six rounds. He usually rode with only five, the hammer resting on an empty chamber to keep from discharging as he went about his chores. Now he needed extra firepower. For this he wanted the half-dozen or more pistols he had carried when he rode with Quantrill. A dozen guerrillas could ride into an enemy town sporting the firepower of an entire company of Federals armed only with muskets.

When he'd finished, he drew his Winchester from its sheath and made sure its magazine was full. This was as ready as he could get.

"Give the word," he told Kennard.

"Well now, this is a mite dangerous. We ought to think on it."

Slocum didn't listen to the rest of the foreman's musing. He was afraid to confront the rustlers. Slocum could understand that. He wasn't too eager, either, to face down four men who'd likely open fire at anything that moved across the desert. The difference between him and Kennard was a willingness to push down that fear and do what was right.

He snapped the reins and got his horse down the embankment into the sandy arroyo. He drew his pistol and rode on, not caring if Lonigan and Kennard backed his move. This was the right thing to do, and Slocum wasn't going to turn his back and ride away from cattle thieves.

The soft footing prevented his horse from making the kind of approach Slocum would have preferred—at a gallop. Better to not let the rustlers get the idea they were under attack. Surprise was the only thing in his favor, and the soft crunch of his horse's hooves against sand and gravel sounded like cannon fire to him.

When he saw four figures ahead, he let out a whoop and pushed his gelding as fast as it could run in the sand.

The attack accomplished its purpose. The rustlers spooked. They were mounted and herded a dozen head of cattle ahead of them. Two lit out, charging up the crumbling banks on either side of the arroyo where it was shallowest. Slocum heard their hoofbeats receding in the still night. That left him two outlaws and a dozen head of cattle.

The beeves almost killed him.

One rustler got to the front of the small herd and fired several times, getting the cattle to stampede. They were contained by the high arroyo walls and had only one direction to go—straight toward Slocum.

Slocum got off a quick shot that probably didn't do anything but frighten the cattle even more. The lack of footing that had hindered his horse kept the stampede from being all that dangerous. The cattle ran only a few yards and then found the going too difficult. Still frightened, they were dangerous beasts, but Slocum was in no danger of being trampled.

He worked his way around the knot of frightened beeves and found himself caught in a cross fire. One owlhoot shot at him from atop the embankment. The other in front of him began firing a rifle. Slocum bent low and got his horse moving forward. This put him out of range of the outlaw who had already gained the rim of the arroyo. It also caused him to ride smack into the muzzle of the rustler still in the dry river-bed.

The long tongues of flame leaping toward him and the hiss of hot lead past the brim of his hat were simultaneous. He was almost close enough to smell the outlaw's breath. Slocum kept low, raising his six-shooter only when he had a chance at a shot. He hit the outlaw's horse. From the way it reared and then stumbled, it wasn't a fatal shot but it would slow the rustler down if he tried to run.

He did.

Slocum fired as he rode after the man on the wounded horse, then his six-shooter came up empty. He tucked it away and got his rifle from the saddle sheath, but by the time he got it cocked and to his shoulder, his target had evaporated. Using his knees, Slocum steered his gelding from side to side in the arroyo but saw nothing of where the rustler had gone. Rather than ride into an ambush, Slocum drew rein and lis-tened hard. No sounds reached his ears except the frightened noise from the cattle behind him.

Reluctantly, Slocum wheeled about and returned to find Lonigan and Kennard busily shooing the small herd out of the arroyo.

"You saved the Circle Bar K a pile of money, Slocum. They woulda made off with ten head," Kennard said. "I'll see that the boss gives you a little extra for this. Maybe a cow of your own."

"Thanks," Slocum said. "You need a hand getting the cows back to the main herd?"

"Me and Lonigan can do it but—"

Slocum worked to reload his six-gun.

"You're coming with us, ain't you, Slocum?"

"Long Drink, there are four outlaws out there. They lit out to every direction of the compass, but one of them's on a wounded horse."

"You're not going to track him, Slocum. Not in the dark!" Kennard sounded downright frightened at the prospect.

"Might be I want a second steer. That'd be almost a herd, wouldn't it? Two beeves?"

"Look, Slocum, you don't have to."

"There might be a reward," Lonigan said, sucking on his teeth. His head bobbed as he thought on it a little more. "Rustlers this bold might have big rewards on their heads. You ever work as a bounty hunter, Slocum?"

"Hate the sons of bitches," Slocum said. "Almost as much as I hate cattle thieves."

"What are you going to do if you catch him?" Kennard asked.

Slocum hadn't thought much on this since there hadn't been much time to reflect on the future.

"Take him to Fort Huachuca, I reckon. Can't believe the Army likes rustlers."

"That's what I'm gettin' at, Slocum. You take him there and the Army'd let him go. The boss and them's not on good terms," Kennard said.

"That's right. The boss said they tried to cheat him on a deal. Circle Bar K was sellin' cattle to them, mostly them what just upped and fell down, but the quartermaster didn't much care. Then a new one came in and refused to pay for what they'd already done et."

"Shut up, Long Drink," Kennard said, irritated. "What I'm sayin', Slocum, is that there's no point riskin' your life for nothing."

"Might be I'd just string him up."

Kennard laughed harshly. "You'd have to take him into the mountains to find a limb strong enough or a tree tall enough."

"This'll be a bridge I'll cross when I get to it, then," Slocum said.

"You want me to ride along? You know. Just in case? To keep you company?"

"No thanks, Lonigan. I can deal with rustlers on my own."

"Don't go, Slocum. I can't be responsible if you get yourself shot up."

"Nobody but me's responsible for what I do. And don't think I'm likely to be the one getting shot."

"You might not have a job waiting if you go traipsin' off like this. It's against ranch policy to take the law into our own hands."

Slocum looked hard at Kennard, then laughed.

"In Arizona Territory? The nearest marshal is over in Tombstone, 'less you call that no-account drunk in Benson a lawman."

"Stay, Slocum. Please."

Slocum wondered what Kennard's problem was, unless he was part of the gang. Or maybe he just had a yellow streak a mile wide, and it hadn't showed up before now.

"I'll be back when I finish tracking down the rustlers. Keep that cow you promised as a reward well fed, will you, Lonigan?"

"Kin I have it if you don't come back?"

Slocum laughed at that as he rode off. Lonigan and Kennard started arguing and that was the last he heard of them as he descended back into the arroyo and began his hunt for the rustler's trail.

He found it just before dawn.

2

The blood trail grew larger until Slocum knew the rustler's horse couldn't go on much longer. By noon he topped a rise and squinted through the desert's heat shimmer to see a man slogging along with a saddle on his shoulder and a rifle in his other hand. It didn't take Slocum much to fit everything together. The horse had finally died, leaving the outlaw on foot.

Slocum drew his Winchester and levered in a round. The metallic click as it cocked and slid a new round into the chamber carried farther than he would have liked. The rustler dropped his saddle and whirled around, bringing his own rifle to his shoulder. He got off a round before Slocum could fire.

The range was too great for an accurate shot. Slocum didn't waste any lead firing back. He put his heels to his horse's flanks and trotted forward, keeping his rifle ready for use the instant he came into range.

"Give up," he shouted. "You're on foot, and I'm not going to quit tracking you!"

"Go to hell!" The outlaw fired several more times and then ran. Slocum wasn't sure where the rustler could go, but since he wasn't being shot at, it was time to gallop. He reached where the rustler had dropped his saddle and quickly found the man's trail.

The rustler headed for a hill, intending to use the attitude to get a better shot at Slocum. He never got the chance. Several quick rounds from Slocum's rifle caused the man to pull up short. He turned and raised his hands. Slocum drew rein a dozen paces away. There was nowhere left to run, and Slocum had the drop on him.

"Don't shoot!"

"Lose your rifle!" Slocum warily waited for the man to comply. He bent and gently placed the rifle on the ground, but when he stood, he had a derringer in his fist. He fired both barrels, but Slocum bent low and the slugs missed. "That was a damned fool thing to do. Any reason I shouldn't just leave your corpse for the buzzards?"

"I ain't done nuthin'!"

"You're a murderous cattle-stealing son of a bitch," Slocum said.

"I never did no such thing!"

Slocum stood in his stirrups and got a better idea where he had ridden while following the man's trail.

"The fort's not five miles that way," Slocum said, pointing with his rifle. "Start walking."

"I can't!"

"You were making good time carrying your saddle. Think how much faster you can walk with it slung over your shoulder—and knowing I'll put a bullet in your damned heart if you don't step lively."

"You got the wrong man. I didn't steal no Circle Bar K cows."

This cinched it for Slocum. He had the right man, as if there could be any question. During the fight in the arroyo he had shot the man's horse. The trail of blood led straight here, though he hadn't seen where the horse finally died.

"Walk. Fast. I want to get to the fort before sundown so I can get me some chow."

Slocum said nothing in reply to the man's protests the entire distance to Fort Huachuca. He hoped the man would stop his yammering when the fort was in sight, but if anything this caused an even more impassioned plea to be let go.

"You have a reward on your head?" Slocum asked. "Is that why you don't want to be turned over to the Army?"

"I ain't done nuthin'," the man said.

"Only steal ten head of cattle. Might have been twelve, but a couple were missing from your little herd."

Slocum shut his ears to the new outpouring of alternately threatening and begging for mercy. He wanted nothing of what the man had to offer.

"Hello!" Slocum called when he got within hailing distance of the fort. Like many Arizona forts, the walls were adobe and only waist-high to keep in the livestock. The sentries provided the first line of defense, although a couple Apaches could slit their throats and be inside the fort walls, if they were so inclined, before anyone knew it.

Slocum guessed that the Apaches weren't much of a threat at the moment since the guards responded slowly, and when they did, they weren't overly alert to the situation.

"You two wantin' into the fort?" A youngster, hardly shaving from the look of his face, came through the opened gate, his rifle resting on his right shoulder. Slocum could have cut him down before the soldier knew there was trouble.

"Got a rustler to turn over to your commander," Slocum said.

"I ain't—"

"Shut up," Slocum ordered. He kicked his prisoner and sent him sprawling. "Get the officer of the watch so I can turn this owlhoot over to him."

"A rustler? Reckon I can do that. He don't look like a rustler."

"What's a rustler supposed to look like?" Slocum had to ask.

"Well, he ought to have cows all around him and—"

"What's going on?" A lieutenant marched up and stared at the outlaw, then at Slocum. "You have a reason for pointing your rifle at this man?"

Slocum explained the situation.

"Very well, sir," the lieutenant said. "We'll deal with this. Major Tompkins will want to speak with you. You're looking mighty tired. You can get some water and a plate of beans in the mess."

"Much obliged. You see that this owlhoot gets locked up in the stockade?" Slocum stared straight at the young soldier when he spoke. The youngster jumped to obey, only to be called on it by his lieutenant.

"You obey me, Private, not a civilian."

"Sorry, sir."

"Get the prisoner to the stockade." The lieutenant shot Slocum an angry look, pivoted, and marched off. Slocum followed to the base commander's office. The lieutenant hadn't waited for him. Slocum didn't bother knocking as he went in. The lieutenant was in earnest conversation with a man who looked old enough to have been a general. At one time, during the war, he might have been. His option to being reduced in rank was to be mustered out. The look of a career officer was hard to erase, no matter the rank.

"So you brought in a rustler, eh?"

"I did, Major," Slocum said.

"Whose cattle?"

Slocum hesitated. The way the major asked put him on guard.

"Circle Bar K cattle. Ten head for sure and maybe two more. Him and three others rustled the beeves last night, but his partners got away."

"So you tracked him down?"

Slocum said nothing.

"Is Leonard Conway still the owner of Circle Bar K?"

"He's the one who pays me fifty cents a day and chuck," Slocum said.

"Quite the cheapskate, old Conway," the officer said. "Why don't you get on over to the mess and get yourself some decent cavalry food? Then you can be on your way."

Slocum thanked the officer and had no trouble finding the mess. The only things on the post that stank worse were the latrines. The food matched the smell, and Slocum had a bellyache when he finished, but he decided it was what he had needed. It had been a long spell since he had eaten.

He went out onto the steps to build himself a smoke. The young guard came marching by. Slocum called out to him.

"You get the rustler locked up all good and proper?"

The private looked at him and frowned. Then he brightened.

"You been gettin' some chow. That's why you didn't hear, I reckon."

Slocum stopped rolling his cigarette and stood.

"What haven't I heard?"

"The major let that fellow go. No evidence, he said."

"He let him go because they were Circle Bar K cattle being stolen," Slocum said angrily. After the second step toward the major's office, he stopped and wheeled about on the private.

"Is he still on the post? The rustler?"

"Oh, no, he's done gone. Bought hisse'f a swayback mule fer next to nuthin' and lit out when the major told him he was free to go."

Arguing with the cavalry officers accomplished nothing. Slocum got to his horse, mounted, and headed out. It was twilight, but the stars were as bright as a cloudy day, allowing him to pick up the mule's tracks easily.

The man was making a beeline for the border. Once he had

figured this out, Slocum rode faster. A broke-down mule was no match for the speed of the gelding. Slocum spotted the outlaw within fifteen minutes of leaving Fort Huachuca.

Within twenty he had the rustler at gunpoint again.

"I should have listened to my foreman," Slocum said. "He told me the soldiers wouldn't hold you."

"There's no evidence," the rustler said. "You better let me go. If Major Tompkins finds you, he'll have you in stocks for this. I'm a law-abidin' citizen!"

"The only law you know comes out the end of a gun," Slocum said, sighting in.

"Wait, no, wait! I did it. Don't kill me. I confess!"

"I know you did it. You knew whose cattle had been stolen without me telling you. There are a half-dozen other spreads in the area but you knew Circle Bar K head had been rustled because you did it."

"Let me go and I kin pay you. Ain't got much left. A few dollars."

"You can tell it to a judge," Slocum said. He lashed the man's hands behind him and turned toward the northeast. If the cavalry wanted nothing to do with a cattle thief, maybe the law in Tombstone would.

It took three days to get to the edge of the dusty boomtown.

"I'm telling you, you'll be sorry if you don't let me go."

Slocum looked at his prisoner and considered doing just what he asked. Only Slocum would add a bullet to the part about letting him go. He had grown increasingly aware of how much of a snake the rustler was. He hadn't bothered asking his name since he didn't want to know. Even if there was a reward on the man's head, Slocum wasn't inclined to collect it. He was doing everyone in Arizona Territory a favor by seeing the outlaw locked away in the Yuma Penitentiary for a good, long time.

"Let me have a drink. Just one. Tombstone's got more damn saloons than any other town between San Francisco and Kansas City. If they're gonna lock me up and throw away the key, you owe me that much."

Slocum saw the man's conjecture about the number of watering holes might be right. Along Fremont Street he saw that about every other business was a saloon. He turned down Fifth and passed Allen. If there had been dozens of saloons along Fremont, there were even more here. Finding the jail wouldn't be all that hard since it would one of the few buildings that didn't have a saloon in it.

As soon as he heard the cell door clank behind the outlaw, he would wet his whistle. It had been a dry, long four days. It would take him another couple days to get back to the roundup to find if Kennard had a job waiting for him or had fired him as he had hinted.

It didn't matter. Slocum would collect his wages and move on if the job at the Circle Bar K Ranch was over. He seldom stayed anywhere as long as he had in Arizona. With summer coming down the tracks like a runaway locomotive, the Front Range up in Colorado might be a better place to spend the summer. Or Wyoming. There were plenty of ranches there. One of them had to be in need of his services as a cowboy.

"There, by the courthouse," Slocum said. He yanked on the rope he had fastened around the man's neck. The rustler fell hard to the ground. Slocum waited for him to get to his feet. "Good thing your mule wasn't ten hands tall."

"You son of a bitch," the rustler spat out. Then he choked as Slocum pulled him along. Slocum kicked open the door and shoved his prisoner in. The deputy behind the desk reached for a sawed-off shotgun on the desk in front of him.

"What's goin' on?" the lawman demanded.

Slocum explained. The deputy scowled, then picked up the shotgun and poked it into the rustler's ribs.

"You git on in there while I find the marshal and see what needs doing."

"What needs doing is to get him in front of a judge and jury for cattle rustling."

"The Circle Bar K is a mite out of local jurisdiction," the deputy said, pronouncing the word as if he had just learned it. From his look, he was a failed silver miner. He had a gimpy leg and had probably been injured in a mining accident. Waving around a shotgun as town deputy was probably the best job he could get if he wasn't picking away at the silver chloride ore underground.

"The Army down Fort Huachuca way don't want to be bothered—"

"For a reason. They know I'm innocent!"

The deputy kicked the door between the office and the cell block shut with his heel.

"I'll let Marshal Sosa know. You be in town for a spell?"

"Long as it takes me to get a drink."

"The Crystal Palace is a right classy place," the deputy said, longing in his voice. "Truth is, 'bout any of the gin mills can serve you a decent beer and a sandwich. Competition is brisk." He spoke the latter words with precision, as if repeating what he had heard someone else say. Slocum doubted the deputy had ever experienced an original thought in his life.

Slocum walked out in the gathering heat of the day and went up to Allen Street to choose. He could have tried the Crystal Palace but Saloon Nineteen was closer. He went in, ordered a beer along with a beef sandwich, and was working on his second beer when the deputy came in, his gimpy leg dragging a little.

The man seemed surprised to see Slocum.

"Thought you'd be on your way by now," the lawman said uneasily.

"You made Tombstone sound too appealing. When does the marshal want me to swear out a complaint against the rustler?" By the deputy's expression Slocum knew something was wrong.

"Well, you see, it's like this. He said there ain't any evidence. One man's word against another. The marshal did say that Mr. Childress he wasn't gonna file false arrest charges against you or nuthin'. That sounded mighty charitable of him, if you ask me."

Slocum stared in disbelief. What did it take to put a rustler behind bars in Arizona Territory?

"You let him go?"

"No, no, not me," the deputy said. His eyes darted around like a mouse looking for a woodpile to hide in. "I had nuthin' to do with it. The marshal, he was the one what let Mr. Childress out. But he didn't have no other choice."

"Why not?"

"He had a lawyer." The deputy looked around, and then leaned closer to Slocum. "Tombstone is filthy with them cocksuckers. There's an entire street filled with their offices. Rotten Row we call it."

"Where did Childress go?"

The deputy shrugged.

Slocum drained his beer and left the saloon, marching straight for the jailhouse. He reached the small building in time to see Childress shaking hands with a well-dressed man wearing a bowler.

"Childress!" Slocum roared.

Childress went for his pistol. Slocum was faster. He had his Colt Navy out and firing before Childress cleared leather. The man in the cutaway coat leaped away, bellowing incoherently. Slocum focused only on the rustler. The outlaw wasn't much of a gunman, struggling to skin his six-shooter out of his holster.

"I swear, you're a dead man if you get your hogleg out," Slocum shouted. "You're going back to jail where you belong."

Childress looked up to the man in the bowler.

"Sir, there must be a mistake. My client is—"

Slocum swung his pistol and caught the man alongside the head, knocking him down. He pointed his six-gun at Childress and said coldly, "Inside the jail. Move!"

Childress's hands were shaking and he looked like he was

going to cry, but he obeyed. He went inside and headed straight back for the cells. Before Slocum could congratulate him on knowing where he belonged, he heard a whistling sound and then he crashed to the floor, out like a light.

3

"You lock him up and keep him locked up!" Childress shook his fist at Slocum's motionless body. When he went to give him a kick in the ribs, both his lawyer and the marshal stopped him.

"Don't do anything that'll land you back in jail," Jackson Pine said, putting a restraining hand on his client's shoulder. Childress tried to pull away, but Pine was stronger. He bore down hard, digging his fingers into a nerve.

"You let go of me, you damned shyster," Childress complained. He tried to jerk free, but Pine continued to apply pressure and forced Childress to sit in the straight-backed, rickety wooden chair in front of the marshal's desk.

"You be quiet and let me take care of this. It's what you're paying me for."

"You lock that varmint up, won't you, Marshal Sosa?" Pine said to the lawman.

The marshal looked at Slocum and nodded slowly.

"Don't have much love for his boss. He works for Conway over at the Circle Bar K Ranch, right?"

"That's what I've heard. After all, who else would slander

my client with such malicious charges? Conway is infamous in this part of Arizona for his vile calumnies of all and sundry."

"Save your two-bit words, Counselor," the marshal said. "You want to help me drag him into a cell?"

"That's your job, Marshal," Pine said. He rubbed his sweaty hands against his trousers, not wanting to touch the dusty cowboy.

"I will!" Childress started to stand but Pine pushed him back and shot him a disapproving look. Childress subsided.

"I'll prefer charges later, if you don't mind." The lawyer touched the side of his head and winced at the tender spot under his fingers. The pistol barrel had not broken the skin but had left quite a bruise. Gentle probing made it out to be the size of a silver dollar.

"You, too?" the marshal asked Childress.

"Certainly." Pine spoke up before Childress could speak. "My client is the one who has the civil case against him, as well as a criminal one."

"Yeah, right," Marshal Sosa said. "You two clear out. I don't want him seein' the pair of you and goin' crazy. The cell'll hold a gorilla, but this one has the look of a man whose anger sorta overflows, if you know what I mean."

Pine gingerly touched the bruise on his temple. Nodding hurt like the dickens. He reached down, took Childress by the arm, and pulled him to his feet. Before the man could take a step in the direction of the cell where Slocum was already locked up, Pine shoved and sent his client stumbling out into the hot sun.

"You don't have to treat me like that. Touch me again and I'll rip your damn fool head off."

"Mr. Childress, do you understand power?"

"What are you goin' on about?"

"It's like this," the lawyer said, taking a deep breath before he continued. "Out on the range you live by your wits. I have no doubt that you were rustling cattle—wait!" Pine held up his hand to forestall the predictable outburst. "I don't want to know. As your lawyer, I can present a better case in front of a jury, should it come to that, if I have not heard a confession from your lips."

"What are you—?"

"Be quiet and I'll tell you. On the range, your six-shooter and your wits keep you alive. In Tombstone they mean nothing. Less than nothing since if you tried to use either your three-pound weapon or your pea brain, you'd end up in jail. Or worse."

Pine paused. He was heartened when Childress didn't try to put in his two cents' worth.

"I know how to get things done in Tombstone. The courts are more powerful than you can ever imagine. A single piece of paper will put a noose around your neck—or remove the rope. I am in charge of all that."

"You're only one of a couple dozen lawyers in town."

"Try not to sound so petulant. You are right. There are more than thirty lawyers for a town of a couple thousand. Not a one of us is starving. What's that tell you?"

"You're all crooked."

Pine laughed.

"We don't like to think of ourselves that way. Crooked implies we break the law. Rather, we *use* the law. Bend it, twist it, pervert it on occasion, but it remains the law and it is my servant. I command it to do things you could never dream of doing. And it is all legal, unlike driving off someone else's cattle in the hope of reaching Mexico before they catch you."

"Why'd you get me out of jail? I can't pay very much."

"I see sterling qualities about you that I can use."

"Sterling? You mean silver?"

"Exactly," Pine said, slapping Childress on the back. "I need an assistant to help me get title to one of the richer silver mines in the area." He turned down Toughnut Street and pointed. "The mines in town—underneath the town itself—are rich. When Schiefflin made the discovery that brought this filthy little town to prominence, I knew my destiny. Prospectors rushed in and claimed the best spots, but some of those mines weren't sold to large companies."

"There are a passel of leathery old geezers who think they'll get rich workin' their own claims," Childress said, contempt obvious in his tone. Pine knew he could use that arrogance to his own benefit and Childress would never know what was going on.

"Quite so. And some of them have failed to retain legal representation to secure their claims."

"So you're gonna steal one of them mines using the law?"

"It won't be stealing if a judge agrees to my legal brief. One miner in particular has been less than meticulous about filing the necessary deeds to his mine."

"I don't know what you're sayin', but I think I'm likin' it more and more."

"I'm sure you are, Mr. Childress, I'm sure you are. Let me buy you a drink while I explain what needs to be done." Pine started to put his arm around the rustler's shoulders, then took a half step away. Bugs crawled up and out of the scruffy man's collar. Pine rubbed his hands against his trouser legs and led the way into the nearest saloon. He didn't bother to note which it was. At this time of day, the miners weren't off their shift yet and only a few who were out of work loitered about.

"I worked up a mighty big thirst, what with Slocum draggin' me halfway across the desert the way he did."

Pine motioned to the barkeep for a half bottle and found a table toward the rear of the long, narrow saloon so he could sit with his back in the corner. Childress had no trouble flopping down opposite him, his back exposed to the door. When the bottle came, Pine poured. Before he could get himself a shot of whiskey, Childress had downed his and clicked the glass on the table, demanding another. Pine poured a second, then tended his own drink.

He sipped and made a face. The bitter taste was hardly disguised by the gunpowder put in to give the raw alcohol color. Trade whiskey would be the death of him unless he got better-paying clients and could drink the good stuff most saloons kept hidden away for special customers.

"It ain't Billy Taylor's Finest but it'll do," Childress said, pouring himself a third shot while Pine nursed the first.

"It can be," Pine said, his voice low and conspiratorial. He decided this was the proper way to approach Childress for his cooperation. If there appeared to be something illegal about what he suggested, Childress would be more comfortable with that rather than the simple and quite legal act of serving process on Ike Tarkenton. But just because it was legal didn't mean it wasn't going to be dangerous. The crazy hard-rock miner was more likely to shoot than to listen, no matter how exquisitely drafted the court papers were.

Childress was the perfect one to serve him with the court summons.

"You sayin' if me and you team up, there's money in it?" Childress looked sharply at him. Pine nodded. "Might be that's not such a bad thing. I was gettin' mighty tired out of stealin' a couple head of cattle and then gettin' robbed by them Meskins. A fifty-dollar cow'd only fetch five south of the border. Like as not, they wanted to pay in pesos."

"That's not bad if it is a silver coin," Pine pointed out.

Childress snorted.

"Them *ladrones* ain't never seen real specie. All they got's paper money, and it's worth even less than greenbacks on this side of the border."

"Why deal with them?" Pine bit his lower lip. These weren't questions he ought to be asking a client who might still end up in front of a jury to be tried for rustling.

"Ain't got nuthin' else to do. None of them fat ass ranchers'll hire me to do an honest day's work. So I steal from them. Especially from the Circle Bar K since ain't nobody in Arizona that likes the owner."

"I've heard Conway is a man of few words—and those tend to be cuss words."

"Damned right, and he don't make no bones about tellin' you what he thinks of you. Serves him right gettin' his beeves stolen."

"I need to know that I can trust you to do what you're told," Pine said. He peered past Childress at a burly man who had sauntered in. He wore his six-shooter low on his hip and had the look of a gunman.

"If there's money in it, I'll do whatever you ask of me."

"Your current legal bill is one hundred dollars."

"What! That's highway robbery! All you done was get me out of jail."

"I convinced the marshal to drop rustling charges," Pine said. "More than this, I took Slocum off the street and got him out of your hair so you'd be free to do whatever you want." Pine touched the bruise on his temple and winced. If he had the time, he'd make sure Slocum rotted in prison for buffaloing him the way he had. However, there was no reason to let Childress know that. Let him think everything he'd done was for the benefit of the client.

Pine saw this wouldn't be too hard. Childress's only thoughts were of his own well-being. He viewed the world as if it were a brightly reflecting mirror with himself in the center of everything.

"I won't pay!"

"You won't have to if you're in my employ," Pine said. "I'll forget the hundred dollars if you collect what's due me from that gent. The one just knocking back a shot of whiskey."

Childress swung around in his chair and gave the man a once-over.

"He's big. That don't scare me."

"It ought to. He's very good with his six-shooter. I don't know if he is a hired killer, but he might be. His name is Simonetti. I never learned his first name." As he spoke, it occurred to Pine that he didn't know Childress's first name either. He shrugged it off. Such details never mattered in the long run. He didn't intend to have Childress working for him more than a few days. That would be all it took to get Ike Tarkenton to agree to an amicable settlement—even if it took some serious persuasion on Childress's part to bring it about.

"What's your beef with him?"

"I got him out of jail, much as I did you. The charges against him were more serious and required paperwork signed by a judge. I sprung him, and he refused to pay."

"You outta collect before you get him out of jail."

"I realize that now. But if I have you doing my . . . collecting . . . that's a moot point."

"Mute? He don't sound like no mute. He just ordered hisself a whiskey loud enough for me to hear."

"Never mind. He owes me five hundred dollars."

"A galoot like that ain't got five hundred of anything," Childress said.

"Perhaps not, but it would be interesting to find out."

"If he ain't got it, kin I kill him?"

Pine was taken aback at such savagery and almost reconsidered putting Childress into his employ. Then he saw the wad of greenbacks Simonetti flashed as he paid for his drink. Pine sat a little straighter, and his inhibitions against violence faded. Simonetti had lied to him and taken advantage of him. Dragging the matter through court would only cause Simonetti to hire another attorney to defend him and burn through that roll of money.

"He's got the money, and it's by rights all mine."

Childress started to stand, but Pine reached across the table and pushed him back down. Childress turned angrily on him.

"Calm down. I want the money. Don't hurt him, unless it's necessary." Pine wondered if this was realistic. Simonetti was twice Childress's size and probably meaner. He moved like he was always ready to throw down and get his six-gun out and blazing away at anyone foolish enough to call him out. Simonetti was a one-man disaster waiting to happen.

"Of course it's gonna be necessary. You want the money or not?"

Pine leaned back and gestured for Childress to do as he pleased. The lawyer intended to sit here, or maybe go to the bar where others could see him so he couldn't be blamed for anything that happened. For all he knew, Simonetti would leave Childress dead in the middle of the street.

He watched Childress push through the swinging doors and go out onto the boardwalk. Several minutes passed, and he began to frown. Childress might have hightailed it to get away from the hundred-dollar charge he had levied against him. The kind of citizens he dealt with were basically crooked. Childress might even think it was funny to run out on a hundred-dollar debt. Pine had come across worse thieves in his work since he'd ridden into Tombstone almost six months ago.

A young boy ducked into the saloon and looked around. Pine saw the way the boy's eyes turned wide when he stared at Simonetti. The boy overcame his fear and hurried to where the giant of a man stood drinking. After getting Simonetti's attention by tugging on his sleeve, the boy spoke rapidly. His voice was too low for Pine to hear what he said, but it galvanized Simonetti. He pushed the youngster out of the way and stormed from the bar.

For a moment the sudden departure caused a furor among the other patrons. Pine didn't miss how the boy climbed up on the brass rail, grabbed the mug of beer Simonetti had been working on, and quickly drained it himself. He fell off the brass rail, hiccuped, and then left the saloon. The boy's gait was already a little tipsy.

As curious as he was, Pine forced himself to remain at the table. After a few minutes, he grew anxious and called out, "Who wants to get into a poker game?"

"Lady Jane's not gonna be in 'til six. You can play faro then."

"I want to play now! And it's got to be poker, not faro." Pine intended to cause as big a commotion as he could so they all remembered he was inside the saloon, not out taking care of Simonetti.

Or maybe witnessing Simonetti killing Childress.

"I've got a deck of cards. Who's got some money?"

The patrons exchanged glances. One man started to join him but another—a miner from the cut of his clothing—grabbed his arm and whispered urgently. The potential card-player backed off and ordered another beer, pointedly not looking in Pine's direction.

What the miner had said didn't matter to Pine. These men would remember him being in the saloon, and that's all he wanted. An alibi.

Less than ten minutes later a commotion outside drew the men. The barkeep went to investigate and ducked back inside, eyes wide.

"I don't believe it. Somebody's gone and shot Simonetti. They plugged him in the back."

This caused immediate whispering as the men began speculating on who might be responsible. Pine sat a little straighter when he saw Childress appear in the doorway leading to the back room. While the patrons and barkeep were crowded around the door leading to the street, Childress slipped into the saloon and took his chair across from Pine.

"Here you are," Childress said, a sneer curling his lip. "Five hundred." He tossed a wad of greenbacks large enough to choke a cow onto the table.

"You fool, don't show the money like that. People will figure out what happened." Pine grabbed the thick roll of bills and tucked it into his jacket pocket. The bulge was obvious, but he doubted anyone in the saloon would notice. He hesitated, then asked, "What happened?"

"He gave up the money." Childress worked on another shot of whiskey. He slammed the shot glass onto the table and bellowed, "Bartender! Another bottle. No more of that tarantula juice. Give us the good stuff you got hid away behind the bar."

"Childress . . ." Pine began. He clamped his mouth shut when the barkeep came over.

"I thought you left." He scowled as he stared at Childress.

"Took a leak out back."

The barkeep looked over to Pine, who said, "He's been here except for that."

"Coulda swore he was gone longer. You gents are slowin' down drinkin' that bottle."

"I was havin' a damn hard time pissing. I think I caught me somethin' from one of your whores."

"Don't go sayin' a thing like that," the barkeep said sharply. "It gets out that any of my pretty waiter girls got the clap and nobody'd come in, not even for a drink."

"Might be some other place then," Childress said, backing off his outrageous claim. The barkeep set the bottle on the table and left, muttering to himself. The crowd returned and began discussing the killing in louder voices.

"What did you do?" Pine felt a mite desperate.

"Nuthin' you didn't tell me to do. He objected to handin' over the money he owed you, so I took it. All it took was a bullet in the belly."

"He drew first, right? He threatened you?" Pine's desperation grew.

"Yeah, that's what happened, Counselor. That's what the gimpy deputy called you, wasn't it? Now what do you want me to do about this silver miner who won't leave your mine?"

Jackson Pine settled his nerves, took a drink, and then began telling his new employee what he wanted done.

4

Slocum wondered why his head felt like it was going to fall off his neck when he hadn't been drinking. At least, he didn't remember drinking that much. The taste of beer lingered in his mouth, but he hadn't been in Tombstone long enough to tie one on that would give him a hangover like this.

He rolled onto his side and then crashed to the floor. This brought him fully awake. Pushing up, he banged his head against the cot in the jail cell. He swung around, sitting on the floor, and took in his situation. The iron bars were a little more than arm's length away. Above him, high in the wall was a narrow barred window. Even if it didn't have strong bars across it, the opening was too small for him to crawl through should he successfully pull apart the bars. Forcing himself to stand caused more pain in his head. Even his shoulder ached.

"You hit the floor twistin' to the side," the deputy said, looking in on him. "Since you was out cold fer so long, you don't git supper."

"Why was I hit?" Slocum remembered Childress and the

lawyer and then being hit from behind. It made his head ache all over again.

"Now, that's a matter 'tween you and the court. The marshal, he said to keep you locked up until hell froze over. I don't know who you done made mad, but it's somebody mighty powerful."

"I just got to town," Slocum said.

"You're a real fast worker, then. Most times, it takes a week or more 'fore a drifter finds himself in your position."

Slocum dropped to the cot. It creaked ominously under his weight and then began swaying. He leaned back against the cool adobe wall and tried to get everything straight in his head. The pain was subsiding. Fading to a dull ache didn't let him concentrate too well, though.

"He's a rustler. You know that. Why'd you let him go?"

"Ain't my call. I seen his like before and yer prob'ly right. If Childress ain't a rustler, then he's done somethin' else. Ain't my call. It's up to Marshal Sosa who's locked up and who he only runs outta town. If it was left to me, you'd be ridin' out of Tombstone and Childress would be locked up. But—"

"It's not up to you," Slocum finished for him.

"It ain't up to me," the deputy confirmed.

"What's bail for whatever I'm charged with?"

"That's the funny thing. Not ha-ha funny but weird funny," the deputy said, pulling up a chair and tipping it back so he could lean against the wall with the front two legs off the jailhouse floor. "Usually Marshal Sosa's got a number in mind. Post bail, get the hell out of town, and never come back 'cuz there'll be a bench warrant out fer skippin' out. But with you, no bail."

Slocum couldn't bribe his way out of jail in any case. He didn't have more than a few dollars in scrip riding in his shirt pocket. Pressing his hand down, he felt the outline of the thin wad of greenbacks there. The law hadn't bothered taking his money, which he counted as both fortunate and careless on the marshal's part. Lawmen seldom got paid enough. Robbing those they locked up was usually considered part of their salary by the town fathers.

"What am I charged with?"

"That's the other part of this bein' so funny. Nuthin' was entered on the record. See?" The deputy pointed to the desk in the outer office. "That there's a record book where Marshal Sosa keeps all the names of those he locks up. 'Bout the only ones who don't get writ down are politicians. And lawyers." The deputy spat, accurately hitting a cuspidor in the far corner of the room.

"Who's Childress's lawyer? The one I cold-cocked?"

"That there's Jackson Pine. Don't know much 'bout him and don't much care to. Just another of them shysters with offices along Rotten Row."

"Might be an apology would get him to drop charges."

"I tole you. There ain't no charges against you."

"Then let me out."

The deputy laughed.

"You got a real good sense of humor for a man who might end up over in Yuma Penitentiary. It don't work that way. You got the look of a fellow who knows that, too."

Slocum closed his eyes and willed away the pain in his head. Whoever had hit him from behind had driven the butt of a pistol smack into the back of his head. Since the deputy wasn't fessing up to it, Slocum guessed that the marshal was responsible.

"Where's Sosa? I want to talk to him."

"He's out keepin' the peace, him and his number one deputy, Mike Eakin. In a mining town like Tombstone, that's a real chore. Eakin don't have problems gittin' around the way I do, so he gets to makes the rounds with the marshal." The deputy got up and hobbled to the desk in the outer office. Slocum guessed the man's bad leg kept him from a lot more than just making the rounds with Sosa. It might even be that Sosa had an army of deputies to accompany him. From what Slocum had already seen of Tombstone, that wasn't out of the question.

Slocum refused to believe he couldn't break out of this cell. With the deputy sitting in the chair, insisting to talk his ears off, Slocum had to be more careful how he examined the lock, the hinges, the door itself, and the way the entire wall of bars was fastened to the walls. If he had a stick of dynamite, he might be able to escape. After close to an hour of listening to the deputy's nonstop drivel, Slocum came to the sorry conclusion that there wasn't any easy way out of this cell. He was in here until the marshal let him out.

Or he went to court on charges of hitting a lawyer over the head.

As if reading his mind, the deputy said, "It's not as much of a crime as you'd think. Pine knows better than to ask for a jury trial. Hell, he'd have every man convictin' *him*. Sorry, you're in here 'til the marshal decides to let you go."

Slocum lay down on the cot, the deputy's endless drone putting him to sleep. The ache in his head faded, and he finally drifted off to a deep sleep only to come upright and reaching for a six-gun that wasn't at his hip when the outer door slammed hard.

The deputy shot to his feet and blocked Slocum's view.

"You don't want to do this," the marshal said. The answer was indistinct, but Slocum knew whoever spoke was hardly speaking English. "You have to clear it with the judge." More soft whispers Slocum could almost overhear. Sosa grumbled and argued a bit more, then called over his shoulder to his deputy, who stood only a couple feet away, "Let the buzzard out of his cage."

"Yes, sir, right away, Marshal." The deputy produced a key from the depths of a coat pocket and hastily opened Slocum's cell door. In a low voice, he said, "I didn't know you had such powerful connections. Sorry if I offended you any, Mr. Slocum."

Slocum didn't know anyone in Tombstone that he hadn't

hit over the head with his pistol barrel or who had locked him up. He stepped past the suddenly deferential deputy into the outer office. Marshal Sosa stood like a schoolboy caught throwing spitballs in class.

Slocum stared hard at the small Chinese woman in the corner of the room. She wore a jade green dress, intricately embroidered with gold thread, and had her hands hidden away in the voluminous sleeves. She bowed slightly—hardly more than an inch bob of her head in Slocum's direction—then faced the marshal.

"He is the one."

"I didn't know he worked for you," Sosa said. He gave Slocum a quick look that combined fear, hatred, and . . . envy. It made no sense, but Slocum wasn't going to argue.

"You got me out of jail?" he asked the woman. She nodded slightly again. He tried to judge how old she was and failed. She could have been thirty or she could have been sixty. There was a timeless quality about her that made him worry he had just gotten himself into a worse situation than assaulting a lawyer and getting locked up for it.

"If there's anything I can do, Mary, you let me know," the marshal said.

She said something in singsong Chinese. Slocum didn't understand and neither did the marshal, but a bulky Celestial immediately entered the office from out in the street. He took his hands from his sleeves and pointed. Slocum couldn't help noticing how calloused those hands were and how powerful.

"You ever work on a railroad?" Slocum asked the huge Celestial.

"No talk, go, go," the woman said. Slocum shook his head and was grabbed by Mary's bodyguard and lifted up onto his toes. He stared not at the man but at the woman.

"I want my six-shooter. The marshal has it in the top drawer of his desk."

Sosa was already opening the drawer with the gun by the time the woman looked at him. Her dark eyes communicated more than words ever could. When she looked back, her bodyguard let Slocum down.

Taking the Colt Navy, Slocum strapped it on and settled it before following the bodyguard from the office. Outside, he turned, blocked the man, and held the door open.

"Much obliged," Slocum told the woman.

"Come."

"Where to?"

"Hop Town." Mary walked strangely, as if each step was only a quarter of what it ought to be. Slocum had seen hifalutin women in Saint Louis wear skirts so tight they couldn't take a decent step, but Mary's dress—Slocum had to think of it as a gown since it was so elegant—didn't restrict her legs. He remembered hearing a Chinese in San Francisco tell about how women in his country had their feet bound to keep them small. Slocum hadn't believed him, but there hadn't been any Chinese women to study then.

"What's that?"

"My town," Mary said. "No more talk."

Slocum considered his chances of simply walking away, finding his horse, and riding from town. He decided they weren't too good. Her bodyguard watched him with the cold look of an executioner. The farther they went, the more Chinese he saw. All of them bowed in Mary's direction. This and the way the marshal had deferred to her told Slocum the deputy had been right. He had acquired himself a powerful patron. He just didn't understand how any woman, and a Celestial at that, gained such recognition in a mining boomtown.

Mary went into a butcher shop. Two Celestials looked up, meat cleavers in their hands. She ignored the blood on the floor and pushed aside curtains concealing a small back room. A single comfortable chair in the middle of the room was obviously hers. Slocum stood with the bodyguard directly behind him.

"You owe me," she said.

"Reckon so. You know I don't have money, but you don't want that, do you?"

Her dark eyes sharpened as they fixed on him. A small smile curled her lips.

"I chose well. I am China Mary. Nothing happens in Hop Town without my approval."

"Nothing?" Slocum tried not to smirk. China Mary was a madam running a whorehouse or two for the miners. That explained her power. In a boomtown with few women, she had to see immense business for her girls. Along with the miners came their silver. Along with the silver came power.

"Do not be stupid. It is not the way you are, Slocum."

"Nothing," he said, agreeing with her. She nodded once.

"Ah Sum will go with you."

Slocum waited. China Mary didn't elaborate so he asked.

"Fairbank is railhead. Package stolen there. Return it to me. You will find thieves and return package to me."

"Ah Sum knows the package when he sees it?"

"You bring back package. All is forgiven. I keep package. You ride away."

"When was it stolen?"

"One week."

"What's in the package?"

"Go now. Your horse is outside. Ah Sum will guide you." She looked away, silently telling Slocum the interview was over. Or was it a royal audience? He had never thought on talking to a king or queen but it couldn't be much different than talking to the ruler of Hop Town.

"Let's ride," Slocum said to the bodyguard, who pointed to the door. Outside and around back Slocum saw his horse tethered to a rail next to another that cost ten times what his gelding had. Ah Sum climbed up and waited for Slocum to mount. The bodyguard pointed and waited for Slocum to ride, following behind.

"This the trail to Fairbank?" Slocum asked after they had cut across barren desert for a half hour. He expected a road or at least a trail to the railroad depot supplying Tombstone. Whatever the mining town needed was shipped in, then loaded on wagons for the final trip across Goose Flats to Tombstone proper.

Ah Sum did not answer. He rode, staring ahead as if he cared about nothing in the world. Slocum let his horse drift away to the side and Ah Sum immediately pointed straight ahead, correcting Slocum's lapse. When they hit a road by twilight, Slocum realized Ah Sum had unerringly guided them across the desert in a shortcut that might have saved a dozen miles or more in travel.

In the distance he saw a tiny knot of buildings. When he heard a locomotive's steam whistle, he knew this had to be Fairbank.

"You don't talk much, do you?" Slocum asked. He sat a little straighter in the saddle when Ah Sum opened his mouth and pointed to a severed tongue. Slocum said nothing more, turning everything over in his head and trying to make sense of it.

The number one chop-chop madam in Tombstone had gotten him out of jail to find robbers who had stolen something from a shipment intended for her. Considering how richly China Mary dressed, he guessed it might be jade jewelry from her country that had been stolen, or perhaps more cloth to make new dresses. He doubted she lived like a nun if every miner in half of Arizona Territory crowded into her whorehouses.

Why she hadn't asked the marshal to send a deputy or two out on the robbers' trail was a question he couldn't answer. Even the sheriff of Cochise County would be beholden to her. For all that, Ah Sum looked capable enough to find the thieves on his own. He was big and strong and utterly loyal to his mistress. China Mary didn't trust Slocum enough to send him out on his own without Ah Sum as a chaperone.

They rode into town. Slocum went straight for the railroad

depot. After he had dismounted, he asked Ah Sum, "How long ago was the package stolen?"

The Celestial held up both hands, showing eight fingers. Slocum went up the steps and into the depot where the ticket agent dozed. The old man came awake with a start when Slocum rapped sharply on the glass window. The agent pushed open the window.

"What kin I do you for, mister? The train's not leavin' for another day. Got to do some work on a steam cylinder."

"I need to know about a robbery eight days back."

"Craziest thing I ever did see. The robbers busted into the mail car and rummaged through four sacks of mail. Only took one and left the rest."

Slocum considered this for a moment, then asked, "Were any of the sacks left opened?"

"Four of 'em. Don't know why they didn't tear into the other three."

"Because they found what they were looking for," Slocum said.

"What might that be?" The old man looked hard at Slocum.

"Can't say. Did the local marshal try to track them?"

"He did but gave up after a mile or two into the desert. Don't get me wrong. Old Sammy's a decent enough fellow but actually tracking and catching road agents is beyond him."

"Did the railroad send out a detective?"

The ticket agent snorted, wiped his mouth, then spat into the corner of his office.

"No reason. Nobody fessed up to losin' anything. Stealin' mail's a federal crime, but the federal marshal wasn't inclined to get his ass into the saddle to come out. Not that I blame him much. What's a stolen bag of mail when you got real crime poppin' up all around the territory? Heard tell Prescott's a hotbed of criminal activity. It's also a damn sight cooler when summer starts poundin' away at the desert."

"Which way did Sammy go when he went after the robbers?"

"Toward the river. To the west is the San Pedro. You familiar with it?"

Slocum nodded. He had ridden along the river farther south. It was as crazy as everything else in Arizona Territory. Some places it flowed on the surface and in others it went underground for miles. That didn't stop the trees and other vegetation from growing, but there wasn't any water for horse or man in some stretches.

"Much obliged," Slocum said.

"If you want a ticket on the train, be back here by noon tomorrow!"

The offer tempted Slocum, but he went out to a silent Ah Sum, who watched him with the same eyes a vulture might, waiting for its prey to die.

"I got a start on the trail. Let's go."

Ah Sum pointed to the sky. The sun had set and the stars were twinkling high above.

"I can track at night," Slocum said. Mostly he wanted to get out of Fairbank so he wouldn't have to answer questions about having a silent Celestial staying behind him like a shadow.

He rode along the edge of Fairbank until he found a track running south and west in the direction of the San Pedro River. There wasn't any reason for the robbers to cut across country if they wanted to make a quick getaway. He trotted along the trail for a mile or so, then drew rein and stared hard.

Ah Sum clapped him on the shoulder and pointed ahead.

"Not yet. I think our hunt's over."

Slocum dismounted and pushed through thick undergrowth. A flash of white had caught his eye. He found the ripped-open mail sack on a mesquite limb. Scattered on the ground were the contents, hundreds of letters in white envelopes.

He began gathering the letters and stuffing them back into the mailbag. There might be a reward for the return of the U.S. Mail. As he worked, Ah Sum paced back and forth like a caged tiger. In addition to the letters, Slocum found two small packages. He stood and took these to the Celestial.

"Either of these what you're looking for?"

Ah Sum glanced at them, then swept his powerful arm in an arc that knocked the packages from Slocum's grip.

"Reckon they're not. Let's keep looking."

It was as Slocum had feared. The package China Mary wanted was the only thing missing from the mailbag.

"Let's keep riding," he said. Ah Sum grunted, nodded, and got onto his horse. It was going to be a longer search than Slocum had expected.

5

When Slocum awoke in the morning, the first thing he saw was Ah Sum sitting across from the dead campfire, staring at him. The Celestial had his hands tucked away in the voluminous folds of his padded jacket. Those folds moved slightly, as if stirred by inner winds. Otherwise, Ah Sum might have been chiseled from some sallow stone.

Slocum stretched and sat up. He looked around where they had made camp the night before. The mailbag he had found was tossed over near the Chinaman. Slocum wondered if Ah Sum had gone through the contents again, just to be sure the package his mistress wanted wasn't still there. He doubted it. Ah Sum did not look like the sort who ever made a mistake.

Silently, Slocum built a new fire and got it blazing. He put a coffeepot on to boil while he went hunting for something to eat. In spite of being close to the river with all its undergrowth, Slocum couldn't find anything worth shooting. When he returned, Ah Sum was gobbling up rice he had fixed using the boiling water in the coffeepot. Slocum threw out the rice water and refilled the pot. He needed coffee, not rice.

Ah Sum continued scooping the sticky rice into his mouth

using two fingers. When he finished, he cleaned his hands by rubbing them against his jacket. Then he sank down and once more turned into a statue.

Slocum drank his coffee and boiled some oatmeal for breakfast. As he ate, he decided the oatmeal wasn't that different from the rice, but he preferred his own victuals.

"Ready?" Slocum finished packing his gear and saddled his horse. By the time he mounted, Ah Sum was astride his horse and impassively watching. Slocum had seen a cat with the same look as it followed a mouse. The thought didn't make him feel any more comfortable.

Walking slowly along the trail, Slocum kept an eye peeled for anything to hint that the outlaws had come this way. He knew this was the right direction but more than a week had passed. If the robbers had China Mary's package, they wouldn't be inclined to stick around. What bothered him the most was how single-minded the robbers were. There had to be money in some envelopes in the mailbag slung behind him. There had to be money in the mail car as well, but they hadn't bothered with it. They had wanted one thing only.

What was in China Mary's parcel?

"Why would the robbers stay around here?" Slocum asked aloud. Ah Sum looked hard at him but otherwise didn't even nod or shake his head. "They had something they intended to sell to somebody else. Is that it?"

Ah Sum remained stolid with not so much as a flicker of emotion in his dark eyes. In spite of his poker face, the Celestial betrayed just enough to Slocum to know he had hit the target. He worked over this possibility and was about to ask Ah Sum another question when he pulled back hard on the reins, causing his horse to rear.

They had ridden down near the San Pedro River. At this spot the water flowed briskly. His horse's nostrils flared. If his acute sense of danger hadn't stopped him, he would have thought the horse only scented the water.

Slocum went for his Colt and had it out and cocked when

he heard a grunt followed by a dull thud. He swung around in the saddle to see Ah Sum pull a hatchet out from the folds of his sleeves. His first hatchet had been thrown with devastating accuracy, and he'd driven it deep into an ambusher's forehead. The thud Slocum had heard was the sharp blade splitting open the owlhoot's skull.

"There're at least two more," Slocum said. He jumped to the ground and went to kneel beside the dead man. Slocum searched his pockets and took out a few dollars. He tucked them into his own pocket. The dead man wasn't going to need them, and Slocum deserved something for all his trouble.

"There's nothing on him. How big is the package?" Slocum looked up at Ah Sum. The Chinaman sat astride his horse with his hatchet in his hand. He turned his head slowly as he listened.

Slocum didn't hear any movement in the brush along the riverbanks. The dead man had been stationed here as a sentry to warn the others. Gripping the leather-wrapped handle of the hatchet, Slocum pulled it free. For a heart-stopping instant, he thought the dead man sighed. Then he realized it was only air gusting out of the man's lungs. He had been killed so fast he hadn't even exhaled before he died.

Slocum silently handed the bloody ax back to the Celestial. He put his finger to his lips and pointed up the riverbank. If he had posted a guard here, that's where Slocum would have his main camp. The sentry's death had been so quiet he doubted anybody in the camp would know anything was wrong yet.

In spite of making his way to the camp as silently as any Apache, three men were waiting for him with six-shooters leveled. Slocum hit the ground as the first blast of hot lead seared above his head.

He didn't have a clean shot so he held back. He fought three men and had only his six-gun. The odds weren't with him, so he'd have to change that or end up mighty dead mighty quick.

"You ain't stealin' it. We won't let you!" The robber do-ing the shouting only meant his words as a diversion. Slocum heard movement to his left, rolled onto his side, and fired three times. Then added a fourth slug to finish the job. The outlaw crumpled to the ground.

"What is it you think I intend to steal?" Slocum shouted his question to give himself time to reload. If he held the remaining two at bay just long enough . . .

He looked up into the muzzle of a rifle pointed at his head. The outlaw grinned. A scar on his upper lip turned it into a sneer.

"Looky here. I got myself a sneak thief."

"You got the drop on him, you shoot him, you dumbass!" The other outlaw sounded irked.

"You heard what my crazy partner said. I ain't got no choice but—" The outlaw's rifle discharged, but the bullet missed Slocum by a foot. "Damn, what hit me?"

The outlaw turned and Slocum saw a hatchet embedded in the man's shoulder. He lifted his Colt and fired twice, both bullets hitting the back of the man's head. He tumbled for-ward, his forehead blown away in a spray of blood as the slugs exited just above his left eye. Slocum swung his six-gun around when he heard a small sound, but it was only Ah Sum coming to retrieve his hatchet.

Slocum motioned for the Celestial to circle while he en-gaged the surviving outlaw.

"We can dicker," Slocum called. "Your life for the pack-age. It can't be worth that much."

"Like hell it ain't," came the surprising reply. "I'd die for it. I'd die without it!"

Slocum heard the pounding of horse's hooves and knew the outlaw fled. He scrambled to his feet but did not rush into the camp, fearing a trap. Stampeding a couple horses to make it sound as if he hightailed it might let the owlhoot set up another ambush.

Changing his direction, Slocum circled and found the rope

strung between two trees. Three horses nervously pawed at the ground. Unless there had been a spare horse, only one had left the camp.

Slocum pushed closer until he could look around the thick trunk of a cottonwood to see a smoldering campfire. Four bedrolls were still spread out, three recently slept in, showing how fast the outlaw had left camp when he heard Slocum coming. He moved to a different tree to get a better look at the camp and decided it was empty. His quarry had fled.

From the opposite side, Ah Sum lumbered into view, a hatchet in each hand.

Slocum stepped out, took in the danger the Chinaman faced, then yelled, "Run! It's a trap!"

Ah Sum stopped but did not dive for cover. He glared at Slocum without understanding what was about to happen.

Slocum put down his head and ran as hard as he could, vaulting the campfire to crash into the Celestial, knocking him backward as an immense explosion lifted them both high into the air.

6

"Don't mind if I do," Judge Rollins said, taking another slug of whiskey from the bottle Jackson Pine had brought as a bribe. "You surely do know how to find fine whiskey." The judge held up the drinking glass filled with two fingers of the amber liquid, sloshed it around, then sniffed almost daintily at it before knocking back the entire contents. He wiped his lips with the back of his hand and carefully put the glass onto his desk, as if he feared it would break.

"A brother of mine back in Kentucky sends a case or two out whenever I ask," Pine said. He lounged back in the chair in front of the desk, studying the judge closely for any sign that there might need to be a more lucrative bribe offered. The hint at a case of decent whiskey went a long way with a man who couldn't stop swilling the trade whiskey served in most of the local saloons.

"Give him my regards when you write to him next," Rollins said. He smacked his lips and looked appreciatively at the empty glass.

"I can send a telegram," Pine said. The small smile on the judge's face told him his bribe had been accepted. He relaxed a little more since he would have been hard-pressed to come up with even a hundred dollars cash money. If Rollins had demanded silver, Pine would have needed to find a different approach.

"I have a great deal of work to do, Jackson," the judge said. "Is there anything I can do for you?"

"Nothing, Judge, except keep the rest of that bottle of fine whiskey safe for me."

"That might be considered a bribe."

"For the next time I come to visit. Just keep it for me."

"Evaporation is mighty bad in this godforsaken desert," the judge said, pursing his lips thoughtfully.

"So be it." Pine got to his feet and started to leave. He stopped at the door, turned, and said, "By the way, Judge. Did you get a chance to sign those papers?"

"What papers are those, Jackson?"

"Might be your clerk is behind with his work. I know how busy you are."

"A judge's work is never done," Rollins said pompously.

Pine patted his pockets and acted surprised. "I just happen to have a duplicate set of papers." He drew the sheaf of documents from his coat and placed them in front of the judge.

"What are these?" Rollins put on reading glasses and held the sheets at arm's length to see the fine print.

"A tax lien, that's all. Mr. Ike Tarkenton hasn't paid property taxes, and I am offering to pay them."

"You left out the date for the first assessment." Rollins looked up over the rims of his glasses.

"That's so you can enter the date, Judge. It's been a full year since taxes were paid."

"Only a year? The city would get more in taxes if it was eighteen months."

Pine seethed. He had to pay the back taxes to seize the miner's property. Rollins was extorting him because that extra money would never be dropped into the city of Tombstone's coffers.

"I must have looked at my calendar wrong. It's good I had you look over the lien before I filed it with the county clerk."

Rollins smirked, entered the bogus date, then signed the papers with a flourish before handing them back to Pine.

"See you in court, Counselor."

"Thank you, Judge." Pine hurried from the room before the crooked judge thought up other ways to extort even more money. More galling yet, Pine had to wire the distillery in Kentucky and pay their sky-high prices to send a case of whiskey. Not for the first time, he wished he did have a brother there to ship the whiskey. His pa and two sisters had died of cholera, and his mother would never stoop to dealing with a whiskey vendor.

He crossed the courthouse lobby and filed the papers. The clerk never questioned the documents in spite of the date from eighteen months earlier being as wet as the judge's signature allowing Pine to seize the mine. He had seen worse—probably that very day. It was how justice worked in Tombstone.

With the legal documents securely in his pocket, Pine stepped out onto the courthouse steps, where Childress waited for him.

"I wish we coulda met up somewhere else," Childress said, looking around nervously.

"Being this close to justice makes you uneasy?"

"I been in too many courtrooms to know there ain't no such critter as justice."

"You are wrong, sir," Pine said. "I have the eviction notice here."

Pine forced himself not to take a step away when it looked as if Childress might spit on him.

"Don't cotton much to legal ways," was all the man said.

"Go fetch our horses over in the livery stable down on Fremont Street," Pine said. "I want to deliver this directly to Tarkenton so I can get the condemnation proceedings under way."

Childress grunted and almost flew down the steps in his

haste to get away from the courthouse. Whistling, Pine went to the bottom of the steps, feeling good with the world.

"You're a miserable, no account, low-down son of a bitch!"

He turned to see another well-dressed man storming down Toughnut Street, fists balled and face a thundercloud of anger.

"Good afternoon to you, too, Jeremy."

"Don't 'good afternoon' me, you snake in the grass." The other lawyer planted his feet and took a swing. His aim was off, but his knuckles still brushed past Pine's face. As he reacted, jerking back, Pine felt a throb in the bruise Slocum had put there with the barrel of his gun. This staggered him more than the actual blow.

"I'll have you arrested for battery! What's got into you?"

"You double-crossed me. You said we would split fifty-fifty on the Kensington case. You took it all. I want my cut, you—"

"Not so loud," Pine said, looking around to see if any potential clients might be watching. It never paid to air dirty laundry in front of people who could pay you mountains of money later for legal representation. Although he had heard of a few lawyers from along the Row who got into fights regularly and how this increased their business, Pine thought they only skimmed the lowest levels of society for clients. The dregs. The upper class, the ones he aspired to represent, looked askance at such public brawling. Some of the richest men in Tombstone had fought their way up from hard-rock miner to magnate, but more had come from back East with wagons of cash to buy their way into even greater wealth. These were the men he wanted to impress, the very men he wanted to represent.

"Not so loud?" Jeremy screamed. He rocked back, turned his face to the sky, and yelled, "Jackson Pine is a crook. He stole two hundred dollars in fees from me!"

Pine began to worry now because the shouting drew attention, both from the courthouse and from town. Passersby slowed to see what the ruckus was about.

"You're drunk," Pine said as loudly as he could and still maintain decorum.

"I'm a Mormon. I don't drink, you festering pustule. You—" Jeremy launched himself at Pine and knocked him down. Stunned, Pine looked up and saw double. Then he saw nothing. For a moment he wondered if the desert sun hadn't caused a hallucination, then hands helped him stand and he heard several clerks from the courthouse muttering.

One said to him, "Are you all right, Mr. Pine? It was an out-and-out case of him attacking you. You didn't do anything to provoke him. If you need a witness in court . . ." The clerk's voice trailed off, leaving it up to Pine to suggest ways that the testimony might become even better—for an additional price.

"My head hurts like a nest of hornets has moved into it."

"Maybe you ought to let the doc look at it. I think he's sober today."

"Yes, right away," Pine said. The crowd slowly dissipated, the gossip already starting. Before Pine could ask what had happened to Jeremy, the others were gone.

From behind the courthouse he heard a muffled shot. He stumbled around, going up the steps and through the lobby. Two clerks poked their heads out, looking worried.

"You hear a shot, Mr. Pine?"

"I don't know. Let me look out back." He still fought to think clearly, but he remembered a little more from the flash he had seen after Jeremy had knocked him to the ground. Going down the back steps, he saw Childress standing over the lawyer, a smoking six-shooter in his hand.

"He tried to hit me," Childress said. "No man gets by doin' that. Nobody."

"Is he dead?"

"He damn well better be or I wasted a damned round

through his damned head." He lifted his six-shooter to fire again. Pine grabbed the man's wrist and forced the gun away. Again he saw the wildness in Childress's eyes and the possibility he would turn the gun on anyone crossing him.

"As your attorney, I'm advising you to get the hell out of town. Go south somewhere in the hills, camp, and try not to be seen. Jeremy wasn't the most beloved of souls in Tombstone but he had friends."

"Law friends?" This time Childress did spit. The gob missed Pine's boot by inches.

"Possibly. A couple of his clients are real desperadoes."

"That don't worry me none."

"Go, ride. Get away and hide out for a few days until this blows over. Nobody will much care about Jeremy, but anything you do right now will only force Marshal Sosa to throw you in jail."

"I'll ventilate him if he tries!"

"This is easier. A few days, Childress. That's all. And I'll be paying you to stay out of sight until we can serve process on Tarkenton."

"Yeah, he has a silver mine you want to steal."

Pine looked indignant, producing a guffaw from the outlaw.

"You steal with a pen. I use a six-shooter."

"Use a horse and ride out of here."

"Not sure I don't prefer that ole swayback mule I rode into town on."

"I traded it away for this horse. Now ride, dammit, *ride*!"

Raising voices from inside the courthouse settled the matter. Childress swung into the saddle and galloped away, going down the steep embankment just behind the courthouse and finding his way through the scrub brush. In less than a minute he had disappeared into the desert.

This gave Pine time enough to compose himself and start practicing his story.

"What's goin' on, Counselor?" Marshal Sosa asked.

"It's my colleague, Jeremy Young. We were discussing a legal matter when he suddenly left and went around the courthouse. I don't know what prompted him to do so, but he did. When he didn't return after a few minutes, I came and saw him like this. He was . . ."

Pine continued to spin his tale, as if he were in court pleading a case in front of a jury. In a way he was.

And he won his case. The marshal did nothing more than order a small boy to fetch the undertaker. No further questions were asked. After all, the dead man was only a lawyer from Rotten Row.

7

The explosion lifted Slocum and hurled him into Ah Sum. It felt as if he were being squashed like a bug between a fly-swatter and a wall.

Slocum landed atop the bulky Celestial with a thud. It dazed him, but the pain on his back brought him around fast. He rolled over and knew his coat was on fire. He kept rolling in the dirt and weeds until the last spark had been extinguished. He sat up. Ah Sum already stood, hatchets in both hands, staring at him with those unreadable eyes.

"The owlhoot planted a stick of dynamite with a long fuse. He expected us to come into the camp, poke around looking for the package long enough so he could blow us up."

Ah Sum looked away for a moment at the deep pit blown in the ground beside the campfire, then looked back at Slocum. He nodded several times. Other than when he threw his hatchets, this was the most animated Ah Sum had been since he had accompanied Slocum.

"Get our horses while I search the camp, just in case he left the package." Slocum got to his feet but Ah Sum didn't move a muscle. Slocum started to repeat his orders, then said, "You search the camp for China Mary's package and I'll get the horses."

When Slocum rode back, he found Ah Sum standing with arms crossed, as if he hadn't moved. The camp had been torn apart, the outlaws' belongings scattered everywhere. A ripped-apart leather bag caught Slocum's eye. The glint of gold coins reflected in the sunlight. He looked at it, then at Ah Sum.

"You see that?" Slocum asked. He got no response from the huge Celestial, so he jumped down and pawed through the pile of clothing until he found the ripped leather bag. Catching one coin between thumb and forefinger, he held it up for the other man to inspect. Ah Sum didn't blink an eye.

Slocum shrugged, gathered the coins, and shoved them into his pocket. He didn't bother counting but he had at least a hundred dollars in specie to show for being shot at by a gang of outlaws. He swung back into the saddle and studied the terrain.

"He went that way, but we ought to be careful. Did you find any more dynamite?"

Ah Sum shook his head.

Slocum thought on this a moment, then said, "He's still got some with him. Maybe not much but enough to blow us to hell and gone. We were lucky I saw the burning fuse when I did or we'd both be dead." Ah Sum didn't twitch a muscle. "I saved your life." No response. "You saved mine and I saved yours. We're even."

Slocum might as well have been talking to a brick wall. He put his heels to his gelding's flanks, tapped the flat of the spurs against horseflesh, and took off at a trot. The fleeing outlaw wasn't likely to slow down and prepare another stick or two of dynamite and then wait to light the fuse. The only reason Slocum could figure that he had any at all was to blow open a safe on the train. Since the mailbags had been stacked up and not locked up in a vault, there hadn't been any need for the explosive.

Slocum wished he'd had time to examine the camp on his own. If these were miners, they wouldn't be anywhere near as dangerous as if they were desperadoes intent on killing and making a living from their thievery. That galled him most about Childress getting away. The man was a cattle thief and ought to have been locked up. From the couple days Slocum had ridden with him as a prisoner, Childress had revealed himself to be a cold-blooded cayuse capable of about any crime.

He stopped thinking about Childress and started serious tracking. The fleeing outlaw had made no attempt to hide his trail—there hadn't been time. But the man had ridden fast and hard, making Slocum wonder if his horse would collapse under him soon.

If they stayed among the trees following the riverbed, the opportunities presenting themselves for an ambush were magnified. Slocum became warier as they rode, and he finally motioned for Ah Sum to ride closer. The Celestial did so.

In a low voice Slocum said, "Keep a sharp eye out for the robber. His horse is all tuckered out by now, so he's going to try to shoot us out of the saddle." When he got no response, Slocum asked, "Do you understand?"

Ah Sum turned his head and gave Slocum a look of pure hatred. The Celestial understood.

"Go to hell," Slocum said. For two cents he'd ride off and never look back, but he felt some obligation to China Mary for getting him out of jail. He could send back some of the gold with Ah Sum for his mistress to repay her, but he had promised to retrieve whatever had been stolen from her. The hunt was increasingly dangerous, but Slocum's honor mattered more than getting shot.

More than because he had given his word, Slocum wanted to find out what China Mary thought was so valuable. Whatever it was, the outlaws thought so, too. They could have pilfered any of the mailbags but had stopped when they got to the one with the Tombstone mistress's package in it.

The tracks in a muddy stretch along the river caused

Slocum to pull up and look ahead for possible ambush sites. The outlaw's horse had started to falter, its gait becoming uneven from fatigue. Slocum turned and finally singled out a clump of brush where a man might lie in wait. He pointed this out to Ah Sum, who nodded once then rode at an angle to get behind any ambusher.

Slocum waited a full minute for the Celestial to get around, then rode forward slowly, his hand resting on the ebony handle of his six-shooter. He drew and fired when the bush shook, then he swung about and started to shoot ten yards in the direction of the river. The outlaw had rigged a piece of string to make the bush into a decoy and Slocum had fallen for it.

"Who are you?" the outlaw asked, his rifle leveled at Slocum. "Tell me what you want."

"The package you stole from the mail car. It belongs to China Mary."

"Of course it does. Who else'd it belong to? You killed the others? My partners?"

Slocum judged how fast he'd have to move to get his six-gun around and aimed before the outlaw could draw back on the trigger. His chances didn't look good.

"Because of the package. You don't have to die for it. Hand it over and you can ride away."

"G-Give it to you?" The man's voice almost cracked with strain. "I need it. I *need* it."

The bush rustled, momentarily distracting the outlaw. The rifle barrel swung the slightest amount toward the bush, giving Slocum the chance to squeeze off a round. Whether his bullet or Ah Sum's hatchet ended the outlaw's life would be something other men could argue over for years. Slocum didn't give two hoots and a holler. The outlaw was dead, maybe from both a bullet in the head and a hatchet in his chest.

"I hear his horse snorting and pawing the ground," Slocum said, dismounting. He walked through the brush to find the outlaw's lathered horse, whites showing around the eyes and nostrils flaring. Approaching slowly, Slocum grabbed the reins

and kept the horse from rearing. He spent a full minute sooth-
ing the horse, then worked his way back and pulled the saddlebags free.

He dumped the contents to the muddy ground. He found
another bag of coins, these all silver. He tucked them away in
his other coat pocket, giving him a bulge on either side. But
the item that caught his eye was about the size of a brick
wrapped up in black oilcloth. Hefting it, he found it lighter
than he had expected.

He rubbed away part of the oilcloth and exposed waxed paper underneath. Using his fingernail to cut through the corner,
a thick black tar oozed out.

"Son of a bitch," he said. He brought back his arm to throw
the package into the river, then froze.

Ah Sum stood with his arm drawn back, ready to release
one of his deadly hatchets.

"This is opium. China Mary sent me to find her opium!"

Ah Sum didn't move a muscle. Neither did Slocum. If he
heaved the opium into the river, he would die. There wasn't
any way the Celestial could miss with his hatchet at this range.
Worse, it wouldn't destroy the opium, so all Slocum would
lose was his life.

"Here," he said, dropping it to the ground. "Take this devil's
venom back to China Mary. I don't care how many men die in
Tombstone from chasing the dragon."

But he did.

8

"You're all thieves, damned thieves, I say!"

"Bailiff, restrain that man," ordered Judge Rollins. He slammed his gavel down repeatedly until the bailiff summoned two deputies from outside the courtroom, who forced the miner into a chair, where he continued to struggle. "Mr. Tarkenton, you will respect this court and show decorum or I'll throw your sorry ass into jail!"

"He's tryin' to steal my claim, Judge," Ike Tarkenton said. He glared at Jackson Pine, who sat impassively at a nearby table, papers in neat stacks in front of him and a law book open with a red grosgrain ribbon dangling from it as a bookmark. "I ain't behind on no taxes. I've always paid, real prompt, too! Look it up!"

"I have examined the records. You are in arrears on the subsidiary and augmentative taxes."

"What're them taxes? Never in all my born days have I heard anything like them bein' owed." Tarkenton stared at the judge in disbelief.

"Your Honor, may I?" Pine stood and struck a pose, one

hand on his lapel and the other making broad sweeping motions he hoped would distract attention from the miner.

"Sure, Jackson, make your pitch to the court. It's got to be better than listening to this . . . defendant."

"Ignorance of all taxes owed is no defense. That is a matter of jurisprudence and tax law we must stand by and obey to maintain order in the community and provide for its public services. It is clear that Mr. Tarkenton has ignored paying all taxes and levies required on his claim."

"The Molly E is my claim! Mine!"

"I have the proper plat survey on this, uh, Molly E Mine, and it clearly shows a section of land to the northeast that has been used to raise cattle."

"I ain't got no cattle. I'm a miner and the Molly E's my property, not yers or anybody else's!"

"Your Honor, please," Pine said.

Rollins rapped the gavel until Tarkenton quieted, then said, "You hold your water, Ike Tarkenton, 'til Mr. Pine's said his piece."

"Thank you, Your Honor. This segment of Tarkenton's claim shows that it is multi-use and therefore not only accessed as a mineral source but also one required to pay taxes for raising cattle."

"I ain't got no cattle," Tarkenton said. "If I did, I'd eat the varmints. I'm livin' on beans and oatmeal. If I had a steak, I'd damn well eat it!"

"Be that as it may, this segment of his land requires that additional taxes need to be paid—and they have not."

"Seems clear-cut to me," Judge Rollins said. "You got anything you want to say, Tarkenton?"

"This is robbery! You might as well hold me up with a gun as spoutin' a law that don't make no sense."

"You are, ahem, two years in arrears." Pine looked sharply at the judge, who smiled. "Pay the taxes or lose the entire property."

"I paid what was owed. I ain't payin' one goddamn cent more to thieves like you!"

"Deputy Eakins, take this man into custody for contempt of court. He will remain in lockup until he apologizes to this court."

"Apologize! I want to beat your damned brains out, you thievin'—"

Tarkenton squawked like a chicken as two deputies dragged him from the courtroom. When the last of his protests faded away, Rollins turned to Jackson Pine and rapped his gavel again.

"When payment of the taxes is made, the Molly E claim will be yours, Counselor."

Pine seethed at the way Rollins had done him out of another six months' taxes. An honest crook stayed bribed, and Rollins had shown himself to be as crooked as a dog's hind leg.

"Thank you, Your Honor. Expect the payment soon." He gathered his papers, closed his law book that had been open to a random page, and started to leave, but the judge stopped him.

"A moment, Mr. Pine. Another case has come to my attention."

Pine sucked in his breath. He knew what was coming.

"I believe Childress is a client of yours? He has been implicated in the death of Jeremy Young, a colleague of yours."

"I have no knowledge of where Mr. Childress is, Your Honor."

"Of course not. Didn't say you did. Just be warned. A warrant for his arrest has been issued. There wasn't anything I could do about that since it seems cut and dried he did the crime."

"I understand, Your Honor." Pine waited until the judge made a vague brushing motion to dismiss him. The lawyers for the next case were already filing into the courtroom, their clients loudly deriding each other.

Pine stepped into the courthouse lobby and looked around, almost expecting to see Childress waiting there. He had enlisted the aid of a dangerous man and that mistake was going to haunt him for a good, long while. Since Childress had come into his employ, he had killed two men. Jeremy was hardly a loss, but his murder caused unwanted repercussions. The way he had gunned down Simonetti to collect the money owed should have been a warning of worse to come, but Pine had needed the money. He only wished he had more of it left after paying off several of his most pressing debts. If he had not been forced by circumstance to pay those debts, he could get clear title to the Molly E Mine right away, but the men wanting their money hadn't been the sort to wait.

He could have set Childress on them.

Pine stood and looked down at his hands. They shook uncontrollably.

"What am I thinking? He's a killer. For two bits and a beer he'd kill me, too."

Pine thought hard on how to use Childress to the best effect. Cutting the man loose right away would forestall gaining the Molly E Mine, but how much longer could he control Childress? Was he even controlling him now? The only chance Pine had of getting rid of the man was for him to simply ride away—or be turned over to the marshal.

That was the more dangerous road to travel since Childress might get out and take revenge. Pine thought harder on the matter as he left the courthouse and went to the stables to get his horse. He needed to examine the mine to be certain Tarkenton hadn't done anything drastic like booby-trap it. The miner might not have thought he would be thrown into jail, but Pine had dealt with other miners who were so suspicious they rigged shotgun traps and even set dead falls to collapse their claims should anyone else venture into them.

He took the road to the southeast, then slowed as he got into the heat of the day. He pulled down the brim of his bowler, but it did little to shield his eyes from the sun. The heat mounted, and it wasn't even summer yet. Pine slowed even more when he saw a trail leading due east off the road, going into a patch of rugged territory where he had sent Childress to hide out. The rustler might have kept riding. Bisbee wasn't that far down the road and would draw an outlaw like him.

Pine rubbed his lips, then took the trail into the patch of badlands, if any part of this godforsaken country could be called worse than any other. Less than an hour into the tumble of rocks and thorny bushes, he got the feeling of being watched.

"Childress!" No response. He called again. This time more than a sluggish wind stirred the undergrowth. Coming out from behind a creosote bush rose the outlaw, a rifle in his hands.

"Didn't expect to ever see the likes of you in this country, Counselor. You might get dust on your boots."

"You stirred up a hornet's nest in town," Pine said. "I don't know when the furor will die down."

"Don't matter much to me, 'cept I can't get into any of them saloons to take a sip of good whiskey."

Pine thought of the bottle he had bribed the judge with. It had been wasted since Rollins screwed him out of a full year's taxes on the Molly E Mine. It would have been wasted bribing Childress for his loyalty, too. Pine's cottony mouth longed for a pull of that good Kentucky bourbon.

"Wish I could help, but I didn't bring any whiskey with me."

"Didn't think a fancy-ass lawyer would have rotgut in his saddlebags," Childress said. Pine noticed the rustler didn't lower the rifle.

"I need to go to the Molly E Mine. You want to ride along to see what I'm angling to get?"

"This the mine you're swindlin' Tarkenton out of?"

"I object to the insinuation that I am somehow hornswoggling him."

"Counselor, you forged the taxes against him." Childress laughed, and it was an ugly sound. "I steal cows. That is being honest. You steal by shuffling papers so fast a three-card monte dealer would get crossed eyes."

"If you want to come along, do it. If not, go back into your rat hole."

"Don't you have a mouth on you," Childress said, laughing again. "I been out here long enough. Time to get me some new scenery. Where's this here mine you're stealin'?"

Pine did not respond. Being accused of thievery by the likes of Childress rankled. While he did Ike Tarkenton no favors, the miner would only squander the money he got from the silver he grubbed from the mine on whores and whiskey. Pine had more noble uses for the money.

"You go on, Counselor, and I'll catch up." Childress faded back into the vegetation. Pine tried to make out where the man went by watching for the movement of leaves or limbs. He couldn't do it. This made him even angrier that human debris like Childress could be better at anything than a lawyer trained to maintain order in society.

He tugged on his horse's reins and got the horse trotting back to the distant road. He reached it, then continued toward Bisbee, only veering away when he saw a crudely painted wood sign declaring that he was on Molly E Mine property and that trespassers would be shot.

"Had quite a sense of humor, didn't he?"

Pine jumped. He hadn't realized Childress had ridden up. How the man did so and while mounted worried Pine a little more than it should have. He had been lost in thought of all the civic good he intended to do with the silver from this mine.

"What do you mean?"

"I seen Tarkenton. He wouldn't be able to hit the broad side of a barn if he was locked inside. How did he expect to defend his mine against claim jumpers?" Childress laughed again.

"Wait, he didn't. He lost it to a legal claim jumper, didn't he, Counselor?"

Pine had nothing to say. He rode on the double-rutted road to a shack about ready to fall down. A strong wind would finish forcing it northward and collapse it. For the moment, it was sturdy enough to live in while Tarkenton worked his claim.

"You want it burned down?"

"Why bother?"

"Bugs. A miner's always got a passel of bugs crawlin' all o'er him. You lie down on any mattress in there and you'll get fleas and worse."

"I'm more interested in the mine," Pine said.

"Always go for the money. Right, Counselor?" Childress swung his leg over his saddle horn and dropped to the ground with a thud. He settled his six-shooter and strutted toward the mouth of the mine shaft.

Pine considered going into the mine with Childress, but a momentary fear of being left dead inside assailed him. But he discarded this as fanciful. What would Childress gain? Killing Simonetti and Jeremy Young had been unfortunate, self-defense, hardly more than accidents or misunderstandings. Pine knew what Childress was and could deal with the rustler. He dismounted and went to the mine.

Childress had gone more than fifteen feet deeper into the mine and stopped to call back, "Can't find no damn miner's candles. You think that son of a bitch worked in the dark?"

"Candles are expensive," Pine said. He looked around the mouth of the mine, thinking Tarkenton might have left his only source of illumination as he worked somewhere nearby and easy to find. Seeing nothing, he went a few feet into the mine and looked for a ledge where the miner might have stashed supplies.

Nothing.

"I'll check his cabin. Might be he used all the candles but was called into town for his court appearance before he could replace his supplies inside the mine shaft." Pine left Childress to poke around in the mine. Without decent light, there wasn't anything he could find.

Pine went to the dilapidated cabin and pried open the door. The creaking door frame made him step back, wary of the building falling down around his ears. Leaving the door open, he went into the cabin. The only light filtering in came through cracks in the walls. Tarkenton hadn't even bothered to cut himself a window.

Turning so he no longer blocked the light from the door, Pine began rummaging around, hunting for candles. He uncovered a kerosene lamp and decided this was the best he was going to find. As he turned, a shadow blocked the doorway.

"Childress?"

"No, you trespassing fool. Is he your hired gun?"

Pine fumbled in his pocket and lit the wick, then closed the chimney so he could see who was speaking.

"Wakefield!"

"Who else would be out here?"

"I don't know why you're here unless Tarkenton hired you to represent him. If so, you're in for a big loss. I've got the tax papers and—"

"Shut up, you two-bit shyster."

"Look who's talking," Pine flared. He held the lamp higher and removed more of the shadow from Colin Wakefield's face. "You're the crookedest lawyer along the Row."

"It makes you jealous, doesn't it?"

He stepped forward but Wakefield did not budge.

"Let me out."

"Like hell. I'll see you in jail for trespassing on my land."

Pine filled the doorway, but the other lawyer wasn't retreating. Behind him stood two gunmen, hands resting on their pistols.

"You're here to steal the mine, aren't you? It can't be anything legal. I've got Judge Rollins's signature on the tax lien I filed against this place."

"All forgeries and trumped-up tax claims. If I have to go to the federal judge down in Bisbee to get Rollins's ass tossed off the bench, I'll do it. He's your lackey, and I'm not letting you steal this silver mine. It's too damn valuable."

"You mean you intend to steal it from me."

"Like you did from Tarkenton."

"It's legal," Pine insisted. He wished he carried a gun. He saw how Wakefield's coat hung open and showed a pistol tucked away in a shoulder rig. Even if the other lawyer hadn't been armed, he had two men with him who were. Pine had seen them around Tombstone but hadn't paid them much attention other than to be sure they didn't need legal representation for their crimes.

They obviously didn't need his legal expertise if they worked for Colin Wakefield.

"You never figured out how things work here in Arizona Territory, have you, Pine? It's not just who can bribe the judges the most, it's also about who can back up their claims with a few ounces of hot lead."

"The law of the gun," Pine said, his eyes darting about.

"How poetic. I like to think of it as 'whoever has the gun, rules.'"

Pine feinted right and got Wakefield moving to block him. As the lawyer got out of his way, Pine threw the kerosene lamp at the two gunslicks. One reacted faster than any man Pine had ever seen, drawing and firing. This made it worse. His slug blew apart the base of the glass lamp and spattered kerosene everywhere. When the wick turned and touched part of the spatter, a tiny puff followed by an explosion knocked the two gunmen back, setting one on fire.

The commotion made Wakefield turn to see what happened. Pine kicked out, tangled his foot between Wakefield's, and sent the lawyer tumbling to the ground. His respite wouldn't be long. Pine lit out for the mine, yelling for Childress.

All he got for his trouble was a fusillade directed his way from both of the men crouched by the mouth of the mine shaft. Wakefield had brought four gunmen with him.

"Childress!" Pine shouted again. He saw a dark shape moving inside the mine and hoped it was the rustler. It wasn't.

Wakefield had brought five gunmen with him, and one had been inside the mine. Childress was probably dead.

Pine began dodging the bullets kicking up dust and ricocheting off stone all around his feet. It was only a matter of seconds before they found the range, and he would be ventilated a dozen ways to Sunday.

He caught the toe of his shoe and fell facedown on the ground. This caused Wakefield's henchmen to miss with their next shots. Then a shot came that sounded different, deeper, throatier but muffled. A scream immediately followed the report. Pine rolled over and looked back at the mine shaft. The gunman who had emerged lay on the ground kicking feebly. The other two stood and stared stupidly as Childress walked out and calmly shot the man on his left and then finished off the one to his right with two more shots.

"Childress! There're two more—three more!" Pine was too frightened to think straight.

"Get the horses, Counselor," Childress said in his mocking tone. "I'll handle this." Childress bent, scooped up a pair of fallen six-shooters, and began blazing away in the direction of the cabin, a pistol in each hand.

The smell of burning cloth and flesh caught on the wind and sickened Pine, but he wasn't going to simply lie in the dust and get himself killed by Colin Wakefield or anybody else. Scrambling, feet kicking up a small dust cloud, he found traction and ran to where they had left their horses. He snared the reins and climbed into the saddle.

At the mine Childress still fired away like a one-man army.

Pine didn't even consider the odds. He galloped to the mine, yanking hard on the reins of Childress's horse.

The rustler dropped the six-guns he had picked up, vaulted into the saddle, and said, "You surprised me, Counselor. You showed some balls comin' back for me."

Laughing demoniacally, Childress raced off. He grabbed his Stetson and waved it above his head like he was riding a bucking bronco. Pine wasted no time following.

He wondered what the hell kind of fight he had gotten himself into—and how he could profit from it.

9

"You know what that is and what it can do to hopheads," Slocum said to Ah Sum. "You know what misery it causes. I've seen opium dens in San Francisco with men so far gone into the opium dreams that they just waste away. Smoking is more important to them than eating."

Ah Sum didn't twitch a muscle. The grip on his hatchets never loosened, and Slocum had the feeling that any shift in this Mexican standoff, however slight, would mean one of them would die.

"I had a friend who died from smoking opium," Slocum said. He swallowed hard as he remembered Cara and how she had slowly descended into the hell of an opium smoker. He had tried to get her back, and she had turned violent. He had loved her and he thought she had loved him, but it turned out the opium was stronger. It had taken her life.

Ah Sum finally moved, indicating Slocum should pick up the brick of opium and hand it over. He kept his arm back and the hatchet ready to cartwheel through the air into Slocum's head if he didn't obey.

Slocum carefully dropped to one knee and fumbled about

for the opium, all the while keeping his eyes on the Celestial. He felt the slick oilcloth and slipped his fingers underneath the package, then stood as slowly as he had knelt.

Holding it out, he made Ah Sum come to him for it. The Chinaman never relaxed his vigilance for an instant. Slocum intended to drop it and force Ah Sum to look down. In that instant he would act. Before he could do it, the opium was snatched from his hand with impossible speed and Ah Sum stepped away.

"You smoke opium? Do you chase the dragon?"

Ah Sum gave no flicker of understanding of what Slocum said, yet he had to know. He lowered his hatchet and cocked his head to one side, indicating it was time for them to return to Tombstone. Slocum had done what China Mary had asked.

"I'll go on from here," he said.

Ah Sum made a grunting sound that showed his displeasure with that. He gestured using his hatchet. Again Slocum considered how fast he could draw and fire. Once more Slocum discarded the idea that he was faster. It often took several bullets to kill a man. Slocum had heard of a bank robber shot fourteen times who was still able to make a getaway. Two others of the gang had nursed the man back to health, split the take three ways, and the last Slocum had heard, the robber was running a general store in Peoria. He didn't get around as well as he had before the robbery, but there was no need to be all that spry running a legitimate business.

No, Slocum could fire and hit Ah Sum but the Celestial would have his hatchet flying in the same instant. He might even throw his second. Slocum had seen how the Chinaman could use either hand when he reacted. Either—both—would be far deadlier than a single shot unless Slocum got lucky and hit the man's head or drilled a .36-caliber bullet through his heart. Even then, reflexes were hard to stop and Ah Sum was *fast*.

Slocum would bide his time.

They mounted and rode slowly away, leaving the robber's body for the insects and coyotes. He reckoned he had gotten all the gold off the gang that they carried. It was little enough pay, he knew, to be guarding a five-pound block of opium on its way to cause untold misery among the Tombstone miners.

After several hours of riding, Slocum pleaded the case to make camp, eat, and rest for the night. At daybreak the next day they were on the trail again and reached Tombstone by sundown the following day.

He sat astride his gelding, looking down Fremont Street. The saloons were already filled with miners seeking a moment's relief from the aches and pains of their occupation. He had more than a few of his own after being in the saddle for almost five days. As the lure of a shot of whiskey caused his mouth to water a mite, he felt a sharp poke in the ribs. Ah Sum pointed toward Hop Town and China Mary's butcher shop.

Reluctantly, Slocum rode away from the raucous cries and the sometimes shrill laughter of the soiled doves working the saloons. He could use a little companionship to go along with his whiskey. Enough gold rode in his pockets to have his pick of the women. He'd heard that some at the Crystal Palace or the Bird Cage Saloon weren't half bad looking.

As they approached the butcher shop, shadows began moving toward them. A half-dozen Celestials seemed to float out of hiding, their feet never touching the ground as they drew closer, as silent as ghosts. One took Ah Sum's horse without so much as a word being exchanged. Slocum handed his horse's reins to another, who bowed slightly in his direction and backed away, head lowered.

The butchers still worked, although it was long past sundown now. The white men in Tombstone were drinking away their wages. The Chinese continued working. Slocum pushed aside the curtain and went into the backroom with the single chair. China Mary sat there, as if she hadn't moved since she had sent him and her bodyguard out to recover the stolen opium.

Ah Sum stepped forward, bowed deeply, and handed the oilcloth-wrapped package to his mistress, the brick resting in both outstretched palms.

"You have done well," she said. Her fingers restlessly stroked over the brick, as if it were a cat and she tried to elicit a purr or two from it.

"I don't like the idea of dope," Slocum said.

"You drink."

"I need it to kill the pain sometimes."

"Opium does that also." She held it up, then extended her arms. "Take it."

Slocum didn't move.

"I don't understand. You're giving it to me?"

"Ah Sum will show where to deliver it. When it is given, your obligation is over, John Slocum."

He ought to have felt relieved, but he didn't. There were a hundred deaths wrapped up in this innocuous-looking package. China Mary sensed his reaction.

"Go. If you do not like what is done, return and we will discuss it more."

Ah Sum nudged him in the ribs with the haft of his hatchet. Slocum took the opium from China Mary and walked out, Ah Sum following closely. Outside the night was turning cooler by the minute, but the chill he felt had more to do with the package he carried than it did the desert's temperature.

The Celestial pointed back toward the heart of Tombstone. Slocum wondered if the Chinese were allowed to operate their opium dens so close to the saloons. In San Francisco and elsewhere with large Chinese populations, they were always segregated and kept away from white men, although those were the heaviest users of the drug.

Ah Sum steered him past the busiest part of Tombstone down Fremont Street and to the far northeast corner of town, where he could hardly hear the loud music and laughter from the saloons. He stopped and stared when he read the sign. Ah Sum nudged him, then gave him a poke in the ribs that downright hurt.

"There? You want me to deliver the opium there?" Another poke in the back got him moving forward. Slocum clutched the package and opened the door.

The odor of carbolic acid hit him immediately. A man sitting at a desk writing furiously in a journal looked up, adjusted his glasses, then took them off.

"Not often I get a patient who comes in on his own feet." He stood and came around the desk. "What can I do for you? Gunshot? No? Headache from too much whiskey?"

Slocum stared at the man.

"You're a doctor," he said.

"Name's Fritz Gottschalk. Some in Tombstone might not think I'm a doctor, but I'm better with humans than I am with horses. Now, what can I do for you?"

Slocum held out the brick of opium and said, "I was told to bring this to you."

"What is it?" Gottschalk reached out, touched the oilcloth, then grabbed. "China Mary got it!"

Slocum felt his belly knot up. The doctor was young, not more than thirty, and looked to be in good physical shape, but anyone this eager to get opium had to have a habit the size of the Rocky Mountains.

"I delivered it for her. I'd better go." Slocum started to leave when the door leading deeper into the surgery opened and a lovely woman with flame-red hair stepped out.

"What is it, Doctor?"

"Claire, she got it. China Mary got it for us." He held the opium up like it was tribute to some pagan god. He hurried past her into the back room, leaving her alone with Slocum.

"He's mighty eager to get a smoke," Slocum said. He didn't try to hide his disgust. The woman turned on him, her emerald eyes fixed on his. Her lips pulled back into a thin line as she almost spat the words.

"That's not for him. It's for my father."

"That makes all the difference in the world," Slocum said. This surgery hardly looked like an opium den, but then this wasn't one of the tunnels of the rat warren under Chinatown in San Francisco.

"He has cancer. My father has cancer and is in incredible pain. The opium dulls the pain. He . . . he probably won't live but at least his last days won't be spent in terrible agony."

"I didn't know," Slocum said awkwardly. "I apologize, Claire."

"Miss Norton," she said coldly. "You may call me Miss Norton."

"Apologies, Miss Norton," Slocum said. "All I was told was to recover the opium and deliver it here. I thought it was for a dope addict. China Mary didn't tell me it was for medicine." He started to go but the young woman caught his arm.

"Please, wait. You found the stolen opium? Thank you. You didn't have to do that, sir."

"Slocum, John Slocum. And yes, I did." He didn't want to get into the details.

"She's the only one in Tombstone who'd help him because . . . he's not very well liked."

This stopped Slocum dead in his tracks. From what he had seen in the short time he'd knocked around Tombstone, being liked wasn't all that common, but she made it sound as if her father was a complete outcast.

"What's he got? Leprosy?"

This produced a small laugh.

"Worse," she confided. "He's a lawyer."

"I can understand folks not liking him, then. I pistol-whipped a lawyer named Pine and got myself thrown in jail. If it hadn't been for China Mary, I'd still be there."

"Oh, I doubt you would have ever wanted to hit my father. He takes cases none of the others will. *Pro bono*."

"What's that?"

"For free. He represented China Mary and won for her a . . . respite from illegal taxes."

"She runs whorehouses. She can pay."

"I know what she does. My father does, too, but he arranged for her to bring in her brother from San Francisco. The mayor put on a terrible tax to keep the Chinese from immigrating to Tombstone. This was before she was the undisputed ruler of Hop Town."

Slocum marveled at how this town operated. Every boomtown had its own laws and customs, but Tombstone worked in ways he couldn't begin to fathom.

"He continues helping those in Hop Town who can't pay. No other lawyer will take a case from one of the Celestials. And he wins. He's such a good lawyer he makes them all look like idiots." Her grin was open and appreciative.

"That must irk about everybody."

"Everyone along Rotten Row." She smiled even more. "I see you've heard the name. My father's practice is at the far end of the rest of the lawyers' offices."

"You don't look like you belong here," Slocum said. "You have the look of . . ."

"Civilization?" Claire suggested. "I've only recently arrived here to take care of my father, after he fell ill. I was living in Boston."

"If your pa dies, you'll go back to Boston?"

Claire looked startled at the question. She started to speak, then clamped her lips together and chewed on her lower lip for a moment as she thought.

"I have not thought that far ahead. My mother died several years ago. That was when my father moved here to find new purpose in his life. I don't know where a similar quest will take me."

"I'd better go report to China Mary that the opium's been

delivered," Slocum said, not knowing what else to say. He felt that Claire wanted to keep talking. She had probably been cooped up in the doctor's office for days or even weeks as she tended her pa and hadn't been able to talk with anyone but Fritz Gottschalk.

Slocum opened the door and ran smack into someone coming in. He backed away, and his hand started for the six-shooter in its holster.

"You!" both he and Jackson Pine said simultaneously.

Slocum gave the lawyer a quick once-over and wondered where he had been. His dapper clothing was in tatters and more than one cut on his hands and face showed he had encountered something more damaging than getting a pistol barrel rammed against his head.

"Mr. Slocum mentioned you two had met," Claire said, obviously enjoying taunting Pine.

"He ought to be rotting in jail."

"And you ought to be rotting along Rotten Row," Slocum said.

"Miss Norton," Pine said, taking off his bowler and making what he obviously thought was a courtly bow. Slocum wanted to use his six-gun on the lawyer again and see how he reacted to that.

"Since you're not here to see me, I can only assume you came to consult with Dr. Gottschalk."

"I would go anywhere, anytime to see you, Miss Norton."

"You—" the woman began.

"You don't need to get those cuts patched up. You're doing just fine. You're not even bleeding much on the floor," Slocum said, moving so that he stood between the lawyer and Claire.

"What I do is none of your concern, Slocum. Seeing Claire is—"

"Miss Norton," Slocum corrected. "When you address her, you'll call her Miss Norton."

"You can't tell me what to do. How'd you get out of jail

anyway? I'll have a word with Marshal Sosa about releasing you without a court hearing." Pine's anger grew. The hotter under the collar he got, the more Slocum liked it.

"That's a right good idea. Go talk to the marshal," Slocum said. He stepped forward and forced Pine back. "Right now."

Pine sputtered, put his bowler back on, and left grumbling to himself.

"Thank you, Mr. Slocum," Claire said. She put her hand on his arm.

"I'll be glad to get rid of him anytime you want."

"Yes, for that, too. But thank you also for bringing the opium. This might be the first night in a very long time that my father's been able to rest without pain."

"If there's anything else I can do, let me know." Slocum started out but again Claire put her hand on his sleeve. As he turned, she kissed him squarely on the lips. She backed off, blushed, and then hurried into the room where her father was being tended.

Slocum decided fetching the opium had worked out better than it had any right to. He stepped out into the night and discovered he was alone. Ah Sum had gone back to China Mary.

He was free.

10

The night before, after leaving the doctor's office, Slocum had gone to the first saloon he saw and had knocked back several shots. Somehow, as thirsty as he had been before, he didn't really taste the trade whiskey as it ripped and tore at his tongue, throat, and gut. All he could think about was Claire Norton and how he had saved her father a whale of a lot of pain.

From the sound of it, her pa didn't have long to live. Slocum found himself wondering what she would do when he died since this wasn't a town for a refined woman like her. Boston was a world away, both in distance and culture. Slocum had never been there but had heard the stories of how society had afternoon teas and genteel dances and otherwise sat around in polite discussion.

Even as Slocum had thought of that, a fight had broken out, forcing him to take his whiskey and stand back so two miners could crash into the table, breaking it into flinders. His bottle was in danger of being knocked around by the fight so he left then, finding himself a soft pile of hay at the rear of the livery where he could sleep near his horse.

Morning had come and Slocum stared at his gear and horse and considered riding on. He had a job at the Circle Bar K Ranch—or thought he could get it back if he didn't. Leonard Conway owed him for saving ten head of cattle, and the foreman had given him a cow of his own. That ought to be enough to ride herd once more. If it wasn't, Slocum figured riding west was as good a direction as any to leave Tombstone.

He should have ridden out, but instead he walked back to Dr. Gottschalk's office. He hesitated at the door, not sure what to do. He could go in and—then what? Ask after Claire's father? That seemed too contrived. Or he could find some ailment for the doctor to tend. For the first time in months, Slocum had money to pay for such services.

Slocum paused, hand in the air poised to knock on the door when it opened. Slocum wasn't sure who was more surprised, him or Claire Norton.

"Mr. Slocum! You startled me."

"Sorry, didn't mean to scare you."

"What are you doing here? Have you come to see Dr. Gottschalk?"

Slocum could have lied. Instead he told the truth.

"I wanted to see you again."

"Why?" Claire put her hand to her lips and blushed again. "Oh," she said.

"You're even prettier when you blush like that," he said, making her flush even more. He saw the red go from her cheeks all the way down her throat and probably down lower. He wondered if the tops of her pert breasts also flushed. He thought so, although her lace collar and securely buttoned blouse prevented anything but his rampaging imagination from knowing for certain.

"You are quite the rogue, but you have earned the right to take such liberties."

"Your pa doing better?"

"Quite so, yes, thank you." She closed the door behind her,

closed her eyes, turned her face to the morning sun like a flower blossoming in the new day, and took in a deep breath. Slocum couldn't help noticing the way her breasts rose and fell. She was one fine-looking woman.

"Dr. Gottschalk took what he needed of the opium and returned the rest to China Mary." She sighed. "I admit to sharing your distaste for what will happen to the bulk of the drug, but she offered as much as papa needed. It was very kind of her."

"So she has an opium den somewhere in Hop Town?"

"Yes, of course. How else would she know how to obtain so much of the drug?"

"How'd it come to be stolen? The four outlaws who stole it didn't steal anything else from the train."

"You tracked them down?" Her eyes widened. "That must have been terribly dangerous."

"I owed China Mary, too. This was my way of paying her back. If I'd known what she wanted the opium for, I would have fetched it anyway."

"The shipment was well known to be on the way," Claire said. "It could have been anyone who stole it."

Slocum described the four he had seen—killed—but Claire shook her head.

"It could be anyone, John. Tombstone is seething right now. The anger at how the lawyers are trying to take over is as obvious as the nose on your face. If they can't sue their way into ownership of mines and entire businesses, then they'll do anything they can to make it seem that their theft is legal." She sighed again. Slocum could watch that all day long—and all night, too. "Papa fought them and their crooked schemes, and that's why they all hate him so much."

"Pine didn't seem to have that kind of anger toward him."

Claire looked as if she had bitten into a bitter persimmon.

"He's sweet on me. At one time, I considered him because he has moments of charity hidden away under a veneer of outrageous greed, but increasingly, he's as obvious about stealing through lawsuits and forged documents as any of the others. He's making no attempt to hide that he is no different from the others along Rotten Row."

Slocum thought she sounded a mite disappointed at this revelation of Pine's true nature.

They began walking along side by side. Slocum wished they could head toward a more private spot, but Claire walked down Allen Street, pointing out the various businesses that were being sued by the blight of lawyers.

"One lawyer, Colin Wakefield by name, is the most aggressive. He fancies himself something of a king-maker, if not an outright king himself. The general stores are all being sued by him. He doesn't care if the suit makes any sense. The business has to defend itself and that takes away money they'd use to run their business. Some have laid off employees, but there's a limit to how far that can go."

"If they hire another lawyer, that puts money into the pocket of another shyster." Slocum considered for a moment, then asked, "Could a lawyer agree to defend the store owner at a discount but actually be splitting the fee with Wakefield?"

"I never thought of that, but it's possible. I wouldn't put anything past them." She looked at him with some appreciation. "You have a quick mind, John. It wouldn't occur to anyone but another lawyer to work a deal like you described. That'd be technically called collusion."

"I have many talents," he said. Their eyes locked. She started to speak, then looked away, blushing. "Would you like to see what some of the other talents are?"

She looked back, still blushing, but this time he saw something change in her eyes. Her breath came faster and she stepped a little closer, so her breasts brushed against his chest. Claire looked up and said in a soft voice, "I would. What might these 'other talents' be?"

"They're not ones to show in public," he said.

"Those are the best kind," she said, her breath coming even faster now. "I have a house not far from Dr. Gottschalk's office."

"Do you have a roommate?"

"Not yet," she said, moving even closer. Claire turned suddenly, letting her skirts brush against Slocum's legs. He caught a whiff of her perfume. Or was it perfume? It might have been the musky odor of an aroused woman. He wanted to find out.

He let her get a dozen paces ahead, trying not to look too anxious. A town like Tombstone thrived on gossip, and Slocum wanted to do nothing to besmirch Claire's reputation. She turned east and they walked increasingly deserted streets until Slocum saw a small adobe house standing well away from others. Claire went in the front door but didn't close it behind her. She didn't have to be so obvious in her invitation, but Slocum was glad she was.

He waited a few minutes, then walked up the gravel path and slipped through the door, closing it behind him.

Slocum's eyes went wide when he saw Claire standing in the door leading to her bedroom. She had discarded her blouse and skirt. Wearing only her frilly undergarments, the sunlight behind her shone through the cloth. Her trim body was outlined perfectly. The play of shadow over the peaks and valleys of her body excited him.

"You're beautiful," Slocum said. He unbuckled his gun belt and put it on a table by the door.

"I'm overdressed," she said in a voice charged with emotion. "You should do something about that."

"I'm overdressed, too."

"I'll take care of that. Come here."

Slocum crossed the room and kissed her. For a moment, she resisted, then melted like snow in the spring sun. She flowed closer to him, their contours pressing, meshing, rubbing, striving. Somehow as their kiss deepened, she got his shirt off and unbuttoned his jeans. Breaking off, she stepped back, panting. Her hand went to her throat as she stared at his crotch.

She unbuttoned his fly and released the thick manhood behind the cloth. Slocum gasped in relief since he was getting mighty tight in those jeans.

"You do have talents," she said breathlessly. "I'm glad they're not hidden anymore." Claire moved back a step, but this time, she dropped to her knees in front of him and en-mouthed his manhood. Slocum groaned softly as he felt her tongue working over the most sensitive portion of his anatomy. Her lips closed around him and she sucked. Hard. Then she moved closer, taking ever more of his length into her mouth.

Slocum went weak in the legs as she showed him how versatile she could be. He supported himself against the bedroom doorjamb. Shifting his weight from side to side while her mouth never left him, he kicked off his boots. Then he reached down and brought her to her feet.

"You're right," he said. Her eyes looked at him questioningly. "You're overdressed." His fingers slipped under the neckline of her undergarment. With a single powerful surge, he ripped it open all the way to her waist. He dipped down and pressed his face into the soft valley between her breasts. He continued moving downward, his tongue giving her a taste of the pleasure she had already given him.

"Oh, John," she sobbed out. "I want you so!"

He refused to rush. He gripped her bloomers and yanked again, ripping them off her body, leaving her naked below the waist. The coppery thatch between her legs already glistened with dewdrops from her arousal. He licked and kissed until she went weak in the knees. With a powerful move, he tossed her over his shoulder and bore her backward.

"What are you doing? Oh, oh!"

He dropped her onto the feather mattress. She bobbed up and down once and then her knees spread apart in wanton invitation. Slocum swarmed over her, his weight pressing her downward. He unerringly thrust with his hips. For a moment the thick purple knob on the tip of his manhood banged against her nether lips. Then she lifted her hips the slightest amount. Slocum sank balls deep into her molten center.

They both hung suspended in ecstasy for a moment. She trembled, shivered, and quaked. Then he began withdrawing slowly.

"No, you can't, please, no!"

When only the tip of his manhood remained within her, he paused, caught his breath, and looked into her eyes. They blazed brightly like glowing emeralds. Her fiery red hair spread above her head in a gorgeous halo, and her lips pursed slightly.

Slocum slipped back into her. Claire's eyes closed, and she shuddered again in joy. He stroked smoothly, slowly, building speed until the friction burned at his self-control. Claire cried out constantly and clawed at his arms as passions built within her.

He shared the feelings. Deep down in his loins he felt the tiny spark of sensation turn into fire. The blaze exploded in wild release just as Claire arched her back, crammed her crotch down into his, and began grinding away to take as much of him as she could.

They sank down together on the bed, spent. He rolled to one side and she wrapped her arms around him, placing her cheek on his bare chest.

"John," she said softly. Her breath gusted across his chest hair and tickled. Her fingers moved slowly over his body, but there wasn't any resurrecting the dead—not yet.

"I'm glad I got locked up."

"What?" She twisted around to look at him. "Whatever are you saying?"

"If I hadn't hit Pine and gotten locked up, China Mary wouldn't have been able to get me out to fetch the opium that your pa needed. And our paths wouldn't have crossed."

"Silly," she said, putting her cheek back down. "If all that's true, I suppose I'm glad you were locked up, too." She giggled.

They lay together on the bed for a while until Slocum began to get antsy. When he squirmed a bit too much, she let him go and sat up. He enjoyed the bounce of her bare breasts and the rest of the pert, perky package, but he was getting the feeling something was wrong.

"I feel it, too," she said. "What's not right, John?"

He couldn't see anything wrong between them, so it had to be something more. Something outside this bedroom.

"What about your pa? How's he doing?"

Claire frowned and chewed on her lower lip as she thought.

"He was resting comfortably. The opium took away most of the pain and let him sleep peacefully for the first time in weeks. In fact, Dr. Gottschalk was considering surgery now that he had enough opium to use as an anesthetic. But he wouldn't give a definite answer until Papa regained some strength. The pain had worn him down so much."

Slocum swung his long legs over the edge of the bed and found his jeans. He dressed quickly. During the war he had developed a sixth sense that had kept him alive. If an enemy soldier sighted in on him, he sensed it and had always ducked in time to keep his head from getting blown off. After the war, he had come to rely on this sense to keep from getting into ambushes and outright massacres. It now screamed something was wrong, and he couldn't pin down the feeling.

After he got into his boots, he saw that Claire had donned her blouse and skirt. She looked a bit miffed as she held up her torn underwear.

"It was exciting when you tore it off—"

"Next time I'll do it with my teeth," Slocum said, grinning.

"Promises, promises," she said. She tossed the frilly garments aside. "It is so hard getting decent clothing on the frontier. These came from France."

"I'll buy you more," Slocum said.

"Only if you *don't* rip off my other undergarments the next time," she said. "I hope the wind's not blowing."

"Why?" He strapped on his gun belt and waited by the door.

"I don't want all those miners getting a look at something I want only you to see." She pressed hard against him as she crowded by to go through the narrow doorway. Outside, she turned back, put her hands on her hips, and said, "Well? Are you coming?"

Slocum and Claire hurried from the adobe house, retracing their steps to the doctor's office. He tried to make sense of the uneasiness but couldn't. Late afternoon Tombstone was coming alive as miners got off their shifts and drifted into the saloons. In another couple hours, all the day shifts would be released and serious carousing would begin.

But nothing was out of place that he could see.

"The door's open. Dr. Gottschalk makes a point of keeping it closed. He says it's the only way he can keep his office clean. There's always so much dust blowing around here." Claire started to run but Slocum caught her arm and spun her around.

"Stay here." She struggled but he held her firmly. "Stay," he said firmly. "If there's anything wrong, I'll handle it."

She started to protest, then quieted.

Slocum went to the office door and pushed it open with his foot. The doctor wasn't at his desk, but nothing else seemed out of place—until Slocum heard the sound of someone being slapped. Hard.

With a smooth motion, he drew his six-shooter and went to the door leading to Sam Norton's room. Sounds of a struggle came through the heavy wood paneling. Slocum kicked open the door and got the drop on Childress. The rustler held Norton by the front of his nightshirt. From the long red marks on the lawyer's pale cheeks, Childress had slapped him several times.

"I want to kill you," Slocum said. "But as much pleasure

as I'd get from gunning you down, I reckon it'd be more fun watching you dance at the end of a hangman's rope."

"Slocum," the rustler growled. He jerked around, half dragging Norton from the bed to use as a shield.

Slocum cocked his six-shooter and aimed it directly at Childress's head. There wasn't any way in hell he could pull the lawyer up enough to completely protect himself.

"I'm not going to miss at this range. I should have plugged you when I had the chance, but I didn't know Tombstone was as bad as Fort Huachuca when it came to punishing cattle thieves."

"I need to find out something from him, Slocum. He ain't gonna live. Let me finish and—"

Slocum aimed and fired. And missed. Claire had come in behind him and bumped him just as he squeezed the trigger. Childress let out a squeal like a stuck pig, shoved Norton forward so he sprawled, half out of bed, then turned, and dived headfirst out a small window. Glass broke, Childress screamed and then he disappeared.

"Papa!" Claire pushed past Slocum and rushed to her father's side, helping him back into bed.

Slocum went to the window and shoved his Colt out, ready to end Childress's miserable life. The rustler had disappeared. If it hadn't been for the woman stumbling into him, Slocum would have eliminated a thorn in his side.

And from what he had seen Childress doing to Sam Norton, a thorn in the lawyer's side as well.

11

"You did what?" Jackson Pine stared at Childress in disbelief. "Have you been eating loco weed? You want the marshal to get a posse together and come after you—after *us*?"

Childress snorted in contempt at such an attitude, making Pine even angrier at him. He drew his six-shooter and spun the cylinder, opened the gate, checked the rounds in the chambers, then jammed his pistol back into the holster before saying anything.

"You need to grow a set, Counselor," Childress said. "I done some askin' 'round town, and they all said this Norton was defendin' Tarkenton. All I wanted was to shake some sense into him so he'd give up the case. Without Norton speaking for the miner, you're sure to waltz right on into court and win that claim for your own."

"He's dying of cancer, for Pete's sake." Pine couldn't believe Childress could be so stupid. "There's nothing he can do to stop the juggernaut I've got rolling."

"Some juggernaut," Childress said. "That son of a bitch out at the Molly E Mine damned near killed us."

"I'm going to take care of Wakefield," Pine said. "He used

too much force out there. That'll come back and bite him in the ass."

"He almost blew off our asses. I got partners rattlin' 'round the countryside. They worked with me rustling cattle. You need a couple more guns if you want to go up against Wakefield again. It might take a week but I kin recruit them—for a price, of course."

"This is going to turn into a bloodbath if you keep thinking like that," Pine said, fighting to keep his anger in check. "Fighting in court is just as effective for getting what I want. It doesn't leave dead bodies strewn around town either." Pine didn't add that paying Childress's partners was an expense he could not meet. He hardly had two nickels to rub together until he got the silver mine claim settled favorably.

"Shootin' somebody between the eyes is a lot more permanent. You sue somebody and steal all his money legally, he still has a six-gun and can use it. Shoot him in the face and he's not gonna bother you one whit again."

Pine heard the bloodlust in the outlaw's words. Childress wanted an excuse to kill, but he wasn't going to get it.

"I warned you to stay out of town. What if Marshal Sosa had spotted you? Or one of his deputies?"

"What if they did? I'm a better shot than any of 'em."

"You're sure that was Slocum who stopped you from beating up Norton?"

"How could I mistake him? He's the one what caught me and drug me to this godforsaken town to get locked up in jail. For two days we were on the trail. Hell, I know it was him."

"He defended Sam Norton?"

"He fired at me but some redheaded bitch knocked his gun hand just as he squeezed off a round. Otherwise, I'd be dead. I owe her one. She's a real purty filly, too, so I might give her more than one." Childress made a lewd gesture, then grinned.

Pine glared at him.

"That's Claire Norton."

"The lawyer's wife? He sure likes 'em young. He was an old codger, built like a bird, all frail and breakable."

"Claire's his daughter."

Childress laughed harshly, then drew his six-gun and spun the cylinder again. He sighted down the barrel as he slowly raised it to aim at the lawyer.

"You sound like you got that territory staked out. You object if I squatted on a corner of that claim? Once or twice'd be all the squattin' I'd want. I never do a woman more 'n that 'cuz I'd get bored."

"Leave her alone," Pine said coldly. "You don't have a quarrel with her. If anyone is standing in your way, you ought to deal with Slocum. Leave Sam Norton alone, too."

"You *are* sweet on her. Ain't that a hoot? You'd fight me for her hand—and other parts of her anatomy?"

"Go to hell."

Childress looked fierce, as if he would pull the trigger, then lifted the gun so it pointed at the sky, lowered the hammer, and emitted his mocking laugh.

"Didn't think you had the sand to say that to my face, not when I was throwed down on you. You're all right, Counselor."

"Go get drunk, but don't let the law catch wind that you're in town."

"You don't order me around." Childress's mercurial mood shifted again, turning him angry.

"I have to go and find Judge Rollins. If I can't take care of Wakefield any other way, I'll have you deal with him. You seem to relish the notion of killing lawyers."

"Who don't?" Childress's mood changed once more. He spun and stalked off. Before he reached the corner, he was whistling off-key what might have been "Camp Town Races." Pine pressed his hand into his right hip, hoping vainly a pistol had miraculously appeared there. It hadn't. A six-gun wouldn't do him much good, even if he had one. Only twice before had he even fired a gun and he didn't like either time. The first time he had scared himself and the second he had almost blown off his own foot. He suspected Childress's favored way of gunning down an opponent would be from the back so carrying a pistol wouldn't do him a great deal of good.

Pine walked slowly to the courthouse, forming his arguments as he went. Running afoul of Wakefield the way he had burned him up. A restraining order against the other lawyer might work, but Wakefield had too many hired gunmen to name individually, which was required for such a judicial document. All Wakefield had to do was send one of them around who hadn't been named, six-shooter blazing, and Pine would end up in Boot Hill Cemetery. Legally, Wakefield would not have violated the restraining order and Pine would be dead.

And no one would care.

This thought turned him morose. He had not made many friends since coming to Tombstone. Hell, he hadn't made a single one. The only man talking to him was a bloodthirsty rustler. The other lawyers—his so-called colleagues—worked as hard to swindle him as he did to get what they wanted before he could buy off a judge.

Most frightening was how Wakefield had escalated the rivalry. One lawyer shouldn't threaten another the way he had out at the Molly E Mine. Legal combat in front of a judge was one thing; putting a bullet through your opponent was a different kettle of fish.

He took the steps up to the courthouse lobby as if he mounted the gallows. Inside was cooler, but he had to wait for Judge Rollins to finish with another lawyer's requests, a newcomer from over in San Antonio. Although Pine wasn't supposed to see it, he couldn't help noticing the exchange of a stack of greenbacks. This piqued his curiosity since he wondered what could be worth such a big bribe. As he considered the newcomer, the judge bellowed for him to come in and be quick about it.

"Judge, good afternoon," he greeted.

"I've got a full schedule today, Pine. Get on with it. I can give you five minutes." Rollins made a point of staring at the Regulator clock mounted on the far wall slowly ticking off the seconds.

"I went to the Molly E and ran into a spot of trouble."

"Wakefield?"

Pine tried to assess where Rollins stood on the matter. The judge had either heard or had known about Wakefield and his men going out to the mine from the way he smirked. He doubted Rollins was an honest crook. He wouldn't stay bought. Every decision was always open to change if a higher bid came in. Pine wasn't sure how much higher he could up the ante, yet he needed the Molly E Mine for what he intended to do. Ike Tarkenton was a greedy old geezer. The silver coming from the mine would flow into the proper coffers and benefit everyone when Pine got control.

It was about time for him to develop a civic conscience and do things to aid the citizens of this godforsaken town.

"Of course it was Colin Wakefield. He shot at me and—" Pine bit off the rest of his sentence. Childress still dodged an arrest warrant. It wouldn't do to admit he had even seen the fugitive, much less gone out to the silver mine to estimate what it was really worth.

"And?"

"And he had gunmen with him. He said the mine was his."

"Did he now? He's claiming the mine on the basis of having more guns leveled than you do?"

"Something like that. I need a restraining order on him. On all his men, too."

"How many would that be? I'd need names to put on the restraining order. And you can't expect Marshal Sosa to enforce a vague John Doe order, now can you?"

"I've heard Sosa is planning on pulling up stakes and moving on," Pine said. Rollins shrugged. "What good would the order do if there isn't a marshal for a month or two?"

"Tombstone has gone through such times before. It certainly increased my work when it happened before Sosa was sworn in. The prosecutor might need help, too. Consider that, Jackson."

"I won't live that long," Pine blurted out. "The Molly E Mine belongs to me, and Wakefield will gun me down to steal it."

"The mine is yours when you pay the back taxes. You are merely first in line. Anyone inked in under you on what is becoming quite a list can pay the arrears and take the mine if you are unable."

Pine saw that this was the deal Wakefield had worked. Rollins was straight enough not to remove Pine's name, but if anything happened—a bullet to the back—then Wakefield moved into position at the top of the liens list to steal the mine.

Pine vowed to guarantee that Tarkenton kept it before letting the other lawyer win such a prize.

He left, making sure to identify every shadow in the alcoves around the courthouse foyer. Not only were these potential rivals for the Molly E Mine but Wakefield might also be ballsy enough to gun him down inside the symbol of law and justice for the entire county.

Out in the hot sunlight, he looked around and saw nothing suspicious. Pine shook himself for such paranoia. He might as well eat loco weed as to jump at every movement half seen out of the corner of his eye. Tombstone was a dangerous town, but there wasn't any call for him to believe it was any more dangerous today than it was a week back.

Out in the street, a different goal occurred to him. He cut through town, past Fremont Street, and to Dr. Gottschalk's office. He hesitated at the door, then knocked.

"Come on in," came Gottschalk's irritated greeting.

Pine went in, closed the door behind him, and faced the doctor. Gottschalk scribbled furiously in a notebook. He held up an ink-stained hand and muttered, "A moment. I need to finish this thought before it escapes me entirely. It'll be needed for . . ."

Gottschalk looked up and saw Pine.

"What are you doing here?" the doctor demanded.

"I might be ill."

"Then do us all a favor and die," Gottschalk said. "The Hippocratic Oath doesn't require me to tend to lawyers."

"Why not?" Pine was startled at the doctor's comment.

"I'm not a vet. I don't have to treat rabid dogs. I only have to heal the humans they bite."

"I don't bite, and I'm not rabid. May I see Sam Norton?"

"No."

Again Pine was taken aback at the doctor's adamant denial.

"I want to apologize for the way Childress treated him. I assure you I had no idea he was going to come here, much less rough up Norton the way he did."

"If it hadn't been for Norton's daughter, I'd have had to sign a death certificate for—what's his name? Childress?"

"Yes, Childress. He's got a warrant out on his head for killing a lawyer behind the courthouse."

"Might have misjudged him," Gottschalk said, "but I don't think so. Now get out of my office."

"Please relay my sincere apologies to Mr. Norton. He is, after all, a colleague, and I bear him no animosity."

"That's not what I hear. He's defending Tarkenton against your blatant grab to steal the man's mine. You've got some nerve trying to influence Norton by coming here. What do you intend to say to him? Make some kind of a deal? I'll answer for Sam. No deals. Now get the hell out of my office."

Pine knew better than to argue when a man started getting red in the face from anger. He touched the brim of his bowler, then stepped back outside into the heat. Being thwarted seeing Sam Norton, Pine decided on the next best thing. Or maybe it was *the* best thing. He smiled as he started toward Claire Norton's house. He could apologize for Childress's boorish behavior to her since she didn't have the doctor to intercede.

The house wasn't far. Standing in the hot sun, he felt sweat beading under the brim of his bowler. He took it off and mopped at the sweat with a handkerchief, realizing not all the moisture came from the sun. The prospect of talking to Claire Norton excited him and made him feel like a young buck asking out a girl to the barn dance for the first time.

"Settle yourself, sir," he told himself. "She is a lovely woman and the daughter of a colleague, but she is not unattainable. Why shouldn't she accept you into her house? A successful lawyer, just as her father is—more successful!—and she can certainly do far worse among the eligible bachelors in Tombstone."

He settled the bowler squarely on his head, brushed dust from his coat, and walked boldly to the front door. Even with this bravado, he hesitated to knock. To his surprise he didn't get the chance because the door opened and the vision of red-haired loveliness stood there.

"Good afternoon, Claire," he said in his best courtroom voice.

"Pine," she said. Emotions played across her lovely face, emotions he could not decipher. "What do you want?"

"I'd like to—"

"Go away." She slammed the door in his face.

Pine stepped back, startled. Then anger mounted. How dare she treat him like this! He rapped hard on the door.

"Claire, open up this instant. I want to talk with you."

She opened the door again. This time he found himself staring down the double barrels of a derringer.

"Three, two—"

"Wait!" He saw her finger tightening in the trigger and knew when she reached one, she would fire. "I'm going. There's no need to shoot me!"

He scrambled off the porch and stopped only when he

reached the street running past Claire's house. Pine looked back and saw the fiery-tempered redhead pointing her index finger in his direction. She curled her thumb down as if firing a gun. He was glad she didn't have the derringer in her grip. She would have put a bullet through him if she had.

Pine tried to look cool and collected by tipping his hat in her direction, but she had already slammed the door. He took a deep breath, mopped more sweat, and then turned back toward the south side of town and his office. Steps as heavy as they had been going up to the courthouse, Pine wondered what was going wrong in his life. No one would even accept his apology.

Resolve hardened. He would get the Molly E Mine and show them all. His charity would astound and dazzle. Claire would come running into his arms when she realized how generous he could be. And he would feign indifference, for a little while at least. Then he would take her into his arms and kiss her and—

—a heavy hand shoved him back, bringing Pine out of his daydream.

"What's the meaning of this?" he got out before he saw Colin Wakefield blocking his way in the road. The other lawyer had his coat pulled back to expose the butt of the pistol he had tucked away under his left arm.

"I'm going to kill you," Wakefield said.

"You can," Pine said, "but why not let one of your bully boys do it? Don't you trust them?"

"You got to Rollins and bribed him. I was supposed to get the Molly E Mine."

Pine knew when a man was bluffing and when a man intended to act. As long as Wakefield was talking, he wasn't going to do anything. Pine got his feet under him and swung flatfooted. His fist hit Wakefield's cheek a glancing blow. Since there was no power behind it, the impact startled Wakefield more than it hurt him. He jerked back and lost his balance. Pine knew that he dared not let up the attack. He had fought enough battles in court to understand the principles of war—and that was the way he looked at this dustup.

If Wakefield got his pistol out, one of them would be dead in a flash. Pine knew who that would be and redoubled his efforts, his fists flying. He connected a more solid punch, but Wakefield took it. As he reached to draw his gun, Wakefield stumbled. Pine kicked out and caught him directly behind the knee. He toppled backward to the ground. Pine was on him in a flash.

Using a schoolboy pin, he held Wakefield's shoulders to the ground with his knees. He pummeled the man's face, but none of his punches was powerful enough to do any damage. Pine came to realize he had to do something different. Letting Wakefield lift his left shoulder just a little, Pine grabbed for the pistol.

Wakefield surged and dumped him onto his side. They fought over the pistol, Pine trying to yank it free and use it against Wakefield and the other lawyer trying to keep it in his holster since he was still at a disadvantage.

"Give it up," Wakefield grated through clenched teeth. He was stronger, and Pine felt his own grip fading fast.

Going suddenly limp unbalanced Wakefield again. Pine awkwardly kicked and connected with Wakefield's elbow. The lawyer yelped and gave up trying to draw his pistol, turning his fury to pummeling his opponent.

Pine felt his face getting puffy from the blows landing unchecked. And then there was nothing. For a moment he thought Wakefield had pulled back so he could whip out his pistol. Then he saw Marshal Sosa holding Wakefield in a headlock.

He stood and started to swing. Sosa turned at the last instant and robbed Pine of a knockout punch.

"You both stop, or I'll throw you in jail for a month of Sundays!"

"He attacked me!"

"He's trying to rob me!" Wakefield's explanation was muffled from having the marshal's arm wrapped around his head. Sosa twisted hard and sent Wakefield to the ground. The lawyer fell to his knees, but he fumbled for his pistol.

"Do that and one of us'll end up at Doc Gottschalk's office with a bullet in him." Marshal Sosa was squared off and his hand rested against the hard leather of his holster, his fingers just inches away from drawing his six-shooter.

"I'm an officer of the court. You wouldn't dare throw down on me."

"I'm a law officer and I damn well will. You won't have nobody to plead your case 'cuz you'll be dead. Something tells me Pine will testify for me if anybody's fool enough to charge me."

"I'll get even with you," Wakefield said, glaring at Pine. He turned to the marshal and said, "You just made yourself a powerful enemy, Marshal."

"You can't imagine how that scares me," Sosa said.

Wakefield stormed off.

"Thanks, Marshal, I—"

"Shut up or I'll run you in for public brawling."

"You'd have to arrest Wakefield, too, if—" Pine shut up when he saw the marshal's expression. Sometimes a lawyer had to know when to stop pressing a point in court. He saw that he had reached this point with the marshal.

Sosa grunted, spat, and then stomped off, going into a nearby saloon.

Jackson Pine dusted himself off the best he could and considered how hard it would be for him to learn to fire a six-gun. In court he could beat Wakefield, but that wouldn't matter if he walked around town with a target painted on his back. As much as he hated to admit it, he needed Childress and his bloodthirsty ways about now.

Then he could get on to finalizing his claim to the Molly E Mine.

12

"We're gonna own this whole damn town, me and my tame lawyer."

The words boomed through the crowded saloon. Most of the miners crowded into the long, narrow room paid no heed because they were too busy stoking the fires of their own drunkenness, but Slocum looked up from his whiskey. The sound of that voice was familiar—too familiar. He stood and reached for his six-shooter but a powerful hand clamped down on his wrist.

"Don't start no trouble in here," the bouncer said. He was half a head taller than Slocum's six feet and had shoulders to match his height. In his left hand he clung to a slung shot, letting it dangle down in such a way that told Slocum he knew how to use it. Rather than have his wrist crushed or his head bashed in by a bag filled with lead shot, he relaxed.

"I got a bone to pick with him."

"Have another drink. If you got enough whiskey in your gut, troubles just sorta melt away. Least that's what I've always found." The bouncer shoved Slocum back to the bar. He stood behind him for a moment, waiting to see if he was going to have any trouble, then moved on through the crowd to break up a shoving match that was likely to escalate into an elbows and assholes brawl.

Slocum saw the way the bouncer moved and decided not to try anything inside the saloon. He leaned forward on the bar, arms resting on the edge. He put his right hand down flat so it rested only inches away from the butt of his Colt Navy in the cross-draw holster. He could drink plenty good enough using only his left hand.

He lifted his gaze and sorted out the faces in the ever-changing crowd until he spotted Childress. The rustler sat in the far corner of the room with his back to the wall. Slocum was glad he hadn't pressed the matter. Childress had his six-shooter on the table, where he could grab it in a hurry. From the way he poured tarantula juice down his gullet, he would pass out soon enough.

When he did, Slocum could drag him outside and decide what to do with him. Simply putting a bullet into him seemed like the most sensible trail to follow, but if he turned him in to the marshal, Childress might end up at the end of a hang-man's rope for gunning down the lawyer behind the court-house. Somehow, that struck Slocum as a more fitting end to the man's foul life than a bullet cleanly drilling through his heart. He had learned patience during the war as a sniper. Sometimes he would sit all day long in the fork of a tall gum tree, waiting to catch the flash of sunlight off a Federal officer's braid. More than once a single shot had taken out the enemy's commander and turned the tide of battle.

He drank more slowly to keep from getting tipsy. When he took out Childress, he wanted to be sharp and fast and to ap-preciate every instant of the man's disgrace—or death.

"We're gonna own the damned Molly E Mine and that dumbass Ike Tarkenton will be left in the cold," Childress bel-lowed. "Richest mine in these parts. I'll buy this place when I drag enough silver from the mine. I'll stand the lot of you with women and whiskey, too!"

Everything Childress said was filed away in Slocum's agile brain for action later. He remembered Claire saying that her pa represented Tarkenton. With Sam Norton laid up the way he was, Tarkenton had no chance to fight back, either in court or at his own mine.

"Fact is, Tarkenton is a murderer. He shouldn't be allowed to stand trial. He might get off. Them lawyers in this town are sneaky bastards. I say string him up now!"

The call to a necktie party drew some of the miners. Life was boring in Tombstone. A good hanging would liven up their dreary existence. Slocum started to turn but found himself looking smack at the bouncer, who tapped his slung shot against his right palm.

"Who'd join me in bustin' that lowdown snake outta jail and stringin' him up?"

"What's he done again?" asked a miner.

"He's a claim jumper, that's what he is." Childress began spinning a wild tale about how Tarkenton had stolen the Molly E from him. It didn't matter to the drunks listening to Childress that they probably knew Tarkenton, although the reclusive miner might not have made many friends in town. They certainly didn't know Childress since he had just come to town, but the anticipation of watching a man's heels kicking in thin air was more potent that actually thinking.

"Got to go," Slocum said to the bouncer. "You might want to shut that one up. He's stirring up a crowd to lynch a man."

"Long as it ain't inside, what do I care?"

Slocum had to agree with that sentiment. He left the smoky saloon and looked around Tombstone. If he had a lick of sense, he'd get his horse and just leave. He wasn't sure what kept him in town, and he sure as hell wasn't certain why he cared about Ike Tarkenton getting lynched. Long strides took him in the direction of the jailhouse.

He barged in, causing the marshal to look up from a solitaire game spread across the desk.

"What do you want, Slocum? I'm real busy."

"Childress is over at the Mighty Fine Saloon stirring up a crowd to lynch Tarkenton."

"Childress, eh? I'd love to get my hands on him. Can't say things were peaceable in Tombstone before he got here, but we started findin' dead bodies everywhere after he arrived. Mostly, I could care less if he killed every last one of them lawyers, but the judges now, they're lawyers, too, and they stick together."

"Might be a good idea to let the miner go." Slocum looked into the cell block where Tarkenton sat on a cot, head in his hands and moaning softly at his sorry fate.

"That one? Naw, he's got the trembling delirium since I don't allow no booze in the jail. He puked up his guts the first day, then he settled down to that groaning. Fact is, I'm gettin' kinda partial to it. Makes the rest of the noise in Tombstone go far, far away."

"I can bail him out," Slocum said, remembering the gold coins he had taken off the four outlaws who had stolen China Mary's opium.

"Don't care. Judge Rollins said to hold him without bail." Sosa continued to play his cards.

"Are you going after Childress?"

"Can't leave right now. All my deputies are out making the rounds. Until one of 'em returns, I have to guard the prisoner." Marshal Sosa looked up and said, "Don't get any ideas, Slocum. For two cents I'd clap you in the cell next to his. Then you and him could moan out a duet."

"You wouldn't like to hear that, Marshal," Slocum said. He left, thinking hard. The only other person he could ask about this was Sam Norton. Whether the lawyer was up to practicing law and doing something for his client was something Slocum had to find out.

He cut through the middle of town and came out on the far side. He opened the door to Gottschalk's office to find himself looking down the bore of a rifle.

"Sorry, Slocum," said the doctor. He dropped the rifle to

the desk. "I've been plagued today with lawyers and have about decided to kill one if they poked their head through the door again."

"If you kill one, you'd have to cut his head off and mount it on the wall. That'd scare off your patients."

Gottschalk blinked a moment, then laughed.

"You've got a morbid sense of humor, Slocum."

"Who's joking?" Seeing the doctor at a loss for words, Slocum asked, "Is Norton up to me talking to him about a client?"

"You mean Tarkenton?" Gottschalk looked toward the closed back room door and sucked at his teeth, thinking hard.

"He's either awake or he's not."

"It's more difficult for me to say than that, Slocum. I operated on him this afternoon."

"He's dead?"

"No, I think the operation went well. He's recuperating now. I cut into his belly and removed a tumor the size of your fist. If you hadn't brought that opium for me to use as anesthetic, I'd never have tried it."

"He's going to be all right?"

"Too soon to tell. He was awake and alert enough about an hour back, but he's weaker than a day-old kitten. And I don't like to have a whole lot of visitors coughing and sneezing on a patient in his condition."

"I'll stand back."

"Wash up. Here." Gottschalk went to a table and poured carbolic acid into a pan. "Slosh it all over your hands. Even so, be careful about what you touch. I've read some papers done by a French physician, and he has some interesting ideas about what causes disease."

Slocum did as he was told, Gottschalk watching closely. Only then did the doctor open the door into the back room and let Slocum in. In a low voice the doctor warned, "No more than a minute or two. If he weakens, no matter how long you've talked to him, I want you out of there."

Gottschalk didn't close the door. Slocum didn't mind the doctor listening in but wished he could get closer than a few feet to Sam Norton. The man lay sprawled on a bed, one arm flung out. His breathing was shallow and in the darkness Slocum couldn't make out his face, but Norton immediately knew someone had come into the room.

"Who's there? That you, Doc?"

"John Slocum. I brought the opium."

"Claire's spoken highly of you. Is she here?"

"I got a quick question to ask. Tarkenton is your client, isn't he?"

"He is."

Slocum quickly explained what was happening and how Pine and Childress intended to steal the Molly E Mine away from its rightful owner.

"You care about Tarkenton?"

"I want Childress in the Yuma Penitentiary," Slocum said. "He's not only a cattle thief but he's also on a one-man killing spree. The marshal's not able to stop him. Or maybe he doesn't want to."

"Sosa is a good man—for a Tombstone marshal. He's just not committed enough to the rule of law to put his life on the line." Norton coughed. This brought Gottschalk into the room to put a hand on Slocum's arm.

"It's all right, Doc," Norton said. "I can write up a writ of *habeas corpus* to get Tarkenton out of jail, but my hand's shaking too much right now. In the morning. Yes, in the morning." The lawyer's words began to fade away.

Gottschalk pulled insistently on Slocum's arm and got him out of the room. He closed the door with a bang.

"He's too weak to do any such thing, even in the morning."

"Do you think Claire knows another lawyer who'd write up whatever he called it?"

"No. It's about time for you to leave, Slocum. I have a patient in a very fragile condition to tend."

Slocum wished both Norton and the doctor well, then left. The sounds from the middle of town rose, sounding more like a mob than the rowdy, rambunctious miners out on a bender. He walked down Allen Street and saw Childress whipping up the gathering crowd with well-timed shouts and declarations of how Tarkenton deserved to be lynched.

Slocum fingered his six-gun, then decided he'd never get away with it. Deputies were flocking in to break up the crowd, but the few of them against so many men bent on shedding blood told Slocum that Tarkenton didn't have a chance. More than once Slocum had been in a jail where lynch mobs had come, sometimes for him but more often for other prisoners. He didn't hold much with the law, but he cared even less for the mindless mobs looking for somebody to string up.

He cut between buildings, pressing close to the walls to reach Toughnut Street. Dashing along it, Slocum worried about how much time he had. Not much from the sounds coming from a couple streets over in front of the saloon. He stopped outside the jail, thinking fast. The marshal was still inside and likely to be alert now that Slocum had pleaded Tarkenton's case earlier.

He rapped sharply on the door, then ran to the edge of the building before the marshal flung open the door. The barrel of a shotgun poked out and the marshal called, "Who's there? Show yerself!"

Slocum got to the rear of the jail, picked up a rock, and heaved it so it scraped along the side of the building. He didn't wait to see if the marshal came to investigate. Running around, he came out in front of the jail from the opposite direction taken by the marshal. He had very little time before Sosa came back on the run.

Scooping up the keys from a peg on the wall, Slocum went directly to Tarkenton's cell. The miner looked up. His hands shook as he pointed accusingly at Slocum.

"You, you're responsible fer me bein' in here."

"You got that wrong," Slocum said. "I'm the one breaking you out of jail. You should be alive so your lawyer can get you off in court."

"Mr. Norton? Where is that mangy, no good cayuse?"

"He got his belly cut open this afternoon. He's on the mend." Slocum twisted the key hard, got the lock open, and swung back the cell door. "Come on. If you don't, a lynch mob's going to string you up."

"I don't cotton much to Sosa, but he'd never allow that."

"Then stay here for all I care."

"You really know Norton?"

"Talked to him not an hour back."

Tarkenton shot from the cell and said, "Then let's get outta here."

Slocum chanced a quick look out and saw an obviously mad lawman coming around the building. They were trapped inside. Worse, Slocum would never argue Sosa out of being the one to free Tarkenton. An escaped prisoner and a jail breaker, Marshal Sosa had himself a pair of criminals. Slocum doubted even China Mary would get him out since this was a cut on the marshal's considerable pride.

"You kin shoot him," Tarkenton said.

Slocum wasn't going to gun down a town marshal. That would get a vigilance committee hot on his trail. He pushed Tarkenton back behind the door and joined the miner, waiting. If he slammed the door in the marshal's face, it might stun him long enough to slug him and escape. As Slocum tensed, he heard someone call to Sosa.

"Marshal, we got problems. Big ones."

"You're my head deputy, Eakin. You handle it."

"Too many of the drunk bastards, Marshal. You might talk 'em out of lynchin' our prisoner, but I cain't. They'll listen to you, but you might want to hang on to that scattergun while you're talkin'."

Slocum peered through the crack between the door and doorjamb to see Marshal Sosa shifting his weight back and forth indecisively. Then he reached out, closed the door, and ran to help his deputy. Slocum waited a few seconds, peered out through an inch-wide crack in the door, then motioned for Tarkenton to follow.

He closed the door behind them and pointed toward the corral down Fifth Street.

"Get yourself a horse and hightail it," Slocum said.

"What 'bout you?"

"I'll decoy them away. Where are you heading? No, don't tell me. I'll lead them to your mine."

"That's where I was plannin' on hidin' out."

Slocum stared at the miner in the dark.

"That's the first place they'll look for you."

"But you said you'd lead them there."

"Get the hell out of town. Hide somewhere besides your mine. Anywhere else. It doesn't matter. Now go!" For two cents Slocum would have crammed Tarkenton back into the jail cell. The miner read his intent if he didn't make himself scarce.

"I don't know you, mister, but thanks."

With that, Tarkenton ran for the livery stables. Slocum waited to be sure the miner wasn't going to do something dumb like duck into a saloon for a little nip before hitting the trail, then followed the marshal to the front of the Mighty Fine Saloon, where Sosa was having no better luck controlling the crowd than his deputies had.

"Disperse," Sosa yelled. "Get on back into the saloon and get likkered up. There's no call to lynch nobody."

Slocum saw that the marshal lost any authority he had when someone came running up and yelled, "He's gone. There ain't no prisoner in the jail. He escaped!"

Slocum knew he had only a few seconds to get Tarkenton to safety. The anger at the marshal robbing them of their lynching seized the mob.

"He went to his mine," Slocum bellowed. "Where else would he go? He's running for his mine!"

Then he stood back and let the mostly drunk crowd rush to find horses and ride out of Tombstone, heading for the Molly E Mine. Slocum hoped that Tarkenton remembered that he wasn't supposed to hide out there.

After the crowd had turned into a posse intent on finding Tarkenton, Slocum went looking for Childress. He had a score to settle with the murdering rustler.

13

The lynch mob thundered past Jackson Pine, forcing him to press his back against the bakery shop wall. He choked on the dust and then brushed himself off when the last of the mob had disappeared. He shook his head in wonder. The populace of Tombstone acted like some stampeded cattle herd at times, and he never quite understood that, though he used it to sway juries when he had need to.

He finished dusting off his bowler and had settled it onto his head when he saw Childress standing half hidden in shadow beside a saloon. A quick look around convinced him the marshal and his deputies were nowhere to be found, and that it ought to be safe to talk to the rustler. The lawmen might have ridden with the mob tearing out of town, but Pine wanted to keep it private whenever he spoke with his hired gun. Childress still had an arrest warrant out on him, and as an officer of the court, he was obligated to turn the man in, even if he both worked for him and was his client.

Pine tasted bile when that thought crossed his mind. Hired gun. This made him no better than Colin Wakefield. Still, the fight with the other lawyer had convinced him he needed

Childress more than ever. If only he could guide his blood-thirsty ways in productive directions . . .

"Childress!" He waved and then looked around guiltily. Childress was leaving, and he wanted to talk with the man.

"Well, well, if it ain't my counselor. You see that? The lynch mob?" Childress laughed. "I done it all. I stirred 'em up and got 'em on the trail after Tarkenton."

"Why are they leaving town?"

"Tarkenton busted out of jail," Childress said.

"How'd that happen? He wasn't smart enough to dupe the marshal. Did Norton get him out?"

"I don't know for sure but I'm thinkin' how it might have been Slocum what busted him out."

Pine clenched his hands into tight fists. They hurt from the fight he and Wakefield had earlier, but he would willingly get into another bare knuckles engagement with Slocum. He wasn't sure but he had a feeling in his gut that Slocum had turned Claire against him. What a drifter, a cowboy, a stupid, uneducated man could offer her that a university-trained lawyer like him could not was beyond his ability to understand.

"We need to corral Tarkenton and get him back in jail. It would be good if Slocum was in the cell next to him."

"I been askin' 'round town. Seems China Mary is his guardian angel. She's—"

"I know who she is," snapped Pine. "Norton represents her and her whores when they get arrested."

"Might be better to take care of them more permanent-like."

Pine looked hard at Childress. The man smiled almost angelically. He might have been commenting on the preacher's Sunday sermon, but his suggestion spelled the deaths of two men. A few minutes earlier Pine might have objected, but now the deaths of his two biggest stumbling blocks became more logical.

"What do you have in mind?"

"Arizona Territory is mighty big. The desert is cruel. Folks disappear all the time. Might just be two more might ride into the desert and never be seen again."

"Buzzards get hungry," Pine said, playing with the idea and examining the consequences from all directions.

"You oughta know."

Pine looked at the rustler sharply. He didn't care what a lowlife like Childress thought of him, but he didn't have to be so blatant in his disrespect.

"It might be better if Tarkenton is found dead and it looks like Colin Wakefield did the deed."

"Wakefield? You want to frame another lawyer? That's rich."

"I believe in the law of minimum effort."

"What's that?" Childress looked at him suspiciously. "Sounds like a way of getting out of work."

"Not so much avoiding the unpleasant but making the most of an opportunity. If you can remove Tarkenton and make it look like Wakefield did it—or ordered it—then it makes gaining the deed to the Molly E Mine all the easier. One act rather than two. Minimum effort. Understand?"

"What about Slocum? I got a real yen to put a bullet in his gut and leave him out in the desert to die real slow."

"I don't care what you do to him," Pine said. A picture flashed through his mind of him shooting Slocum rather than Childress. He pushed it away. He fought his battles within the law. If the law let him swindle and steal, the law needed to be changed. It wasn't his problem that the law read the way it did. He used Blackstone like Childress used Colt.

"The mine."

Pine blinked and stared at Childress, not understanding what the man said.

"The damn fool'll head for his mine. That's where the posse went. Somebody in the crowd shouted it out, and they all got the idea Tarkenton would hole up in his mine."

"Nobody's that dumb," Pine said. "If he gets out of jail, the first place the law would look is the Molly E."

"Where'd you want me to hunt for him?"

Pine opened his mouth, then clamped it shut. He didn't know anywhere else to go but the mine. Tarkenton was a solitary soul, doing nothing but digging out silver from his mine, coming into town for a drink and supplies and then returning to dig even more of the precious metal from the ground. He had no friends that Pine had ever heard of, attended no church services, probably didn't even frequent the whorehouses.

Pine swallowed hard. It might be himself he was describing.

"We ride, me and you, Counselor?"

"I'll get my horse," Pine said.

He trotted back past the Mighty Fine Saloon, where Childress waited for him. The man wiped beer foam off his upper lip.

"Figgered there was time for one more drink."

Childress didn't wait for Pine to give the order. He dug his spurs cruelly into his horse's flanks and shot off like a Fourth of July rocket. Pine followed, not wanting to push his own mount to such a pace. He'd rather get there eventually on horseback rather than having a dead animal under him. In less than a mile Pine overtook Childress. His horse was lathered and its sides heaved.

"You see any of the gunmen with Wakefield?" Pine asked. "You think you can take them, if you have to?"

"If the money's good enough, I'll cut down the entire town of Tombstone."

"Too many have tried that, and it doesn't work. You have to pick at it like an ant working on a chicken carcass. Tear off a bit here, a bit there. Eventually you have the entire chicken. You try attacking it all at once and you'll get eaten alive."

"My way's better," insisted Childress. "A couple shots and

Wakefield loses a couple bodyguards. The ones he's got left will up and leave. I know their kind. I see 'em all the time. Their loyalty's only money deep. When Wakefield reaches the point where he can't pony up enough to pay them, they'll be history."

"You make it sound easy." Pine was dubious.

"It will be. Give me the word." Childress coughed in what he thought was a genteel fashion. It sounded more like he hawked up a gob. "'Course, these things cost. Plenty."

"How much plenty?" Pine asked.

"Fifty percent of Tarkenton's mine. I read the assay report filed on it with the land clerk. I can use a few hundred ounces a month to do some right fine things."

"I'm sure," Pine said dryly. He had his own vision of how to use the money, and he doubted Childress shared even an instant of it.

"I cut down Tarkenton, Slocum, and all of Wakefield's guards for the money."

"Not Wakefield, too?"

"I figger you want him for yourself. Right, Counselor?" Childress laughed his soul-chilling laugh. "When I talked with you that first time, I knowed we was meant to be partners. We're gonna be rich, Counselor, rich!"

"There's the posse," Pine said. "They're milling all around."

"Let's join the fun. Might be they'll take care of Tarkenton for us. You still owe me if they already strung him up."

They rode closer to the Molly E Mine and saw a dozen men prowling around, waving their six-shooters in the air and occasionally firing them. Pine looked for the man in charge but couldn't find anyone.

"He in his cabin?" Childress asked. "If he is, you might burn it down with him in it."

"Wait!" Pine's command fell on deaf ears. The cry went up that Tarkenton hid in the primitive cabin. Within minutes the cabin was ablaze.

"He'd be squawking like a roastin' quail if he was in there," Childress said, watching the flames licking the sky and then dying down as the last of the wood in the cabin was consumed.

"I wanted that cabin. Now I have to build another one for the workmen when they come out to shore up the mine's timbers and get down to real work."

"No big deal puttin' up a shed like that. Have the damn miners sleep under the stars. That's got to be better than lookin' up all day and seein' nothing but a thousand tons of rock an inch away from your nose."

"He's back in town," someone called. "He duped us. He circled and went back to Tombstone while we're on a wild-goose chase out here."

The posse grumbled, mounted, and within a few minutes had disappeared. Pine suspected they would find a saloon offering free drinks for entertaining stories of the night's ride and that would be it. No lynching, no capturing an escaped prisoner.

"What do we do, Counselor?"

"Pretend to ride off," Pine said in a low voice. "If he's hiding anywhere nearby, he'll come out and we can bag him."

"Shoot him?" Childress pressed.

"Let's see how much trouble it will be capturing him. He might make good bait for Wakefield." Pine's mind raced as he considered ways of using a living Ike Tarkenton to decoy Wakefield and get the other lawyer to make a fatal legal mistake. There had to be precedents he could cite. *Stare decisis.* Something that would forever cut Wakefield off from any claim to the silver mine.

Pine knew he might have to bribe Rollins even more. There were other judges to consider also. He'd bribe the lot of them. The federal district judge in Bisbee liked a well-turned ankle and a willing blonde. The judge over in Benson had a fondness for expensive food. Pine knew a freighter who could bring in iced-down oysters and some champagne from San Francisco. That took care of the judges most likely to deal with probate on Tarkenton's mine.

"I might do up a will," Pine said aloud.

"You fixin' to die, Counselor? If you are, leave your half of the Molly E Mine to me."

"I was thinking how Tarkenton's will might be written to avoid so much legal unpleasantness."

"I don't mind gettin' my hands dirty," Childress said. "But if I'm trackin' you a'right, this will cut out all the legal mumbo jumbo and get us the mine faster?"

"That it will. Don't kill Tarkenton outright. I need him to sign a will."

"Hell and damnation, it can take forever for you to write up something like that."

"It might, but if I have Tarkenton's signature at the bottom of a blank sheet of paper, I can write what I want and take the time to make it airtight."

Childress laughed until he had to hold his sides.

"You're quite a schemer, aren't you, Pine? That's the crookedest thing I ever did hear."

"We're far enough from the mine," Pine said coldly. He didn't think of his tactic as being the least bit underhanded. It . . . streamlined . . . the law. He was going to wrest ownership from Tarkenton one way or the other. This solved several problems in one fell swoop. It was not only better for him, it was best for Tarkenton since it kept him from having to appear in court to defend his mining claim.

"Circle 'round that way," Childress said, pointing to a dry wash. "We follow the arroyo and it'll bring us up a hundred yards from the mine. Unless somebody's got an eye out, they won't see us ridin' up."

Pine took the lead, letting Childress trail behind this time. He turned over one scheme after another but couldn't concoct anything more legally elegant than Tarkenton signing the blank sheet. If Tarkenton could even write. That might

prove a sticking point in court if Wakefield contested it, and
Pine was sure he would, but if the miner could write his
name, it would match with the land deed. Nobody dared call
the land clerk a crook. It was too easy for him to give away
property to adjoining claims or simply to lose the original
documents and throw everything wide-open. Pine had dealt
with three claims the land clerk had purposefully misfiled.
Only appropriate bribes and a public apology for calling him
a "porkchop-eating hog" had brought one of the cases to a
successful conclusion.

The other two Pine had chalked up to experience since he
lost both of them. What he had learned was to never cross the
county land clerk when even the presiding judge was a tad
afraid of his power to misfile.

"We got a fair view of the mouth to the mine," Childress
said. "How long you figger we got to wait?"

"The posse just left. Give him time to see that the dust's settled," Pine decided. He dismounted and found a rock to sit on
where he could watch the mine. The cabin smoldered and sent
fitful, nose-wrinkling curlicues of greasy black smoke sky-
ward. Whatever Tarkenton had stored in that cabin smelled to
high heaven as it had burned.

Almost an hour passed. Childress dozed, but Pine remained
alert. He saw a dark spot moving in a crevice near the mine.
He rubbed his eyes to be sure, closed them tightly, then opened
slowly. He got a better look with his dark-adapted eyes.

"Childress," he called softly. "We got company, and he's
going into the mine."

"What a complete fool," Childress said, shaking himself
awake. He drew his six-gun and started up the hill, not caring
that he made enough noise to scare a rabbit from its hiding
spot. A squad of cavalry charging uphill wouldn't have made
as much noise.

"Remember. He's got to stay alive long enough to put his
John Hancock on this sheet of paper." Pine fished the blank
page out from his coat pocket. He had pen and ink in his

saddlebags. Each of them armed in their own fashion, they made their way up the pebble-strewn slope to the mine.

Pine felt his heart beating faster. He was so close to being the owner of the richest silver strike in all Arizona Territory.

14

Slocum caught up with the posse as they were coming back from the Molly E Mine. He grinned, knowing the lynch mob had been decoyed away by his well-timed shout back in town, but now they were inclined to keep hunting.

Wherever Tarkenton had lit out to, he had to be given a chance to burrow down and pull the hole in after him.

"I saw him," Slocum called. "I think I saw him. Down southwest of town. I came to get you."

"Southwest?" One rider sounded skeptical. Slocum wondered if he could play on this enough to make the entire mob give up and go back to town. He hesitated to offer free drinks outright.

"You men have done a great service to Tombstone tonight," Slocum said. "You ought to go reward yourselves. There's whiskey by the barrel waiting for you in town!"

This sparked enough interest that a half-dozen men broke off from the main knot of riders and started trotting back toward Tombstone. Slocum wondered at the tenacity showed by the remaining half-dozen.

"Aren't you gents thirsty? It was a long ride out and it's a dusty one back to town. You should—"

"We ought to find him. You said you seen him ridin' southwest?"

"I couldn't be sure it was him," Slocum said, wanting to fling out as much doubt as possible. "It might have been someone else. It's dark. How can I be sure?"

"Ah, let's give it up for the night." Four more left, including the man Slocum had tried to convince to go southwest. Two were left, and Slocum didn't like the looks of them. Both were deputies.

"Isn't it a mite unusual for two lawmen to join a lynch mob?" Slocum asked.

"The marshal sent us with them to make sure nothing happened." Slocum recognized the lawman as Mike Eakin, the one Sosa had declared as his head deputy.

"Where's Marshal Sosa?" Slocum didn't want to hear the response he got.

"He talked to the livery owner, who said Tarkenton lit out going north across the flats. The marshal's about the best damn tracker in Arizona. He rode with the cavalry for nigh on a year, following the Apaches. It was Sosa who led Crook down into Mexico after Geronimo."

"Must be good," Slocum said, thinking hard. Even an experienced tracker would have difficulty following a trail at night, under starlight occasionally hidden by clouds, across sunbaked desert. There would hardly be any tracks left to follow if a light wind kicked up. That didn't mean Sosa couldn't nab Tarkenton if he got on the trail quick enough. A lone rider at night would be easy enough to hear and possibly see, if the tracker found a tall enough ridge overlooking the flats.

"The best," said the other deputy. "You come on back to town with us. We got some questions to ask you."

"How's that?"

"Sounded like your voice egging on the mob back in town. And you lied when you said you saw Tarkenton heading southwest. The marshal's sure he went north."

"I could be mistaken. It was dark."

"You ride along with us, Slocum," said Deputy Eakin. "We need to have a long talk 'bout this matter."

Slocum and the two deputies rode in silence for a mile, then he asked, "Is there a road running from Wilcox to Bisbee that doesn't go through Tombstone?"

"Of course there is. We ain't got a railroad, so anything that goes into Fairbank or Wilcox has to be freighted south to Bisbee. The road runs on the other side of these here hills." The deputy jerked his thumb over his shoulder toward the hills surrounding the Molly E Mine.

Slocum felt as if he had just stepped off a high cliff and was falling, falling, falling. Although he had warned Tarkenton not to return to the mine, that was exactly what the miner had intended. He would ride north, find the road down to Bisbee that stretched on the far side of these hills, then come over and take refuge in his mine. It was a long way to ride so the posse arrived first.

If Marshal Sosa stuck to the trail or if he thought about it for even a few seconds, he'd come to the same conclusion Slocum had. Tarkenton was heading back to the Molly E like a carrier pigeon flying home.

"My horse is starting to limp," Slocum said, pulling back hard on the reins. The gelding did a tiny crow hop and stumbled.

"Ain't safe bein' out here alone," one deputy said. "We heard tell of some renegade Apaches sighted in the area with the past week or so. Didn't tell the rest of those cayuses since they'd make so much noise any self-respecting Indian would let 'em ride past unharmed."

"Much obliged, but I'll be fine. This is a well-traveled road," Slocum said, not knowing if it was or not. At this time of night it would normally be as deserted as a cemetery during a barn dance.

The two deputies whispered back and forth and finally came to the conclusion he had hoped for.

"We're headin' on back to town," Eakin said. "If you ain't back by dawn, we'll come lookin' for you."

"Can't ask for more than that. My horse may just have a rock under a shoe. If I pry it out, everything'll be just fine." Slocum dismounted and raised the gelding's right front leg. The horse snorted but did nothing to give him away as he poked and prodded a perfectly good horseshoe. As soon as the deputies disappeared over a rise, Slocum lowered the leg, grabbed the reins, and walked the horse back toward Tarkenton's mine.

He finally mounted and rode the last couple miles until he caught the scent of burned wood. Fearing the worst, Slocum dismounted again and advanced on foot, wary for any trap that might be sprung. When he spotted the lazy spiral of smoke rising from the ruins of the burned cabin, he knew the lynch mob had turned angry at not finding Tarkenton.

He relaxed a little, thinking he might be wrong. Then he caught motion out of the corner of his eye. Continuing to look sideways gave him a better picture of what happened than if he tried staring directly. Two shadow figures moved up the slope from a nearby arroyo. Slocum drew his Colt Navy and waited for them, thinking Marshal Sosa might have a deputy with him.

". . . went into the mine. We can trap him there. Remember, don't kill him until he signs."

"You talk too much, Counselor."

Slocum recognized the voices. He followed their line of travel to the mouth of the mine. Tarkenton might be a miner but Slocum wondered if he had been out in the sun too much and fried his brains. The last place in the world to hide was a mine with a single opening out. He doubted Tarkenton had bored a safety escape or even air holes through the solid rock to keep the air deeper in the mine fresh. Such work would have taken away from the time—and joy—of digging out the silver ore.

He moved faster, coming up behind Pine and Childress. In the dark he couldn't make out which was which, then he caught a glimpse of the pair as Childress lit a lucifer and applied it to a miner's candle. Slocum clearly saw the lawyer's bowler and Childress's ugly face.

"We just walk in and get the drop on him," Pine said. "No shooting unless he opens up on us."

"Listen," Childress said, holding the candle high over his head. Slocum saw the rustler cant his head to one side as he listened to noise coming from deep within the mine. "It sounds like he's usin' a pick on the rock."

"He's still mining the ore," Pine said, a note of awe in his words. "In spite of the lynch mob on his trail, he came back to pull silver chloride from his mine. Doesn't that man think of anything else?"

"Let him get another ton of ore out. That'd mean that much less work for the likes of us," Childress suggested.

Slocum moved closer. When he got within fifty feet, he ran out of places to hide. He either walked straight up on them or he remained where he was, crouched behind a rusted-out ore cart.

A thousand things ran through his head, but the return of the lynch mob was foremost. Pine and Childress had Tarkenton trapped, so it was up to him to extract Tarkenton and get the miner to safety before the entire area was again swarming with men intent on killing him.

Slocum drew his six-shooter and started walking at a steady pace toward Childress and Pine. He didn't know if Pine was packing, but Childress had his pistol out and was ready to use it. Slocum focused on the rustler to the exclusion of the lawyer. He got within fifty feet of them before some tiny sound betrayed him. Pine glanced in his direction and warned his hired gun with a loud shout.

Growling like a mountain lion, Childress spun around and began firing. Slocum returned fire and kept advancing. There wasn't anywhere for him to hide. He had to trust that Childress wasn't too good a shot in the dark. One bullet sang past his ear. Another kicked up dirt at his feet. Slocum kept walking. When he got to thirty feet away, he opened fire again. His range and his aim were better than the outlaw's. Childress let out a gasp and then cursed a blue streak.

One slug had nicked the rustler's leg. Slocum had been aiming to put the bullet in his gut. He kept walking like some elemental force of nature, ignoring the lead flying wildly now. His service during the war had prepared him for such an attack. More than once he had led his company forward when he could see the Federals' rifle muzzles looking as big as his fist straight in front of him. He had never flinched then, and his men had followed him because of his unwavering courage.

The same thing happened to Childress and Pine that had often happened to the Yankee troopers. They saw his inexorable advance and broke. Pine yelped and ran in the direction of the burned-out cabin. Childress ran in the opposite direction, shooting over his shoulder as he went until his hammer fell on a spent cartridge.

Slocum stopped, took careful aim, and fired. Childress stumbled and went down in the dark, still cursing. Slocum had again missed with a killing shot but had brought down the rustler.

His own pistol came up empty. During his attack he had paid no attention to how many times he had fired. Now he was faced with a dilemma. Tarkenton was in the mine. Childress was probably not seriously injured, but Pine had high-tailed it. By now the lawyer might be all the way back to Tombstone.

Good sense dictated that he ought to finish off Childress,

but in the distance came the thunder of horses' hooves pounding against the ground. If the mob had heard the gunfire and returned, Tarkenton would be strung up before Slocum could finish off Childress.

Then the matter was settled for him. Childress began firing. How he had reloaded so fast mattered less to Slocum than ducking into the mine to get out of the line of fire. He took time to reload his own six-gun but now was trapped. All Childress had to do was wait for them to get thirsty and surrender. If it had been the posse returning and not just Pine running away, their situation was even more perilous. There wasn't enough ammo in the world to hold that lynch mob at bay.

Worse, they might get testy and simply blow up the mine, entombing him and Tarkenton. Slocum looked to either side of the mine's mouth and saw the shaky timbers Tarkenton had used. Dynamite wasn't even needed. A rope around one of those supports, a determined tug, and the mouth of the mine would seal itself.

Slocum glanced over his shoulder into the depths of the mine and saw a flickering candle.

"Tarkenton!" No answer. "Tarkenton, we got to get out of the mine. Now!" Still no answer. Reluctantly Slocum backed into the mine, keeping the faint outline in sight and waiting for a dark form to flit across his field of vision. That would be the only target he'd get in the night.

The deeper he went into the mine, the louder the sounds of a pick working on rock became.

"Tarkenton!" Slocum stared at the miner. He had a pick in his hand and worked diligently to chip away ore from the wall. "What do you think you're doing? I told you not to come here since it'd be the first place they'd look for you."

"Can't leave this be, Slocum," the miner said. "Might jist be the richest vein in the whole danged mine. See?" He held up a nugget that gleamed in his hand. "I missed it before diggin' deeper into the hill. I can run a drift here and—"

"You'll have a silver-lined coffin if we don't get out of the mine. Childress is going to kill you if you stick your head outside. I heard horses coming. That might be the lynch mob coming back for you."

"Can't be. I watched 'til they all left. Those bastards burned down my cabin, but with this new find, I kin buy myself a goldarned mansion. Two!"

"We're going to die in here, no matter who's out there," Slocum said, trying to convince the miner of how serious their plight was.

"Ain't the mob. They all went back to town to get drunk. I know them too well to think they'd come back. Hell, there ain't even a reward on my head. I got locked up fer tax dodgin'."

"Pine might be gone, too, but Childress isn't budging. He wants to kill you. I heard Pine say something about forcing you to sign a paper."

"I'd never turn over the Molly E to the likes of Jackson Pine. Let 'em cut off my ears. Won't sign. After findin' this"— he held up his silver ore—"they could cut off my hands and feet and I'd never sign. The Molly E Mine is gonna make me stinkin' rich."

A bullet bounced off the mine walls as it worked its way back toward them. Slocum ducked involuntarily. Tarkenton never noticed as he returned to the serious work of prying the silver ore free from the walls.

"There's no way I can shoot my way out. Childress has position, and even if he is a piss-poor shot, he can't miss. Is there another way out of the mine?"

"Another way?" Tarkenton looked up and frowned. He looked like some strange underground-dwelling creature. The shadows moving constantly over his filthy face turned him into something less than human. His eyes glistened in the light from the miner's candle, and as he grinned, a gold tooth in front reflected enough to give him a totally inhuman aspect.

Slocum fired once. He doubted his bullet came close to doing any damage. Childress would be crouched beside the opening to the mine and just take random shots to drive them farther back.

"I've got to save my ammo if the posse comes boiling in here after us."

"Yup."

"What do you mean 'yup'?"

"There's another way out. 'Course you might not fit so good since you ain't nowhere near skinny as me. I cut an air hole way back in the mine, danged near fifty yards deeper." Tarkenton made a vague effort to point where the air vent was, but he held a silver nugget in one hand and the pick in the other.

"You shinnied the entire way along this air hole?"

"How do you think I chiseled it out? Found a rock chimney and followed a likely-looking vein of ore up it. Halfway I caught sight of blue sky. Only took me a day or so to chisel out a hole all the way to the top of the hill. Improved the air in the mine but never found any silver in that chimney, so I reckon I wasted my time."

"Show me." Slocum saw nothing but darkness at the mine mouth. He backed away, keeping his body between the mouth and the candle flame so Childress wouldn't get a decent target outlined by the guttering candlelight.

Tarkenton grumbled about leaving behind his precious ore, but he began shuffling along, heading far into the mine. He stopped suddenly and pointed up.

Slocum peered at the spot where the miner pointed. It took him several seconds before he realized he was looking up at the night sky, and the tiny dots he saw were stars.

"Get up there. I'll follow."

"You're mighty fat fer that, young fella."

Slocum knew he could always shoot his way out of the mine if it came to that. He didn't like the idea and would be severely wounded if not killed, but at least Tarkenton would be safe.

"I want you to stay out of jail and healthy until Sam Norton mends up."

"Norton's a good man, but he's dyin'."

"Maybe, maybe not. Now get moving."

Slocum helped Tarkenton wedge his scrawny body into the crevice, then turned his face downward as rock and dirt cascaded over him. He stepped to one side, then peered up. The stars had disappeared, but he heard Tarkenton grunting and straining as he made his way up the narrow chimney. After an eternity the stars popped back into sight. Tarkenton had safely reached the top of the hill.

Slocum hoped the miner had the good sense not to go back down the hill and come into the mine again to resume his digging. The lure of silver was more than the man could deny. If he had been an opium addict, the powerful grip on his body and soul couldn't be any greater.

Slipping his six-shooter into his holster, Slocum reached up and ran his fingers around the narrow, jagged chimney. It was as small as Tarkenton had claimed. Before he started, Slocum stripped off his gun belt and used a rawhide strip to fasten it to his right boot so it would dangle down. He'd need all the space around his middle that he could get.

When he found a sturdy enough outcropping of rock, he gripped down hard, pulled himself up as he jumped. And he was firmly wedged inside the narrow rock passage. Barely able to breathe, he considered dropping back but Tarkenton yelled down from above, "The chimney opens up a mite a few feet 'bove yer head."

Slocum hoped the old miner wasn't blowing smoke up his ass. He fumbled around, found a new knob of rock, and began pulling himself up. Now and then his toes found purchase but mostly he had to use his arms to climb upward. Friction between his body and the rock kept him from falling back down, but a sudden widening gave him some breathing space.

Tarkenton had been right about this.

"It gits tighter, Slocum. You sure you want to do this? I ain't the least bit positive you kin make it all the way. I lost a fair amount of skin gettin' out."

Slocum began to fight for every inch he climbed. Just when he thought he would give up, he heard a bullet ricochet along the mine shaft. Childress fired now and again to keep his trapped victims scared. Rather than give up, this doubled Slocum's determination. He lost more than a little bit of skin on sharp rocks, but he finally popped out onto the top of the hill. A cold wind had kicked up. It revitalized him. He hadn't realized it was so hot in the chimney that he was sweating like a pig.

"Lemme help you up," Tarkenton offered. Slocum took the miner's hand and was lifted with surprising strength. He had to stop to pull his gun belt and pistol out of the chimney.

"Now that was real smart of you," Tarkenton said admiringly. "You knowed you'd be pressed 'round the middle. I like a man who thinks ahead." Tarkenton guffawed. "I like 'em since I ain't one of 'em."

Slocum wasn't going to argue that point. He strapped on his holster and drew his Colt to begin reloading it.

"Which way's the mouth of the mine?" He looked around but couldn't figure out what direction he was pointed in.

"Thata way," Tarkenton said.

"Stay here. I'll be back for you."

"Don't be too long. I got metal to pull from this here mine. Yes, sir, the Molly E is gonna make me rich."

Slocum worked his way down the hillside until he came out on a ledge high above the mine. Looking down, he saw a sight that made him grin from ear to ear. The horse he had heard galloping up wasn't one of many—it was only the marshal's. Sosa had the drop on Childress, who argued loudly to no avail.

Slocum had to hand it to the marshal, tracking Tarkenton from town, all the way across a desert that hardly took a print—and doing it in the dark. He had arrived just in time to catch him a wanted outlaw.

Sosa marched Childress off at gunpoint and used shackles from his saddlebags to secure the rustler. Then the pair of them rode away slowly toward town. Slocum simply sat and watched as they vanished into the night.

Luck was finally coming his way.

15

China Mary sat impassively as she heard one of her workers rattling on and in Chinese about the latest problems in Tombstone. Nothing ever changed. Always there was trouble with the girls in the house, sometimes with the patrons but more often with the girls. They were required to be drug-free and often strayed. Dealing with the customers required two distinct paths to tranquillity. Miners were easily removed by the bouncers. More difficult were the politicians and those who had political connections.

Tonight the problems dealt with a judge who chose to become too aggressive.

"Offer him an opium pipe. No charge," China Mary said. "If he enjoys that, perhaps we have a customer for another of our ventures. Support in such quarters will be beneficial when we seek to expand our influence to the other side of town."

The man bowed deeply and backed away, hurrying back to the whorehouse to offer the judge—China Mary didn't care which of several it was—to end the situation properly.

Ah Sum came in and stood stolidly, arms folded. He locked eyes with her. China Mary sat a little straighter in her chair.

"What is it?"

Ah Sum took one hand from a dangling sleeve and motioned to a man who waited in the outer room. He scuttled in. China Mary frowned. The man had not bathed and smelled like an outhouse. His clothing was torn, and he presented the picture of a peasant farmer. She hated peasant farmers. One of the few things in this country she appreciated was the lack of peasant farmers planting rice plugs in flooded fields of shit. Her father had died in such a field. Her three brothers had died in such fields.

"Mistress, I was attacked."

"Describe what happened. You are unworthy to be in my presence but Ah Sum thinks I ought to hear your tale. You may thank him for his generosity later."

"I was attacked. I hid in an outhouse until the killers left."

"Who died?" China Mary fixed her steely gaze on Ah Sum. He showed more emotion than usual, telling her this was not a trivial matter.

"My sister was raped and killed. I tried to stop the killer but another attacked me. I fought."

"Then you got away and hid," China Mary said impatiently.

"That is so. I am worthless. I should have died."

"You should tell me who did this. Do you know their names?" China Mary hoped the man didn't have to identify those responsible. In the past she had found only woe relying on bad memories and poor eyesight. All the towering, bulky Americans smelled of beef, making them more alike than different to the eyes of a Celestial.

"Their employer was called Wakefield."

China Mary sighed. Another war with a lawyer of Colin Wakefield's influence would distract her from more important concerns. She had three new businesses opening, all fronted by Americans. Her money financed their stores and required constant observation to make certain they did not try to steal from her. The American banks would not give loans for the risky new ventures. In the spirit of the Triads, she offered such money. Also in the spirit of the Triads, she tolerated no thievery and immediate repayment of the loan with suitable interest. Even after the loan was repaid, she retained a proportionate share of the business for her trouble.

"Go. I will deal with Wakefield," she said. The man left, bowing and scraping. To her surprise, Ah Sum did not leave. Nor did he look as if the matter was being resolved.

Ah Sum grunted and another man entered. China Mary began to worry now. Ah Sum had summoned her accountant.

"Speak," she said.

"Mistress, Wakefield files tax liens on your property."

"Including the new opium den off First Street?" She had been bold with that, putting the opium den not far from the Bird Cage Saloon. The saloons up and down Allen and Fremont Streets were reserved for Americans and all owned by Americans. Even the Mexicans were shut out from such ownership. By placing a smokers' den so close, she intruded. Not much but a little. To her knowledge, Wakefield did not own any of the nearby saloons, so his interest had to be something greater than restraint of her trade.

China Mary sat quietly, hands folded in her lap as she considered Wakefield and his possible use of bogus tax liens. She knew what Jackson Pine had done to the miner Tarkenton. Another lawyer had taken up the same tactic, only with, to China Mary's way of thinking, greater ambition. Wakefield wanted to control the small empire she had forged in Hop Town.

"He cannot be allowed to close the opium dens," she said. Nothing more was needed. Ah Sum bowed deeply, then left. She felt a momentary relief. There was no more on Ah Sum's mind. That was good. To her accountant, she said, "What are the receipts like? Do we have legal representation to fight off Wakefield's attack?"

"Norton remains ill but the American doctor—"

"He is German," China Mary corrected. Then she motioned for the accountant to continue.

"Norton's doctor has operated on him to great success. Soon, Norton will again be ready to represent us in their courts."

"Good," she said. "Continue with your report of revenue and those city officials who have been bribed. I must know that Wakefield has no authority to get actual tax liens."

The two talked for more than an hour. China Mary's head boiled with figures and profits. Much money could be sent to China for other projects. She might double the flow of opium now that Wakefield intruded so that she would have more for bribes and to counter his illegal maneuvers.

She looked up suddenly when Ah Sum burst in.

"What is it?" Ah Sum grunted and gestured in such a way she could not follow what her trusted lieutenant meant. "Stop! Find someone who can give me the details."

Ah Sum was still breathing heavily. As he turned, she saw two small holes in his padded jacket surrounded by red blossoms of blood. Ah Sum had been shot in the back. She glanced toward an alcove, where a servant waited patiently. She issued orders for medical treatment. Ah Sum was too valuable to endure two bullet wounds.

A pair of Ah Sum's assistants tumbled in, dropped to the floor, and banged their heads repeatedly to show their respect. She waited for them to stop kowtowing before asking, "What happened?"

"Wakefield's men ambushed us," one said fearfully. "We fought. Four of us were killed."

She glanced at Ah Sum, trying to look impassive. The pain wore on him and caused him to wobble. *Even the sturdiest mountain must someday tumble*, she thought, looking at him.

"Why did they ambush you? Where did this happen?"

"Near the new opium parlor on First Street. They moved to rob all the patrons."

China Mary sucked in a deep breath, then released it slowly. Wakefield thought to make it seem that danger awaited any who chased the dragon in one of her smoking parlors. If this worked at the new opium den, he would try it at other locations. The legitimate business would find legal problems with tax liens, but the illegal ones—or the ones like the opium dens that were tolerated, although technically not legal—would be attacked in such a way that customers would seek other diversions.

"What of the whorehouse?"

"They tried to burn it down. Ah Sum fought them. They rushed away." The man speaking glanced toward the increasingly pale Ah Sum.

"I know of his wounds. He will be tended. There is no further threat?"

"Wakefield's men died also. Seven of them. Many ran off."

"So this is only a pause in a new war. So be it."

She dismissed her henchmen, then said to Ah Sum, "You will allow Mei to remove the bullets. Then you will rest. Your invaluable services will be needed soon."

Ah Sum grunted and pointed. Simply lifting his arm to gesture caused him to wince.

"I will not be without protection," she said. "Norton will soon represent me again." She quieted an even more agitated Ah Sum with, "I will not trust my personal safety to ones such as those who just left." She sighed, closed her eyes, then opened them slowly, having come to a difficult decision. "Slocum will serve me well. Again."

16

"I cain't stay here," Tarkenton complained. "I got to get on back to the Molly E so I can—"

"Get your head blown off," Slocum finished for him. "That's if you're lucky. You might be hanged. Or worse."

"What's worse 'n bein' hanged?" Tarkenton asked suspiciously. "I heard tell of a band of Apache around here what skinned men alive and left 'em in the sun to writhe about and die eventually." The miner shivered at the hideous picture he conjured up. "That's worse 'n bein' hanged. Cain't think of anything worse."

"Worse than that," Slocum said. "How'd you like to be done out of the Molly E Mine and you couldn't do a thing about it?"

"You mean have the mine stole out from under me? I'd never let that happen. I'd—" Tarkenton stopped and stared at Slocum. "I'm beginnin' to see what you mean. If I was in jail and Pine stole the mine, I'd know 'bout it and there wouldn't be a damned thing I could do."

"That's right," Slocum said. He looked around the barren stretch of desert south of town he had ridden into. There weren't a lot of places where a man could live, but this spot near the road leading down to Bisbee looked likely enough to keep Tarkenton alive for a day or two.

The miner went to the edge of the murky pond and stared at it.

"That's nuthin' but mud."

"Use a cloth to filter out the mud. Drink what comes through. It'll be better than the spring up at your mine. That tasted like it has arsenic in it."

"Might be. Lot of heavy metal there. If it'd tasted like silver, I'd've thunk up this filterin' scheme on my own fer when I took a piss." He looked dubious as Slocum began work using his bandanna to show the miner what to do.

"You stay out of sight. We're close to a mile from the road leading south. There might not be many who even know of this watering hole."

"Them Apaches do. They know where ever' drop of water in Arizona Territory is."

"Stay hid for a couple days and not even the Apaches will find you," Slocum promised. "Most of all, keep out of sight if anyone from Tombstone comes this way. They're likely to be part of that lynch mob."

"Might work for Pine, too. That varmint and his hired gun tried to kill me."

"Don't you forget that. The marshal might have Childress locked up, but Pine got away."

"Ain't afraid of him."

"You ought to be since he's the brains behind the scheme to steal your mine. I'm going into Tombstone to find out what's going on." Slocum had no reason to mention he was more than a little anxious to see Claire Norton again, too, for reasons that had nothing to do with Tarkenton's damned Molly E Mine.

"If you see that Jackson Pine, you put a bullet in him for me, will you?"

"I'll think on it. Real hard," Slocum said. "You stay here."

He glared at the miner until Tarkenton wilted and looked like a whipped mongrel.

"I will," Tarkenton said reluctantly.

Slocum mounted and stared at the miner, wondering if he would remain hidden here for even a few hours. The man had one thought only in his thick head and that was pulling silver chloride ore out of his mine. Slocum knew the only reason he bothered helping the miner was that Sam Norton represented him.

And Slocum wanted to stay on Claire Norton's good side, not that he had found a bad one yet.

He rode due west and then angled up toward town, following the same path he had when he had brought Childress to Tombstone that first time. It seemed like a lifetime ago, but it was only a week or so back. By the time he trotted into town, the sun had set at his back and the saloons roared with boisterous drunken song. A new melodrama had opened at the Bird Cage and miners lined up, jostling one another, to get to the front of the line. An occasional brawl was taken out into the street but no one paid a great deal of attention. They were mostly inside the saloons having too good a time knocking back beer and shots of whiskey and talking to the pretty waiter girls.

Slocum licked his lips, wanting a taste of what the miners shared but knew he had other more immediate concerns.

Riding through town, he left behind the rowdy streets lined with saloons and worked his way past Dr. Gottschalk's office. He glanced in and saw the doctor sleeping at his desk. He kept riding, out to the edge of town where the Norton house stood silent and alone. A single light burned in the narrow window. Slocum dismounted and tied up his horse, then went to the door. He hesitated, then knocked.

It took Claire a few seconds to open the door. When she did, she opened it only a crack. He saw her lovely green eye peering out. When she recognized him, she threw open the door, and he found himself with an armful of warm, willing woman.

"Oh, John, you're back. I was so worried. I heard about the lynch mob and the marshal and Tarkenton and . . . tell me all about it!"

She pulled him into the house and shut the door behind them. She paused to catch her breath, then smiled almost shyly and locked the door.

"Do you really want to hear about Tarkenton and how Marshal Sosa arrested Childress?" he asked.

"I most certainly do," she said. Claire reached up and began unfastening the grosgrain ribbons of her nightgown. "In the morning."

He watched as she ran her slender fingers over every tie, then carefully, slowly pulled until the bow came apart. She started at her slender neck. The first tie revealed more of her throat and just a hint of the deep valley between her breasts. The second tie opened and Slocum caught sight of the snowy slopes. The third and fourth opened, causing a vee to open all the way down far below her breasts. As she moved about, swaying like a willow in a gentle summer breeze, the nightgown parted and covered strategic portions of her body.

"You're the most beautiful thing I've ever seen," he said.

"You say that to all your women, don't you, John?"

There was only one answer he could give to such a question. He stepped forward, took her in his arms, and kissed her. Hard. Their lips crushed together. For an instant, she stiffened and tried to force herself away. Then she melted and flowed and their bodies fit together perfectly. He ran his fingers through her hair, tangling the coppery locks.

She gasped when he moved from her hair and stroked down her back. To her waist. Lower. He cupped her firm buttocks and squeezed down hard enough to pull her into his body. Claire began moving, trying to position herself better. Her legs parted, and she curled one around Slocum's thigh so she could stroke up and down against his jeans like a cat rubbing itself against a post.

"So nice," she said, "but I want more. Give it all to me." She reached down and pressed her hand into his crotch so there would be no question what she was asking.

He kissed her again, going from her lips to her ear and then down to the hollow of her throat. She threw her head back and sighed. When he reached the valley between her breasts, she was shaking all over. He slipped and slid his tongue about from one hard nub to the other and then worked his way down even farther, taking his sweet time and tormenting her with feathery kisses and soft caresses. When he reached the lowest ribbon Claire had left tied, he began worrying it with his teeth until it parted, exposing her deep navel. He pressed his tongue into it and worked it about until she sobbed with need. Then he moved still lower.

He caught the last ribbon tie in his teeth, reared back, and pulled it free to reveal a rust-colored patch of fleece between her legs. A quick lick along her nether lips caused her to lean forward, bracing herself on his shoulders. He reached around her thighs and lifted her bodily from the floor, spinning her around and carrying her into the bedroom, where he dropped her onto the bed.

Claire fell back, her nightgown billowing open all the way down her front. She looked at him with lust-glazed eyes.

"Hurry, John. I need you so."

He hurried. He got his gun belt and boots off, then his shirt and jeans. And finally he stepped to the bed where she lay.

Claire reached out and took his rigid manhood in her hand. She looked up, their green eyes locked, then she dipped forward and took his tip into her mouth. He felt some of what he had already given the woman. Tiny sparks flew down his length and ignited in his loins. He had been hard before. Now he became a steel rod.

Moving closer, he began exploring her body with only his fingertips. Light touches and deep gazes, he examined every inch of silky smooth bone-white skin until he found the spots to press and stroke that excited her the most.

He knew he had found a special spot on her hip when she stiffened and lay back on the bed, eyes closed. Her body shook and her legs went straight.

He reached down to her inner thighs and parted them. As she relaxed, he moved forward, kneeling between her spread, raised legs. Claire reached down and found him. She guided him inward. Slocum moved slowly, relishing the tightness, the heat, the feel of a woman all around his length.

Propping himself up on his hands, he moved forward with authority. He sank deep into her and paused. She rotated her hips under him, stirring him within her like a spoon in a mixing bowl. Then he pulled out. She gasped and squeezed down with her inner muscles, trying to prevent him from abandoning her like this. He was too powerful. He slid back until only the tip of his shaft parted her nether lips. But he did not remain there long. He thrust back, faster this time.

He built the speed and desire in both their bodies with his deliberate, potent strokes. Claire gripped his upper arms and curled up to meet his every inward stroke. Then she sank back and abandoned herself to complete physical and emotional release.

Slocum was not far behind. The fiery tides built within him and then raced along his length to spill forth. When he was spent, he rolled to the side and let Claire snuggle closer.

For a moment such as this, he would risk anything.

"So tell me," she said. "Everything."

"It's not morning yet," he teased.

"I expect to find other ways of passing the time until sunrise," she said, "but you're not ready for them yet. So tell me. Is Ike Tarkenton safe?"

"I've convinced him to stay out of sight." Slocum didn't have to tell her how improbable it was for that situation to last, considering Tarkenton's insane desire to do nothing but dig silver ore from his mine. For a day he might stay hidden, then he would ride out. Maybe to his mine, possibly into Tombstone. Either destination might be all it took for Pine to jail him—or worse.

After he'd finished telling her how he and Tarkenton had escaped the mine through the air shaft, she drew back and studied him critically.

"So that's where the cuts and scrapes came from. I was afraid you'd gone off with some floozy."

"Who treated me this rough?" He saw Claire's speculative look. "As rough as you'd treat me?"

"That's something we can explore, John," she said softly.

"Did you hear anything from the marshal after he got back to town with Childress?"

"He put a double guard on him so he couldn't escape. The saloon owners don't like this since that means one fewer lawman to patrol the streets, but Sosa is not giving in. He's been humiliated by too many escapes."

"Does he suspect me of having anything to do with Tarkenton busting out the other night?"

"He might. He hasn't said. He's certainly not posted a reward for you charging you with aiding and abetting a jail break."

"Tarkenton won't stay put too long, and Childress is like a stick of dynamite with the fuse burning down fast to the blasting cap. There's no telling what Pine might do to get him free. Your pa's got to start filing papers to help Tarkenton hang on to his mine."

"Papa is doing better, but he is still weak after the surgery. Dr. Gottschalk said he is giving him less opium for the pain to keep him from becoming addicted. This makes Papa feel worse so it's hard to tell how soon he would be able to go to court again."

"A day or two?"

"Oh, not that soon." Claire pressed her cheek against his bare chest. "And don't you ask because he'd try. He is a stubborn man, and if he thought defending Tarkenton in court would get back at Pine, he'd spring from his death bed and race the Grim Reaper to the courtroom."

"What caused the feud between your pa and Pine?"

Slocum felt the woman tense and move away from him a little. He refused to let her slip away like that. In a moment, she gave in and stopped trying to distance herself.

"It goes back to when Pine came to town. He approached Papa about becoming his partner. Knowing Pine, it was probably the other way. He wanted Papa to be his partner."

"I don't know your pa that well but I can imagine he tossed Pine out on his ear."

"On his ass," Claire said, giggling, but it was a nervous giggle that told Slocum there was more to the story. He didn't have to be a mind reader to know what it was. He had seen the way Pine acted at the doctor's office. He was sweet on Claire, and she wanted nothing to do with him. The offered partnership had been nothing more than a way to get in good with her, and like the astute lawyer he was, Sam Norton had seen through it right away.

That made the lawyer's stock rise in Slocum's opinion.

"If the marshal would start at one end of Rotten Row and go to the other, arresting anyone who was a lawyer, he could improve Tombstone a hundred times over."

Claire giggled again and then said, "But my papa would be in jail with them. Knowing him, he'd represent them in court. And win!"

"What about Wakefield?"

"He's just plain wicked. The man doesn't have a soul. Look what he's trying to do all around town."

"What's that?"

Slocum listened with half an ear as Claire detailed the shady dealings Colin Wakefield engaged in. As far as he could tell, they weren't any worse than what Jackson Pine was trying to do to Tarkenton, but Claire made them sound worse somehow. When she'd finished, she was almost out of breath.

"I think he wants to own the town, but he wants to do it by controlling everything that's illegal."

"Do you reckon those four who robbed the train of China Mary's opium shipment worked for him?"

"He hangs out in the lowest dives in town. I wouldn't put it past him. If he had gotten the opium, he might have tried to ransom it to Dr. Gottschalk in return for Papa's confidential files."

"What's in those?"

"Why, details of every case he's defended. When he came to town, he worked for some of the biggest names around. Ranchers, politicians, saloon owners. The more he saw of them and how they operated, the more he began defending their victims. Papa's files must have all kinds of details about illegal activities in Tombstone. You can't defend a man without knowing everything about his enemy."

"Sounds as if Wakefield has a lot to answer for," Slocum said.

This time when Claire moved away, he didn't stop her. He enjoyed the sight of her naked body moving lithely as she dressed. It took her a bit longer to dress than it did him, but he still strapped on his six-shooter about the time she worked on the buttons for her shoes.

"What are you going to do, John?"

"I need to poke around and see if I can't send a rat or two scuttling out where I can shoot them," he said.

"Be careful," she said. Claire gave him a warm kiss, but it was nothing like those she had lavished on him before.

Or it might just have been that he was distracted, thinking about how to flush out Wakefield—and Jackson Pine.

17

Slocum found a spot at the corner of Fremont and Second Streets, where he could lean back in a chair, pull down the brim of his hat, and watch what happened along two of the busiest streets in Tombstone. Two deputies made their patrol up one side of the street and down the other, barely paying attention to Slocum. He was heartened by this since it meant trouble was slowly disappearing in town.

With Tarkenton hiding out, Pine and Wakefield weren't likely to be out gunning down anyone who moved. Slocum considered going to see if Sam Norton was doing better, but decided to avoid the doctor's office for the moment. If he were Pine, he'd have a man posted there watching to see who came and went. For all he knew, Pine might be there himself hoping to catch a sight of Claire. When he had run the lawyer off before Norton's operation, it had been obvious from the expression on Pine's face where his emotions lay. He was smitten with the woman. Slocum had confirmed this when he had lain beside Claire in bed and heard her tell of how Pine had wanted to partner up with her father.

The legal combination had to be less a concern to Jackson

Pine than having his would-be partner's daughter come into the office every day. It was an obvious play for her affections.

Slocum tensed as the thought occurred to him that Pine might kill Sam Norton on the premise that Claire would turn to him in her moment of sorrow. It was twisted and it was exactly what the lawyer would do. After overhearing Pine's scheme out at the Molly E Mine, he was convinced that Pine was capable of about anything underhanded or outright illegal. At least Childress had been unable to force Tarkenton to sign the blank sheet. It didn't take Slocum much guesswork to figure out what would have been written above the miner's signature.

How many others had fallen for the same scheme?

Slocum rocked forward, settling all four chair legs on the boardwalk so he could lean out and see what Marshal Sosa was up to. The lawman argued with a man standing just inside a saloon a few doors down. When Wakefield stepped out and began poking the marshal in the chest with his index finger, every jab emphasizing a point, Slocum knew he had to get closer to find out what had got Wakefield so riled.

He stood, stretched, and sauntered down the boardwalk, trying not to appear too anxious. When he reached the end of the boardwalk, he was only twenty feet from Wakefield and Sosa.

". . . illegal incursion into my territory, Marshal. You have to agree." Wakefield jabbed Sosa just above his badge with his finger, like he was stabbing the marshal with a small knife. Slocum saw the marshal's face tighten. Every poke pushed him just a little closer to throwing the lawyer in jail—or maybe just drawing his hogleg and drilling a .44 slug into Wakefield's gut.

"You need to show me how that's illegal. I don't cotton much to opium dens, and keepin' them in Hop Town is a good thing, but it's not illegal to put one next to your saloon."

"It's not my saloon," Wakefield snapped. "I represent the

owner, that's all. It's a legal relationship, not an ownership one."

"That's not what I heard."

"You heard wrong," Wakefield said. He started to poke Sosa again, but the marshal grabbed the lawyer's wrist and shoved his hand aside. "You're making a mistake siding with that Chink whoremonger."

"China Mary runs a brothel, and there's no doubt she controls the opium in town, but I get less trouble from her than I do you. And you're supposed to be an officer of the court."

"That's a damned lie, Marshal. I'm law-abiding. She must be in arrears on some of her license payments. Why don't you look into it and find out how you can shut down her opium dens? There might be a bit of a . . . reward."

"A bribe, you mean," Sosa said.

Wakefield's sneer would have caused Slocum to bust out a few teeth behind it if it had been directed to him. Sosa ignored it.

"You'll come around eventually to my way of thinking, Marshal. It won't be long before I own the Molly E Mine and am rolling in silver. I'll own this town."

"You might own the town someday, Mr. Wakefield, but that don't mean you'll ever own the people in it—or the law." The marshal spun and stalked off. Slocum turned and pretended to interest himself in a couple bolts of yard goods in the window of the general store.

The marshal passed Slocum without so much as a glance in his direction. Wakefield went back into the saloon, but Slocum was more inclined to find out what Sosa was up to. The lawman sounded as if he couldn't be bribed, at least by Wakefield. That made him as close to an honest man as Slocum was likely to find in Tombstone. Although it might be a matter of Wakefield not finding the right amount, Slocum had heard actual outrage in Sosa's voice. That gave him some hope that Tarkenton might be saved from both being lynched and having his mine stolen away through legal she-nanigans.

Slocum walked along, hunting for the marshal, only to hear a boot scraping on the boardwalk behind him.

"Don't bother turning 'round, Slocum. I've got a six-shooter aimed at your spine."

"How are you, Marshal?" Slocum considered what to do. He had been careless for an instant and let the lawman get the drop on him.

"I'm huntin' fer the varmint that let Tarkenton out of jail. In my book, that's a crime. Might even think it was as bad a crime as what Tarkenton was locked up for."

"If he hadn't escaped, he'd be danglin' from a tree limb somewhere."

"Doubt that. The way that mob acted, they'd just as soon tied a rope 'round his neck and dragged him a mile or two."

"All the better that he hightailed it."

"I'm not so sure 'bout that. The Molly E Mine is a bone of contention with them lawyers. Get that squared away and everyone'd be happier and a whole lot more peaceable."

"Except Tarkenton. It's his mine they're wanting to steal."

Sosa snorted.

"What's he know? He's a hard-rock miner."

"That doesn't mean he ought to be robbed, even if you think it is for the public good."

"To hell with the public good. I'm thinkin' it'll be for *my* good. All this squabblin' is drivin' me crazy."

Slocum almost laughed. He was right about the marshal. He had an honest core, but that didn't save Tarkenton's mine or keep Ike from being the guest of honor at a necktie party if those misdeeds brought some peace and quiet to Tombstone.

"What are you going to do?"

"You got sprung by China Mary to do somethin'. I don't know what and I don't ask. But if I lock you up, I think maybe Tarkenton would come around. You and him look to be part-ners."

"Do I look like I'd be partners with a miner?"

"Cain't hurt lockin' you up for a day or two."

Slocum wondered how long he would stay alive inside one of Sosa's cells. Childress was there and Pine would get him out eventually. Considering how close Pine and Childress had come to killing Tarkenton, the lawyer might take a shot at him while Childress was still locked up, just to give his henchman an alibi. Pine was that devious.

"You don't need to do this, Marshal. I haven't done anything wrong."

Sosa laughed harshly as he reached around to slip Slocum's six-gun from its holster. He had rammed the barrel of his own gun into Slocum's spine to keep him from getting any ideas about putting up a fight.

"A man like you's done nuthin' but wrong. I just need to find what it is. You have wanted posters with your likeness on them, Slocum?"

Slocum hoped that the constant turnover in the marshal's office had caused all the old wanted posters to be burned to make room for new ones. Sosa might have a poster on Slocum for killing a federal judge. Or maybe not, since that had been a while back right after the war. Georgia was a long ways off. Still, Slocum hadn't ridden the West and remained pure as the wind-driven snow. More than once he'd robbed a stagecoach or a train to keep body and soul together when there hadn't been any other jobs available. He had no idea what Sosa might find if he looked.

"Go on, get in there," the marshal said, prodding Slocum into the cell adjoining Childress.

"Now don't that beat all," Childress said, opening an eye as he lay back on his cot. "I wondered when you'd turn up in here. You're the one that's the damned outlaw, not me."

"Shut up," Marshal Sosa said mechanically.

"What are you locking me up for?" Slocum asked. "I haven't done anything."

"Suspicion," Sosa said.

"Of what?"

"Whatever's been goin' on 'round this town," the marshal said. "You gotta be responsible for some of it."

Slocum glared at Childress, who was smirking.

"Wasn't me who went out to the Molly E Mine to kill the rightful owner," Slocum said. "Has your partner tried to get you out yet?"

"Partner?" The marshal perked up and looked at Childress. "When I caught this varmint, he was alone."

"Pine hightailed it before you got there," Slocum said.

"How do you know that, Slocum? You weren't there. Or were you?" Childress demanded. "See, Marshal? He knows what happened to Tarkenton. He was the one what busted your prisoner out of this jail. He's a low-down criminal, he is!"

"He's got a point, Slocum. You seem to know a powerful lot about what happened at the mine. If Tarkenton was there, this means you were the one that got him out of this jail."

Slocum clamped his mouth shut. He had said too much and would likely pay for it with a long stretch in jail. The only way he would avoid the charges of breaking out a prisoner was if Tarkenton stayed clear of town and was never caught. The miner would blurt out everything if he fell into the marshal's hands again.

A sudden gust of hot air blew through the cell block. The marshal spun around to see who had come into the outer office. He closed the door between the cell block and his office behind him.

"You're gonna die, Slocum. You so much as mention Pine and you're a dead man."

"You'd've gunned me down a long time ago if you'd had the chance." Slocum sat on the cot. He looked at Childress and said, "I'm smart enough not to turn my back on you."

Childress roared like a grizzly and began shaking the bars. Slocum noted how there wasn't so much as a tiny clank, warning him the bars were too secure to ever break through without the serious use of tools. He didn't have even a rock in his boot, much less a crowbar or rasp.

If Slocum had had a short stick, he would have poked Childress just to see him get angrier. Bear baiting could be fun, as long as the bear didn't break free.

"Shut up," Sosa said, coming into the cell block. He held the keys in his hand and came straight for Slocum's cell. "You're free. Get the hell out of here."

"Who sprung this bastard?" Childress shouted. "I'll kill him, too!"

Sosa glared at Childress but his real anger was directed at Slocum.

"I don't like havin' my authority circumvented."

"A judge sprung me?" Slocum asked. He got no answer.

He stepped into the outer office and knew who his benefactor was—again. Ah Sum stood quietly, his fathomless eyes fixed on Slocum. On the marshal's desk lay a scrap of yellow paper covered with a precise line of inked letters. Slocum couldn't read what had been said, but the note had been signed with the initials CM.

"Get out of here," Sosa said.

Slocum took his six-shooter and slipped it into his holster. Ah Sum pointed. Slocum saw how the giant Celestial moved and guessed he had been shot up. The wounds hadn't yet healed.

Slocum left without a word to the marshal. Outside, he took a deep breath. The hot, dry air smelled of freedom. Then Ah Sum bumped him with his shoulder and got him moving toward Hop Town. Slocum knew the way to the butcher shop, robbing Ah Sum of the chance to shove him again. Without breaking stride, Slocum went through the door and past the butcher with the meat cleaver in his hand, poised to make a downward chop. Through the curtains to the room with only the single chair in it, a single chair where China Mary sat.

"What do you want of me?" Slocum demanded.

"You are angry," she said, "even after I released you?"

"You want something. Otherwise, you'd let me rot in the calaboose." He expected the woman to argue or at least make some show of denying the charge. China Mary did nothing of the sort.

"We understand one another," she said. She reached in the folds of her rich brocaded coat and drew out a packet of greenbacks. Using both hands, she placed it on the floor in front of her feet, then sat up again.

"That for me?"

"You are to do a job for me. That is your payment."

"What do you want me to do?" Slocum's heart raced. He suspected he knew, but he wanted to hear it.

"Kill Colin Wakefield."

If he could have bet the money on the floor, he would have doubled his money.

18

"I'm not a hired killer," Slocum said. He stepped forward and kicked the stack of bills back in China Mary's direction. Her eyes never left his. She nodded slightly.

"You owe me for again releasing you from jail."

"The marshal could never have held me," Slocum put out. "He locked me up to see what rats would come scurrying out of the woodpile."

China Mary frowned slightly. Slocum knew she didn't understand what he meant. He didn't bother finding a different way of telling her the marshal was using him as a cat's-paw.

"I work for myself. I have no love for Wakefield or any of the lawyers in this town. The only one I'll work for is Sam Norton since he stands up for miners like Tarkenton."

"You will need to stop Wakefield to help miner," China Mary said.

"Might be, but I won't be paid money to kill another man. If I cut down Wakefield, it's because I want to."

"Very well," China Mary said, bowing slightly in way of dismissal.

Slocum spun and left, pushing through the curtains. Ah Sum waited on the other side, a hatchet in his hand.

"You won't need that," Slocum said. "I'm on your side." He hesitated, glanced over his shoulder into the audience room. China Mary had stood and walked slowly toward another door, leaving the money on the floor. For her, that stack of greenbacks meant little. Her coin was the same as that of the lawyers—power.

Slocum stepped outside, wondering what the hell he was going to do. He didn't have a dog in the fight, but he had saved Tarkenton and felt an obligation to the miner. That might be nothing more than keeping him alive, but Slocum wanted to save the Molly E Mine for him if he could. The only one in town sharing that goal was recovering from surgery at Doc Gottschalk's. Slocum cut through the middle of town. Although it was only early afternoon, the saloons were already filling with customers. Piano music filled the air, vying for supremacy over the boisterous shouts of miners working themselves up to getting drunk.

He walked a little faster when he reached the doctor's office, but slowed when he got to the door standing open. Slocum rested his hand on the butt of his six-gun as he peered inside. Dr. Gottschalk wasn't at his desk. Slocum pushed the door open with the toe of his boot and slowly took in the rest of the office. Empty. A quick move took him inside so he could look behind the door.

He started to call out, but something felt wrong. Slocum drew his pistol and used the barrel to open the door to the inner room. Sam Norton lay on the bed. There was no question he was very dead. A knife had been driven into his chest.

Slocum backed out and checked the area around the doctor's office but saw no one. The killer was long gone. Only then did he return to the inner room and examine Norton's body. Slocum caught his breath when he saw a bloodstained scrap of paper impaled on the blade and a bit of ripped cloth stuck in the guard.

Leaving the knife and the bit of cloth in place, he tugged the paper free and held it up in the dim light. A silent fury burned inside as he read what the crudely written note said. Slocum spun, bringing his six-shooter up as he heard footsteps in the outer office.

"Who's in there?" Gottschalk stuck his head in and saw Slocum with the gun trained on him. "What's going on, Slocum? You shouldn't disturb Sam. He's—"

"Past being disturbed," Slocum said bitterly. He stepped away so the doctor could see the body. Gottschalk let out a gasp, then rushed forward.

"He can't be dead. I saved him. Damn you, Sam, I *saved* you." Gottschalk pounded on Norton's chest. The dull thuds told the story. Nothing would bring back Samuel Norton.

"I just got here but didn't see anyone," Slocum said. He tucked the bloody note into his pocket. "You want to take the knife out of him?"

"We need to get the marshal."

Slocum started to agree, then froze. The note had claimed Childress as the author of Norton's death, but the rustler was still locked up in the jail. Or was he? Had Sosa let him out? That meant Pine might be involved. Or Pine might have killed Norton and tried to shift suspicion to Childress. Slocum shook his head. It was beginning to ache. That didn't make sense since Pine knew Childress was locked up.

But the rest of the note made perfect sense, if Pine was the killer. The note said that Claire had been kidnapped and that anyone following would end up like Norton—a knife through his heart.

"I'll fetch Marshal Sosa, but you ought to look real close at the knife. There's something caught in the guard."

"You've got sharp eyes, Slocum." Gottschalk tugged the knife free and held it up to get a better look. He grumbled, went to the window, and raised the shade. "Sam doesn't need dim light to sleep anymore." He turned the knife around so that he saw the scrap of cloth ripped from a shirt.

Slocum compared the pattern with the nightshirt Norton wore. The killer must have accidentally cut a piece of his own shirt. Reaching out, Slocum put his hand onto the dead man's chest, then mimicked lifting the knife high and bringing it down.

"I see how the killer could have cut his own cuff." He duplicated the motion.

"So he held Sam down, then stabbed him? Sam was too weak to fight."

"He might have been asleep," Slocum said. He looked closely at the doctor as he asked, "Have you seen Claire?"

"Not for a couple hours. I had to deliver a baby over in Hop Town. She said she'd come by to check on Sam, so I didn't think twice about leaving him. He was doing so well. I *saved* him, dammit!"

"Put the knife where it'll be safe. The cloth caught in the guard might be all it takes to convict Norton's murderer."

"I'll wrap it in paper and put it in the center desk drawer. You go get the marshal. I want Sam's killer bad, Slocum. I want him so bad I . . . I'd open the trapdoor under him on the gallows, Hippocratic Oath be damned!"

"Do what you have to," Slocum said. He left but found himself torn between telling Sosa what had happened and getting his horse and starting to track down Norton's killer.

Too many questions burned in his head for him not to go to the jail. A small crowd had gathered, the men jumping and pushing, each trying to get a look inside. Slocum grabbed one man on the edge of the crowd and spun him around.

"What's the fuss?"

"Ain't ye heard? The marshal's done been kilt!"

Slocum bulled his way through but was stopped by Deputy Eakin at the door.

"Don't want you pokin' 'round, Slocum," the deputy said, barring his way. Slocum tilted his head so he could see the marshal back in the cell block. A cord had been looped around his neck, strangling him. Then the cord had been fastened to the iron bars.

"Childress?"

"That's the way it looks. He used a strip of rawhide to strangle the marshal. Can't say how he got the keys 'less Sosa had 'em with him. Can't say why, but that might be how it played out."

"I want Childress," Slocum said.

"Me and two other deputies do, too. You keep your nose out of this or I swear, China Mary can talk her yellow face blue and I won't ever let you out of jail." He tapped his chest showing he wore the marshal's badge now.

"Where would Childress go?"

"You tell me. You was the one what brought him in for cattle rustlin'." The new marshal made it sound as if Slocum had brought the plague to Tombstone. In a way, he had.

"Where's Jackson Pine?"

"Ain't got no idea. Ain't got any proof he had anything to do with Childress's escape neither." Deputy Eakin—now Marshal Eakin—grabbed an onlooker by the collar and dragged him back. The crowd was growing unruly and wanted justice for Sosa. Alive, they opposed the lawman. Dead, he became a symbol.

Slocum backed away and his place was immediately taken by three curious miners wanting to see the dead marshal. They might live with the threat of constant death but it was still a sideshow attraction for them seeing a corpse. The town gossips would buzz about it for days until something even more outrageous happened to occupy their time and conversation.

Slocum wanted that to be how he saved Claire Norton and brought Childress back to town, belly down over the back of his horse.

He hurried down Third Street to the livery stable and wasn't too surprised to see the owner sprawled out at the rear of the barn. He knelt and pressed his thumb into the bloody knot on the side of the man's head. He groaned, then weakly fought to push Slocum away.

"Take it easy," Slocum advised. He got a bucket of water and dashed it in the man's face. Sputtering, cursing, the stable owner sat up, fists ready for a fight.

"Come here, you mangy mongrel. I'm gonna thrash you good. You can't steal my horse!"

"Settle down. Here, take a drink." Slocum found a bottle of whiskey on a bale of hay. A couple shots remained in the bottom. He uncorked it and handed it to the man.

"Who the hell are you?"

"I came for my horse and found you."

"He hit me. The son of a bitch hit me. He was tryin' to steal a couple horses and he hit me."

"Childress?"

"Who?"

"The man Marshal Sosa had locked up."

"Don't know 'bout that." He described Childress close enough for Slocum to believe that, after strangling the marshal, Childress had come straight here to steal a couple horses. That turned Slocum even madder as he realized how Childress had plotted not only Norton's death but Claire's kidnapping. He hadn't stolen a single horse. He had wanted a second one for her to ride in case he couldn't find another horse for her near the doctor's office after knifing her pa. Childress intended to get back at everyone he could—and he had.

Slocum wondered if Claire's kidnapping had been aimed against him or against Jackson Pine.

"How long ago did he wallop you?"

"Can't say. Can't be more 'n an hour." The man touched his head and winced. "You find any more liquor 'round here? That's my hired hand's stash."

"Find it yourself. I've got me a killer and horse thief to find."

"I'll have Sosa whip up a posse. He owes me plenty since I take care of his horse for nuthin'. He owes me."

"You'll have a hard time collecting that debt," Slocum said as he led his gelding from a stall and began saddling it.

"Why's that?"

"Let's just say you've got a headache, and that's better than what Sosa's feeling right now."

"I dunno 'bout that. My head's gonna bust open any second."

Slocum led his horse outside and stepped up. Putting his heels to the horse's flanks, he trotted to the edge of Tombstone and then stopped. He started to go after Childress and then realized he didn't have a ghost of an idea where the rustler might have taken Claire. Slocum stood in the stirrups and slowly looked around. The Sonora Desert was a mighty big place.

19

Arizona Territory stretched out arid and burning hot in all directions. He could guess where Childress might have taken Claire, but chances were good he would be wrong. Slocum sat for several minutes, thinking about what he knew of the rustler and possible places he might choose to hole up in. After long reflection, Slocum figured out what he really knew.

Nothing.

He turned his horse back toward Tombstone and rode for the edge of town where Rotten Row stretched. The buildings might have belonged to any business, but one sign after another proclaimed legal services could be had. For a price. There were dozens of them. Slocum wondered if anyone had considered how a single good fire could remove much of the blight on Tombstone. He decided the lawyers were only one of many problems facing the boomtown and that as many of those willing to shoot himself a lawyer would be opposed by those who would gladly hire one to defend his rights.

It took him only a few minutes to find the office he wanted. Slocum tethered his horse, made sure his pistol rode easy in his holster, then went into Jackson Pine's office. For some reason he was surprised to see the man at his desk, frowning as he read a paper clutched in his hands.

"Be right with you," Pine said. He looked up when he heard Slocum's six-gun cock. "What the hell, Slocum? You can't barge in here and threaten me like that."

"Looks like you're wrong on two counts," Slocum said.

"I'll have you locked up again. The marshal might pay more attention to China Mary than he does the law, but there has to be a judge who will issue an arrest warrant for you that'll keep you locked up."

"Which marshal are you talking about?"

Pine reared back and looked at Slocum as if he had been out in the sun too long.

"Marshal Sosa might not be the most diligent lawman but he's better than many Tombstone's had in the past."

"You figure your court order includes finding him a burial plot?"

"Y-You killed him?"

"Childress did when he escaped." Slocum watched the lawyer's reaction. Pine had shown he could lie with a straight face, but this time real shock washed over him. He started to speak, clamped his mouth shut, then more carefully chose his words.

"You think I had something to do with it?"

"He killed Sosa. Strangled him to death. Why the marshal would go into the cell block with the keys is something of a poser. It might be that you strangled Sosa and gave Childress the keys to get free."

"I did no such thing!"

"It's not too clear what happened," Slocum allowed. "There might have been someone helping him. Maybe not."

"Certainly not in my case. I . . . I found myself a bit relieved that the marshal arrested him. Childress was proving to be a real handful and had developed a tendency to, how should I say this? He would venture out on his own path ignoring my advice. With him in jail, I could concentrate on other matters and not worry about what mischief he might get into."

"Matters like stealing Tarkenton's mine?"

"That is under litigation. I am sure I will prevail over any argument Norton makes. He is something of a sob sister and prone to emotional appeals. I base my cases on the letter of the law."

"Even if you have to forge the documents. I heard what you and Childress tried to do to Tarkenton. Sign a blank sheet, write a deed to the mine so it looks like he sold it to you."

Pine looked a little guilty, and Slocum knew this was the truth. It had been his choice to wrest the Molly E Mine from Tarkenton.

"How much of a fight in court do you think Norton will put up?"

"Not enough. His cases are usually weak, but that comes from his choice of client."

"If it went to trial today, you'd win," Slocum said. "Norton's dead. Shot through the heart."

"I didn't do it! I know nothing about any of this." Pine's eyes narrowed. "You're lying. None of this is true, is it? What do you want from me, Slocum?"

Slocum shook his head slowly.

"Sosa is dead. So is Norton. And Childress isn't in his cell any longer. All that's the gospel truth."

"You're lying. This is some trick to make me—do what? What do you want, pointing that six-gun at me? I'm not giving up on winning title to Tarkenton's mine."

"You might need all the silver in the Molly E if you want to ransom her."

"What *are* you talking about?"

Again Slocum saw irritation rather than smugness in the lawyer's words.

"Childress kidnapped Claire Norton after he killed her pa with a knife through his heart. I figured he was following your orders." Slocum watched all the blood drain from the lawyer's face. There was no actor—or lawyer—who could fake the utter shock Slocum read. He didn't have to be any kind of poker player to know everything he had told Pine came as a complete surprise to the man.

It also made sense that a man like Pine might think he could use Childress, only to find he had roped a cyclone. Used to prevailing in court, Pine probably thought manipulating Childress would be as easy.

"Claire?" Pine struggled to regain his composure. "You said Norton was shot. Your story changed, so you're lying."

"I'm not under oath. I wanted to see how much you actually knew." It pained Slocum to admit it, but the lawyer had shown no hint of knowing anything about Norton's murder or Claire's kidnapping. "You don't know where Childress would go to earth?"

"I . . . no. The first contact I had with him was getting him out of jail after you brought him in for rustling. I didn't even check the marshal's files to see if there was a wanted poster on him. A defense attorney shouldn't know such things before he goes in front of a jury to plead a case. It could only cloud a decent attorney's judgment."

"I don't know about that, but I do know Childress is one dangerous hombre," Slocum said. "Did he say anything about where he might ride if he left Tombstone?"

Pine looked pained and then finally said, "There's nothing I can remember him saying. Why'd he take Claire?" Pine's voice almost cracked with strain. "It can't be ransom, not with her father dead. He is dead?" Pine looked at Slocum with forlorn eyes.

Slocum had his own ideas about why Childress had kidnapped Claire, and they mostly had to do with getting back at him. If Childress wanted to lure Slocum out into the desert into an ambush, there was no better bait he could use. Seeing Pine's reaction told him how much in love with Claire the lawyer was.

"Did you do anything to piss off Childress?"

"That must be it. He wanted me to get him out of jail right away, and this is his way of paying me back for not going straightaway to Judge Rollins to get a release order. It has to be. He can't be ransoming her for money. I don't have any and he knows it."

"What if you were given the rights to Tarkenton's mine?"

Pine looked up. His eyes went wide, and he nodded so vigorously Slocum thought his head would pop off.

"That's got to be it. He wants complete control of the Molly E Mine. He almost said so when we were closing in on Tarkenton. Childress told me he wanted half, and I laughed at him. There was nothing he could do that would deserve that much."

"Killing Tarkenton after he got him to sign a blank sheet of paper ought to have been worth that much," Slocum said. Like a poker player, he watched for telltale signs of emotion. Pine had a tiny tic near his left eye that was twitching to beat the band now. Slocum had run him from anguish to anger and all around every emotion in between.

"That's the way things are done in this part of the country," Pine said with an air of superiority.

"There's no point in keeping her alive unless you own the mine," Slocum said. "Is there any way you can let it out that you finally stole the mine from Tarkenton?" This had its downside because the miner would come storming into town. Slocum wasn't sure how violent a man the hard-rock miner was, but if he thought he was losing his mine, he might beat a man to death with his bare hands. For a shady lawyer swindling him out of the Molly E, he might take time to rip Pine's legs off first, like he was dismembering a chicken.

"Childress wouldn't believe it unless there were hearings. If I simply starting bragging around town, thinking he would overhear, he wouldn't fall for it. There have to be actual court documents issued."

Slocum hated to admit being wrong twice in one day, but Pine was right. Childress was too cagey to simply fall for gossip. He had to admit he'd been wrong about Pine knowing anything about Norton's murder or Claire's kidnapping as well.

"That means she's likely to be unharmed until then," Slocum said, but unharmed more than likely meant not dead. A no-account like Childress could do a powerful lot of unpleasant things to Claire without killing her.

"I'll push harder to get the hearing over," Pine said. He hesitated, then said, "What if I lose? What if there's no mine to trade for Claire's life?"

"Then you'd better think real hard about winning," Slocum said. He left the lawyer stewing in his own juices. Outside in the hot afternoon sun, he considered all the possible hideouts Childress could use with Claire as his hostage. Simply camping out in the desert wasn't likely. There might be abandoned cabins all around, but Childress wouldn't know about them. He and his gang had been rustling to the west some distance on the edge of the Circle Bar K Ranch land. While he might have come this way at some point in his hunt for beeves to rustle, nobody in town had known him when Slocum brought him in as a prisoner.

That meant he knew only the places to hide that Slocum did.

"The mine," Slocum said softly. "The cabin got burned down, but you know that terrain as good as you do anywhere else around Tombstone." This reasoning gnawed at Slocum because Childress really didn't know it, but this was the single place where they both had collided.

He swung into the saddle and headed out of town, angling for the road that would take him toward the Molly E Mine. Slocum knew it was a long shot, but it made sense in a crazy way for Childress to hide there. It would amuse the rustler that he hid out in a place that would be his if his ransom was paid.

Slocum had hardly reached the outer edge of Tombstone when a shot rang out. He drew rein and looked around. A second shot kicked up dust in front of his horse, causing the gelding to rear. Keeping the animal under control occupied Slocum's attention long enough for men to come from hiding on either side of the road.

"You reach for that hogleg of yours and we got orders to shoot you," one man said. Since they hadn't bothered pulling up their bandannas to hide their faces, Slocum doubted this was a robbery. If they had intended to kill him, he would be dead by now.

"What do you want?"

"Somebody wants to see you." The man doing all the talking motioned and one of his partners came over and plucked Slocum's Colt from its holster.

"Reckon I want to see whoever wants to see me."

Surrounded by four gunmen, Slocum rode back to Tombstone.

20

"In there," the leader of the gunmen ordered. He pointed to a side door on an office along Rotten Row. Slocum had almost expected to be brought back to Jackson Pine's office but it didn't surprise him unduly that they had escorted him to Colin Wakefield's office.

Slocum stepped inside, two gunmen close behind him. He walked down a narrow hallway and came out in the main office, where Wakefield sat behind a huge desk.

"If you could grow grass on that," Slocum said, pointing to the desktop, "you could fatten a dozen head of cattle."

Wakefield stared at him a moment, then decided this was a joke. He laughed. Slocum wondered if he sounded as insincere in court. Probably.

"You are a stellar fellow, Slocum. I'm glad my men found you before you . . . rode on."

Slocum looked around for a chair. Other than the one Wakefield sat on, there wasn't one in the room. His gunmen stood in either corner of the room behind Slocum, hands resting on their six-shooters in case he tried anything. Slocum doubted he could get across that huge desk and wrap his fingers around Wakefield's throat before they filled him with lead.

He still considered it.

"I was looking for Childress."

"Oh?" Wakefield seemed uninterested. "I am sure he is around, although if he were smart, he'd be halfway to Texas by now after killing the marshal." Wakefield snorted in contempt. "But what am I saying? Childress is not a smart man. Not like you, Slocum."

"I didn't kill the marshal," Slocum said. "That makes me smarter than Childress."

"That's true, but you have moments of weakness. I want to address those."

Slocum said nothing. Wakefield didn't expect him to reply. If anything, Wakefield wanted to hear nothing but the sound of his own voice. Slocum had seen men like this before, and they always gave him enough rope to hang themselves if he listened long enough.

"Your association with Sam Norton is a mistake. I fully understand the attraction, however, and wish to address that. His daughter is very pretty, perhaps the most beautiful woman in Tombstone. Considering most of the women are whores, that's not too difficult. Those, you understand, who are the prettiest quickly marry rich mine owners or ranchers from the surrounding countryside. That reduces the appearance of those remaining to . . . less than beautiful."

Slocum was right. Wakefield liked hearing himself talk.

"Thinking with the wrong portion of your anatomy places you in opposition to my interests. What can I offer you to convince Norton to, shall we say, underrepresent Tarkenton? Who could place any blame on him if he lost that court ruling? He is still a sick man."

"Norton's dead. Childress killed him." Slocum liked the shock on Wakefield's face. He understood how easy it would be for the rustler to kill another lawyer—him.

"Indeed. I did not know. He must have gone directly to

the doctor's surgery from killing Sosa." Wakefield made a big show of dipping his pen in the ink bottle and scribbling a note on a clean sheet of paper at his right hand. He ended with a flourish and then looked back at Slocum. It had taken all that nonsense writing for him to compose himself. Slocum wondered what he could say next to fluster the lawyer some more. It was hardly fun having two armed men at his back, waiting to blast his spine into splinters, but toying with Wakefield had its rewards.

"You already prove useful. While you were not the agent of removing Norton from the Tarkenton case, you brought me information I had not known." Wakefield glared at the man to Slocum's right rear.

Slocum decided that Wakefield didn't know of Claire's kidnapping and saw no benefit in telling him. The lawyer had something more on his mind, and Slocum knew what it was.

"Women are likely going to be your downfall unless you hire on with me, Slocum. I'll steer you away from all those dangerous females."

"China Mary wanted me to kill you."

"My, you are an open book, aren't you?"

"I figured you knew. There's no reason denying it. I turned down her money for the job."

"Yes, I know that also. That's why I want you to work for me. You and I, Slocum, can make a great team. A thousand dollars a month is a fantastic salary."

"You want me to kill China Mary," Slocum said. The anger on Wakefield's face disappeared almost as soon as it appeared. Slocum had done the same thing as the drunk who blurted out the punch line of a joke, with much the same result. No one liked their punch line being stepped on, least of all Colin Wakefield.

"She wanted me dead. I want to turn the tables on her. You are perfect for this, Slocum. We can fake a shooting, spread the rumor I've been killed, and then you can go to her to claim the bounty on my head. She'll anticipate your report on how I died. When she least expects it, you kill her. A simple, perfect scheme."

"Ah Sum wouldn't like it."

"Oh, kill him, too," Wakefield said, waving away the objection. "Now. I'll pay you two hundred and fifty dollars. That's a week's salary in advance. This should get you—"

"No."

"No? You can't turn down my offer. It is most generous."

Slocum heard the men behind him step closer and knew they were lifting their pistols to shoot him in the back.

"A thousand a month?" Slocum said as if he were weakening. "Show me the week's pay."

Wakefield beamed. He opened his desk drawer and took out a small stack of greenbacks. He placed them in front of him, his fingers stroking the sides to keep them in an orderly pile.

"Not gold? No silver coins?"

"Come now, Slocum, this is money that will keep you in booze and women for more than a week, even if you have quite an appetite for both. By then your next week's salary will come your way and you will realize the virtues of working for me." Wakefield pushed the small stack forward.

Slocum stepped up, reached out for the money, then made a grab for Wakefield's throat. He missed and had to settle for grabbing the lawyer's lapel. He yanked hard and smashed the man's face into the desktop. Wakefield struggled and Slocum lost his grip. He grabbed again and tore part of the jacket lapel before he found himself assailed from behind.

Kicking like a mule, Slocum caught one of Wakefield's henchmen in the belly. The man gulped loudly and sat down on the floor, gasping for air as he rolled onto his side and puked weakly.

Slocum had removed one man from the fight, but Wakefield was more actively fighting back from the far side of the desk. The lawyer took a swing at Slocum, catching him on the chin. The punch wasn't hard enough to do any damage because he was too far away, but Slocum reacted instinctively and recoiled. The other gunman hit him from behind with the barrel of his pistol. His skull was shot full of bright white lights spinning like a dust devil, then faded to black.

Never quite passing out, Slocum continued to fight weakly. He heard Wakefield yelling orders but couldn't quite make out what the lawyer said. Then he was hit on the side of the head again. This time he dropped to his knees, stunned.

Strong hands pulled him to his feet. He tried to walk and didn't have the strength.

"Get him out of here. You know what to do."

Slocum clutched his hands into fists. His left hand curled just fine to strike out, but his right didn't feel right. Through blurred eyes, he saw he had ripped off a piece of Wakefield's jacket. This prevented him from getting his right fist into action.

Another blow landed and removed whatever logical thought had been building inside his head. The hands gripped his arms and pulled him along, his toes scrapping along the floor. Then he felt the texture change. He had left wood floor and now was pulled along in the dirt. Then he grunted as he was heaved up and dropped belly down over his saddle.

"We can take him to that arroyo west of town."

"He'll wash up if it rains."

"Hell, it's gettin' to summer and it ain't never gonna rain for another four months. By then the buzzards and coyotes will have picked his bones clean. Besides, you think anybody'd care about the likes of him if they found him?"

Slocum grunted as his gelding trotted along. He felt himself sliding off but grabbed hold on the saddle and held himself across the horse's back. If he fell off, Wakefield's men might go ahead and shoot him where he lay. He had to recover, think, get a plan squared away in his head before he let them know he wasn't unconscious.

Turning his head slightly, he got a view of the man riding closest to him. The man paid no attention to his prisoner, assuming everything would go well whenever they reached the spot where they intended to kill him. All Slocum could do was thank his lucky stars that they hadn't just gunned him down back in Wakefield's office. The lawyer probably didn't want the blood on his polished wood floor.

When he was ready, he simply let go and tumbled from the saddle, rolling over and over off the road and down into a ditch. He came to rest in such a way that he could watch what the gunmen did. If they simply drew their six-guns and got ready to shoot him, he'd have to change his plan, such as it was. He gripped a rock and held back a smile when the two men began arguing.

"You said he wouldn't fall off," one of them said.

"Like hell. You were gonna tie him down. Go get him."

The argument continued for another few seconds. Then the one who had been ordered to retrieve Slocum came sliding down the side of the shallow ditch, got his hands under Slocum's arms, and heaved.

"Come on, you dumb—"

He never got any further. Slocum swung the rock around as hard as he could. Bones crunched and the man went down like he'd been poleaxed. As he sank, Slocum got his arms around the man to support him. He turned a little to put the gunman's back toward his partner.

"You gonna take all day? You need help?"

Slocum finally wrapped his fingers around the unconscious man's six-shooter. He let the gunman fall, lifted the pistol, and said, "Don't need any help at all." Slocum fired. His first shot hit the mounted man dead center in the chest.

The gunman recoiled and foolishly reached for the tiny spot of blood growing on his breast. Slocum's second round blew away the side of the man's head. He tumbled to the ground and lay still. Deathly still.

Slocum pressed his thumb into the throat of the man he had clobbered with the rock. No pulse. A quick search of the man's pockets turned up a few dollars in coin and nothing else worth taking. Repeating the search on the other dead man, Slocum came out twelve dollars ahead for getting pistol-whipped and almost killed. He retrieved his Colt Navy from the man's belt where it had been thrust for safekeeping.

Their money safely in his pocket, Slocum jumped onto his gelding and rounded up the gunmen's horses. He had three horses now and ought to figure some way of getting the hell away from Tombstone, but Claire was still Childress's prisoner.

He hoped she was. If Childress took it into his head to rape her and then kill her, she was long dead. All Slocum counted on was the rustler's greed. Using the woman as a bargaining chip gave him the chance to own the proven, silver-producing Molly E Mine.

Slocum turned back toward the road that led in the direction of Tarkenton's mine, hoping that Childress was there. After an hour riding, he decided to cut across the country in an effort to make better time. Striking out across the desert would have been more dangerous except for the two horses that trotted behind him. He had two extra canteens and supplies. While the killers hadn't intended to be away long from town, they still carried enough for him to live off several more days. The water in particular was coming in handy as the afternoon heated up fast.

By sundown Slocum realized he needed water for the horses. A patch of green poking up out of the rapidly cooling desert drew him. The San Pedro River ran underground throughout the area and only occasionally surfaced. These spots provided virtual oases for any thirsty traveler willing to make do with muddy pools that could be strained clean to get water.

Slocum circled the patch of vegetation and saw no one. After dealing with Wakefield, he was leery of anyone he was likely to find on the trail. The new marshal and his deputies wouldn't care much about bodies found outside Tombstone, but Sosa's death might have attracted federal deputies eager to cut themselves into the rich pie that was Tombstone.

He didn't let out a whoop of glee, but he felt like it. His luck was changing. This was an honest to God pond, not a muddy swamp needing hours of work to get a thimble of potable water. He rode directly to the pond and let the horses drink. He settled down, removed their saddles, and decided he would leave behind the gear belonging to Wakefield's gunmen. Stretching, he realized how tired he was from the day's events—and he was no closer to finding Claire than he'd been at the beginning of the day.

Dropping his saddle, he turned to pull the gunmen's horses away to keep them from bloating. One horse was gone. Slocum frowned. He hadn't heard the horse leave, and it didn't make sense that it would.

A soft hiss from ankle-high grass being stepped on behind him caused him to swing around, going for his six-shooter. Slocum froze. He stared down the barrel of a rifle held by an Apache brave.

21

"What's the rush, gents?" Judge Rollins lounged back in his chair, lit a stogie, and blew huge clouds of blue-gray smoke into the courtroom. The bailiff coughed and turned away, wiping at his eyes. The judge ignored him.

Jackson Pine stood and said, "The matter might drag on endlessly, Your Honor. My petition calls on the court to settle the matter of ownership of the Molly E Mine right away."

"*I* filed that petition first, Judge!" Colin Wakefield jumped to his feet and motioned in Pine's direction. "My petition takes precedence."

"What the hell difference does it make? You both got a burr up your butt at the same time. You might have copied from one another's papers." Rollins waved the two pages at them. "The only thing I see that's even an itty-bitty bit different is the signature." He shuffled the pages back and forth, then dropped them on the desk in front of him. "And I don't care who signed it. What's the rush, gents?"

Pine licked his lips, wanting to blurt out that he needed to be declared owner of the mine to ransom Claire Norton, but good sense made him hold his tongue. For all he knew, Wakefield had a hand in her kidnapping. He had gotten a ransom note from Childress asking for full ownership of the mine, but that was absurd. Pine was sure Childress would trade the woman for half interest.

"There's no reason for such a productive mine to lie dormant one minute longer than necessary, Your Honor," Wakefield said, striking a pose. His left hand clung to his lapel. Pine saw this theatrical pose and laughed. Wakefield usually pulled it off, but today he had a part of his lapel ripped off. Worse, the cuff of his coat was worn. He might have been in a fight and lost for all the sartorial splendor he showed in the once expensive jacket.

Pine knew this mattered to the judge. Rollins had thrown lawyers out of his court if he didn't think they were properly attired.

"From your petitions, each of you claims the mine. Mr. Pine there says he is the owner because he's going to pay back taxes." Rollins winked in Pine's direction. Or was it only a facial tic? Pine felt his own twitch starting. Something in the way the judge spoke put him on guard.

"And you, Mr. Wakefield, make a similarly powerful claim regarding the Molly E. You go a step further and want the current owner, Mr. Tarkenton, declared incompetent."

"What?" Pine shot to his feet. "I protest such sophistry. There's no call to declare Tarkenton incompetent." He worried that he had not thought of this himself.

"The current owner, Ike Tarkenton, is a fugitive from the law. There seems to be considerable confusion at the jailhouse at the moment because of Marshal Sosa's murder," Rollins said. He puffed a few times to build a bright orange coal at the tip of the cigar, then looked from it to the anxious lawyers.

"Good cigar," he said.

Pine saw how Wakefield smirked at that. Then the judge pulled out a bottle and poured himself a shot of Kentucky bourbon. He knocked it back, licked his lips, and looked over at Pine to say, "Good liquor."

Pine wondered if his bribe of a bottle of whiskey trumped however many of the foul cigars Wakefield had given the judge. It ought to. He had moved heaven and earth to get only the finest. The cigar stank up the courtroom and forced the bailiff to the window to suck in fresh air.

"Gentlemen, you both present compelling reasons to be named owner of the mine." Rollins rocked back in his chair, laced his fingers behind his head, and then dropped the bombshell. "I'll decide when Mr. Tarkenton is present to give the court his version of the truth."

"He's a fugitive!" Wakefield blurted out.

"The matter ought to be settled immediately, Your Honor," Pine said, hoping Rollins only wanted it to appear the fix wasn't in. A bottle of whiskey? He'd make it a case, even if that cost a fortune!

"The matter will be settled, Mr. Pine—when Tarkenton testifies about the taxes and his claim to the mine. It doesn't matter if he is under suspicion for a heinous crime. He's innocent 'til proven guilty under the laws of the United States and the Territory of Arizona. Even if he is guilty, that doesn't mean he can't own property. In fact, he might need to sell his silver mine to pay for a proper defense fighting the myriad criminal charges laid against him."

Pine felt as if he had been punched in the gut. Rollins wasn't an honest crook. He didn't stay bribed. Looking at Wakefield gave him small consolation. Wakefield felt the same. He obviously thought the matter had been settled in his behalf before filing the petition for Rollins to decide the ownership.

A million thoughts flashed through Pine's head. Would Wakefield give him the mine ownership if it was necessary to save Claire Norton? Or would it matter at all to the other lawyer? For all he knew, Wakefield might have sprung Childress and the kidnapping was his way of making sure he got the mine. If Rollins gave it to him legally, fine. If Pine won it in court, then Wakefield could still extort it away, using Claire as the bargaining chip.

But Pine watched the consternation on Wakefield's face. The lawyer didn't even try to hide his dismay and outright anger at the judge's decision. He might not have anything to do with Claire's kidnapping, or he might. Pine needed the ownership settled one way or the other, and Rollins had thwarted the pair of them.

"Wakefield, I'd like a word with you." Pine wasn't sure what he was going to say. Wakefield might agree to a 50-50 split. That might not be enough to ransom Claire, but Pine had to try something. The longer Childress held her captive, the more her life was in danger. He was past wondering what the outlaw was doing to her otherwise.

"Go to hell," Wakefield snarled. He gathered his papers and pushed past Pine.

Pine turned back to the judge, but Rollins rapped the gavel sharply and said, "Bailiff, clear the court and bring in the next case." He refused to make eye contact, which worried Pine even more. Not only wouldn't Rollins stay bribed, but he might be angling for ownership of Tarkenton's mine himself. A quick look at the ore the miner pulled from the bowels of the Molly E told the story. It was one rich strike.

He pushed his papers into his briefcase and left the courtroom, fuming at how helpless he felt. Part of being a lawyer was to win, to feel superior. Now even a nothing of a cowboy like Slocum held a better hand in this legal card game.

Pine stopped on the front steps of the courthouse to see Wakefield stalking back to his office, head down and stride long. If he had ever seen outright anger before, this was it. He would have enjoyed Wakefield's dejection more if he didn't share it himself.

Damn Rollins!

He started down the steps, then froze. He saw a dark

shadow moving near a huge cottonwood tree. The next instant a silver blade cartwheeled through the air, straight for Wakefield. Somehow, the lawyer bent forward at the precise instant that would save his life. The long-bladed knife cut through his shabby coat and warned him of the danger.

Wakefield let out a screech like a barn owl and worked to drag out the pistol holstered under his left arm. He started shooting, but Pine saw that the assailant had disappeared. Only when he had emptied five chambers in his pistol did Wakefield stop to regain control of his emotions. He looked around, saw Pine watching, and made an obscene gesture.

He jammed the pistol back under his coat and walked off so fast he was almost running.

Pine followed only as far as the point where Wakefield had been attacked. He hunted and found the knife some distance away. It had banged into an adobe wall and clattered to the ground. He held it up and looked it over. He recognized the tiny design on the handle as a Chinese character denoting the On Leong Tong. Pine had defended a Celestial once with that chop tattooed on his arm. He had lost the case and the Chinaman had been hanged, but he had learned a thing or two about the Orientals and their community.

Someone wanted Wakefield dead. In Tombstone that had to be China Mary.

Pine slipped the knife into his pocket and headed for Hop Town. As he entered the section of Tombstone reserved for the Celestials and those coming here to partake of the opium pipe or Chinese girls, he felt increasingly uneasy. He doubted anyone would remember how he had failed to get the tong killer off. That had been a year back, right after he came to Tombstone. But the hairs rose on his neck the farther he walked. Unseen eyes watched his every move.

He forced himself not to turn and run. If he did, nothing would happen to him and he would escape alive. But he would never be able to stick his nose into Hop Town again without getting it cut off. He would have branded himself as a coward.

When China Mary's bulky bodyguard stepped from a doorway and stood blocking his way, arms crossed over his broad chest, Pine swallowed hard and felt his mouth go drier than the Arizona desert at noon.

"I . . . I want to see China Mary."

The man didn't budge. His dark eyes remained fixed on Pine until he wondered if there was something more he ought to do. Offering a bribe seemed out of the question. He had nothing that would interest this mountain of a man. Anything else would have to be directed toward China Mary, and what could he offer her in a material way?

Nothing. Unless she wanted his life.

That thought panicked him, but he fought down the fear that threatened to paralyze him and knew he would already be dead in some alley with his throat slit if China Mary wanted that.

Pine stood his ground and forced himself to calm down. After what started as seconds dragged into eternity, the man turned and walked into the store where he had been standing guard. Pine followed without being told. His nose wrinkled at the stench rising from the precisely dismembered hog carcasses. Two butchers stopped their work and watched him appraisingly, as if sizing him up to be turned into cutlets.

The bodyguard held back curtains to a bare room. China Mary sat in a chair. Otherwise, the room was empty.

"Good afternoon," Pine said. "My name's—"

"Jackson Pine. I know of you. What do you want?"

Pine had always thought the Celestials were circumspect, even when they were being insulting. Sometimes even a compliment carried a trace of insult with it, but such bluntness told him he had to present his case fast. He was aware of the bulky guard on the other side of the curtain, although he couldn't see him.

"I think you left this behind." He reached into his pocket, only to find his wrist clamped in a viselike grip. Pressure increased until he dropped the knife onto the floor.

"I only wanted to return it. Your assassin missed Wakefield outside the courthouse."

"I know nothing of this knife or any assassin," China Mary said.

He knew better than to call her a liar, but the attempt on Wakefield's life screamed of Chinese assassins.

"Perhaps I can be of other assistance," Pine said. "Now that Sam Norton is dead, you will need legal representation. I can give that to you."

"What is your purpose in coming here, Mr. Pine?"

He glanced down and saw that the knife on the floor had disappeared. When that had happened, he could not say. Not for the first time since entering Hop Town, Pine felt that events were completely beyond his control. That knife might have missed Wakefield but in this small room it would never miss his back—or his throat.

"Just as I said. I am offering my legal services to you. It seems we both share an opponent and could benefit mutually."

"Please go. Ah Sum will escort you back to . . . your side of town." China Mary stood without another word and left through the other door, leaving him alone.

The powerful hand on his shoulder swung him around and sent him staggering through the curtains, past the butchers still sizing him up and into the street.

It took all his willpower not to run as if all the demons of hell were nipping at his heels.

22

"You want the horses, take them," Slocum said. He knew the Apache would do that very thing because horses were wealth. All he needed was an opening if he was going to save his life. There was no reason for the Apache to simply steal the horses and not gun him down.

The brave made no move to pull the trigger. That gave Slocum a modest amount of hope that he might talk his way out of this pickle.

"I'll give you the saddles, too. Two of them."

"Two?" The Apache looked sharply at him, then frowned. "I take all three."

"Only two. You can have two of the horses. Those," Slocum said, pointing to the mounts he had taken from Wakefield's gunmen. "That one's mine. Not yours."

"I'll kill you! All horses are mine then!"

Slocum wondered why the Apache simply didn't pull the trigger. Unless his magazine was empty. The Indian might be bluffing. But did he dare take that chance? The Apache padded around, his moccasins making the soft swishing sound in the grass that had alerted Slocum. From the way he moved, he was worried about something.

The only thing Slocum could imagine was the cavalry. They were a long way from Fort Huachuca so a patrol had to be far-ranging and intent on finding this particular brave.

"Go on," Slocum said. "Shoot." Slocum stumbled and fell, sitting down hard when the Indian's rifle discharged. The slug tore past Slocum's ear and deafened him from the near-ness of its passage. He told himself to stay out of poker games where he was inclined to bluff his way to a big pot. This wrong guess had almost cost him his life.

"Over. Roll over," the Indian ordered.

Slocum obeyed. The Apache put a knee in the small of his back, then lashed his hands together with a strip of rawhide. Slocum was still shaken from the close brush with death but was possessed of enough foresight to hold his wrists in such a way that the Indian lashed them together ineffectively. Slocum simply twisted his wrists and had enough play to work himself free, given enough time.

"We ride."

"I can't get my horse saddled with my hands tied behind my back. Tell me what your problem is and maybe I can help out. I'm not on good terms with the law right now myself."

Slocum had given the Indian another opening. If the Apache wasn't on the run, the lure of a reward might be enough for the brave to take him into Tombstone to collect the reward. Slocum doubted anything had happened in town to put a reward on his head since he'd left. Wakefield thought he was dead. Pine wanted to enlist his aid in freeing Claire from Childress. And China Mary sought to hire him. He had a lot of people wanting him to be on their side, no matter the deadly game they played.

"No. Not go to Tombstone," the Apache said forcefully.

"If you're on the run, we ought to stick together and watch each other's back."

To his surprise, the brave saddled his horse for him and

then hoisted him up into the saddle. Slocum balanced pre-
cariously with his hands bound behind him but finally found
his seat. The brave went through the other gear and took a few
things. Wakefield's men would never miss any of it. Slocum
had seen to that. But the Indian became increasingly fearful
with every passing minute.

"Ride. Hurry. Now," his captor said, motioning due west.
Slocum had no choice but to obey.

As his gelding fell into an easy trot, Slocum worked on
getting his hands free. The Apache had taken his six-gun but
paid scant attention to his prisoner. He was too busy scanning
the horizon, hunting for whoever hunted him.

Twilight faded into night but still the Apache rode. When
their horses tired, the Indian switched horses, poking and
prodding Slocum with the rifle barrel to mount the other spare
horse.

They rode off, the brave gazing up into the sky to find his
directions every few minutes. Wherever he went, he was in a
powerful hurry. Slocum figured out they were going back onto
Circle Bar K land, or would be in another day's ride. The
Whitestone Mountains to the west loomed dark in the night,
but he didn't have time to wonder about any of the ride.

The Indian pushed constantly, always urging more speed.
Even with four horses and switching off when those they
rode tired, it proved difficult to maintain a steady pace.

Before dawn, exhausted, they switched back to their original mounts and kept riding.

"You're going to kill us both with this pace," Slocum said.
"Let me help you."

"No talk."

"You've got to get someplace by a certain time, don't you?"
Slocum saw he had hit the target dead on. The Apache spun
about and glared at him. "You're a Tonto off the reservation."

"Tonto," the Apache said proudly, thumping himself on
the chest with his clenched fist.

"Strong tribe, brave warriors, kill many enemies in battle," Slocum said. "Where are you going in such a hurry?"

"No talk." He lifted the rifle and pointed it directly at Slocum. Whatever reason the warrior had for not killing Slocum before wouldn't keep him from pulling the trigger now. Slocum fell silent, concentrated on staying in the saddle and worrying at the rawhide binding his wrists.

That put an end to all conversation. They rode for several more hours until Slocum saw that the Indian was tottering astride his horse and almost at the point of falling off from exhaustion. He was hardly in better shape than the Apache, but he had been rested compared to the brave back at the watering hole. The Indian had run a long ways and wasn't going to stop anytime soon.

The Apache snapped awake and looked around in a panic. He stared at the stars, letting a few high, thin clouds move past whatever bright points he used to guide himself through the desert.

"Water," he said, the word almost unintelligible. Slocum felt the same way. His mouth had turned to the inside of a cotton bale miles back. They had drunk all the water and going much farther would be impossible if the horses collapsed under them. The Apache pointed off into the darkness.

Whatever sixth sense the man had led them directly to a small pond. Slocum slipped to the ground and shoved his face into the water, then did his best to drink. He rolled over when the brave approached since he didn't want the Indian to know he had finally slipped free of his bonds.

"Can we rest up a spell? The horses aren't going to last another mile, even swapping off the way we've been doing."

The Apache stared at him a moment, frowned, nodded, and then said, "We rest."

Slocum lay back, trying to get his bearings. It was hard to believe but he thought he had come full circle and once more rode across Circle Bar K land. Did Leonard Conway even miss him? Slocum doubted it. The cantankerous rancher wouldn't miss much of anything other than his steak and eggs for breakfast. It was still nice to know where he could go for help. The rancher wouldn't turn him away if he showed up having been robbed by an Apache. More than once Slocum had heard the rancher rant and rave about Indian depredation on his herd.

Slocum rubbed his wrists and felt the welts acutely. The circulation had returned a long time since. All he needed was to bide his time and wait for the Apache to nod off. When he did, Slocum would have himself a renegade to turn over to the cavalry.

Then he snorted. The brave looked at him.

"Nothing," Slocum said. He wouldn't turn the Indian over to the Army after the way they had let Childress go free. The Indian still stared at him. Slocum had to ask, "What's your big hurry to get here?"

"Squaw, son, they come."

"All of you left the reservation?" Slocum didn't need the man to answer. Of course they had. "You're all heading down into Mexico?"

The brave just stared at him. That was all the answer Slocum needed. He settled down to wait. He closed his eyes, just for a moment, to lull any suspicion. He came awake in a rush when he heard loud commands and saw they were surrounded by bluecoats.

"We got ourselves a renegade Injun, men," the lieutenant said. "Get him in shackles."

"Hold your horses, Lieutenant," Slocum called out. He dropped the rawhide cord and stood. He raised his hands when the soldiers pointed their carbines at him. "You got it all wrong. He's not a renegade. He's a scout from over at Fort Craig."

"What? That's a mighty long ways off." The lieutenant dismounted and looked hard at his captive, then at Slocum. "What're you doin' ridin' with this savage?"

"We're scouting for the colonel, that's what. We got two Warm Springs Apaches off the reservation. We tracked them south of Tombstone and in this direction but lost them two days back. You see them? You'd be doing us a heap big favor."

Slocum saw the lieutenant didn't know what to make of this tall tale.

"Colonel Hatch?"

"None other," Slocum said. "Said he had orders straight from General Crook to get them back on the reservation."

"I didn't hear about any escaped Warm Springs Apaches."

"You're looking for Apaches, aren't you? If you already caught them, good. Me and my friend here can get on back to Fort Craig."

"We're huntin' for renegades," the lieutenant said, but Slocum heard the doubt creeping into his voice.

"You see any riders at all the past couple days? No?"

"We did see two riders yesterday, Lieutenant," spoke up the scout. "But they wasn't Injuns. A man and a woman."

Slocum looked hard at the scout.

"The woman a redhead?"

"We was a ways off, but yeah, she was. Cut quite a figure ridin' along the way she was. They were in a powerful hurry to get somewhere."

Slocum described Childress, but the scout wasn't as sure.

"We was a ways off, as I said. Coulda been like you said. You know 'em?"

"I surely do. They befriended us just outside of Tombstone," Slocum said. "I'd like to thank them, but I reckon they rode north."

"Due west, into the mountains," the scout said. "See yon saddle pass, just this side of the taller hill? They was headin' for it. Or it looked that way to me."

"Do tell," Slocum said, trying not to seem too anxious. He had been wrong about Childress going to the Molly E Mine, but he had been right about him heading for territory he knew.

Childress had rustled cattle in the area for some time and probably knew the watering holes and trails in this part of Arizona Territory better than anywhere else. He had brought Claire here to hide out.

He must have known it would take Pine a week or longer to cheat Tarkenton out of his deed to the silver mine.

"We better escort the two of you to the fort," the lieutenant said, coming to a decision. "We can contact Fort Craig."

"We're not getting anywhere out here. Why not?" Slocum gestured to the Apache not to start shooting. The brave wasn't following much but knew that Slocum hadn't turned him over to the cavalry immediately. He had the good sense to stay quiet.

"Tell me, Lieutenant, is Conway still running the Circle Bar K?"

This brought the officer up short.

"He is."

"Him and Major Tompkins still feuding? I heard a couple scouts from this part of the country talking about that."

"You know Conway and Tompkins?"

"Conway, sure. A patrol from the fort escorted him and his herd to the railhead at Mesilla last year. I'd like to see the old galoot again. He owes me three dollars from a poker game."

"Word is he's not too good a player," the lieutenant said.

"He gets riled up and forgets to pay attention," Slocum said, describing a trait of the rancher perfectly.

"There's no call for us to return to the fort," the lieutenant said. "Sergeant, see that the horses are watered and the men have full canteens. Then form the patrol."

Slocum went to the Apache and said softly, "Don't get spooked. They'll be out of our hair in a half hour."

And they were. When the trailing trooper disappeared from sight, Slocum grabbed his six-shooter from the Apache.

"It was a good thing the soldiers didn't notice you were carrying my six-gun." Slocum held it for a moment, then slipped it into his holster. "I got you out of a jam. Now it's your turn. If you want to find your family and hightail it south of the border, you're going to find a trail for me first."

"Two riders? West?"

Slocum smiled. The Apache had paid attention and understood more than the soldiers about their conversation.

"The man and the woman. Find their trail and put me on it and you can ride all the way to Mexico City for all I care."

"If white man and squaw crossed desert, Billy Wolf will find."

"I'm sure you will, Billy Wolf." Slocum thrust out his hand. The Apache hesitated, then shook on their deal.

23

"Do you want to ride with the body?"

Jackson Pine looked up, shaken out of his reverie by the undertaker's question. He forced himself to get back to the here and now.

"I'll go with Dr. Gottschalk," he said. "If the doctor doesn't mind." Pine looked to the doctor, who scowled. He obviously did not want company on the long ride out to the cemetery, but Pine had put him into an uncomfortable position.

"Get in," Gottschalk said with a tinge of bitterness in his words. "I just hope nobody from town sees you riding with me."

"I don't have typhoid," Pine said, settling into the buggy. He was heavier than the doctor and caused it to tip to his side. He wondered if Gottschalk would try to take a corner on the way out to the town cemetery fast enough to dislodge him. From the way the doctor spoke, it was possible that he carried a grudge.

"I could cure that. I can't do a damn thing about you being a lawyer."

Pine laughed, thinking the doctor made a joke.

"It's not contagious."

"If it were, I'd give up my practice and become an executioner."

Pine realized then that Gottschalk was not joking. He settled down as the doctor snapped the reins and got the horse pulling the doubled weight in the buggy. They rattled over every rock and pothole in the dusty, steep road leading up the hill to the cemetery. Gottschalk answered Pine with grunts and single words when he bothered to even acknowledge his attempt to make small talk.

"Look, Doctor, I had nothing to do with Norton's death. I'm not even certain what happened. I heard he was murdered, that your surgery had nothing to do with his death."

"Just as well since you'd be inclined to sue me for wrongful death," Gottschalk said. "Look, Pine, I don't like you, I don't trust you, and if I was on the stand testifying under oath, I'd swear that you had more to do with Sam's death than meets the eye. I don't know how or why, but you're mixed up in a good man's death."

"I didn't shoot him."

"He was stabbed."

"However he died, I had nothing to do with it." Pine shifted uncomfortably on the hard seat. In spite of badgering the new marshal for information, he had learned very little about Norton's death. He felt a growing anxiety because of Claire and the ransom demand from Childress, but he couldn't confide in the doctor. Or did Gottschalk know she had been kidnapped?

"We're there. Get out."

Pine stepped down and slowly walked the short distance to the grave. The undertaker had pulled up his wagon next to the grave. Two grave diggers slid the wood coffin from the wagon bed and put it on the ground beside the grave.

The lawyer stared at the coffin. Pine. It was made of pine wood. One day he would be in a coffin like that. Pine in pine.

"The reverend's a little late. You want to get started?" the undertaker asked.

"Go on," Pine said.

"He wasn't talking to you," Gottschalk said. "Since Claire isn't here, he was asking me."

"Where is Miss Norton?" Pine asked, hoping to find out exactly what the doctor knew—or suspected.

"Indisposed," was all Gottschalk said. "There's the minister."

"Seems like he's got company. That there's Marshal Eakin with him."

"This is about all the crowd we can expect," Gottschalk said.

Pine looked past the doctor and saw one other group, but they wouldn't be joining the main party. China Mary and her bodyguard stood silently thirty feet away, watching and making no move to get any closer.

He considered going to speak with her again, but the reverend began the ceremony. Pine found himself caught up in the ritual, thinking of Claire as he prayed, and then Sam Norton's body was lowered into the grave. The two grave diggers began shoveling dirt onto the coffin as the minister and marshal stood to one side, arguing. Gottschalk joined them, and they started a three-handed argument. Pine wanted to know what the squabbling was over but knew better than to join them. If Gottschalk didn't chase him off, Marshal Eakin would. The former deputy had no love for Pine after he had made the lawman look like a complete fool on the stand a few months back.

Pine felt a moment of pride at that defense. He had found the precise point to attack to break the deputy's story and had relentlessly pursued it until he'd won an acquittal. He hadn't even bothered to bribe the judge. There hadn't been a reason. Even the prosecutor had realized how weak the case had been and finally conceded.

That had been a fine day for him. Pine knew there would be others.

Finding himself standing alone, he turned to talk with China Mary again, only to see that she and Ah Sum had disappeared. He hadn't seen a carriage or horses, and they were not walking along the road back to town. If he hadn't known better, he would have suspected some kind of Chinese magic had spirited them away.

Gottschalk and the others finished their argument and split, each taking a different way back to town. He hurried to catch up with Gottschalk, but the doctor snapped the reins as he neared and pointedly left him behind. Pine ran a few paces, then slowed and finally fell into a long stride following the doctor back into Tombstone. By the time he got to town, Pine's resolve had hardened. He didn't care if China Mary denied him an audience a thousand times over. The two of them could forge a potent alliance against Wakefield and the rest of the political system in Tombstone. He would have to make her see this.

Pine's resolve faded the closer he got to the butcher shop. When Ah Sum came out, he almost turned and fled.

But the huge bodyguard did not whip out a knife to fling at him. Instead, he motioned for Pine to enter the butcher shop.

Victory! Pine tried to keep from gloating. China Mary had finally come around to seeing things his way. All that remained now was for them to come to an agreement over what needed to be done. Perhaps he could even get a clue to what had happened to Claire. If Childress held her anywhere in town, China Mary would know—or could find out. Her people were everywhere.

"Good morning," Pine greeted China Mary. He wondered if he ought to bow. Since he didn't know how, he refrained. "Thank you for attending Sam Norton's funeral."

"It is not your place to thank me for my attendance. Why were you there?"

The woman's question shook Pine since he had not expected it.

"I have an interest in representing his daughter."

China Mary said nothing, as if she had to think on this matter a great deal more.

"I want to replace Norton as your lawyer. Before, when I made this offer, you were less than receptive. Have you considered what it means in Tombstone to be without a lawyer representing you in court?"

"You are persistent. Why is that?"

Before Pine could put his chaotic thoughts into order—why did he want to replace Norton?—gunshots sounded from the butcher shop. He turned as Ah Sum stumbled back through the curtains. The huge man had hatchets in both hands.

Ah Sum grunted, but China Mary did not stir. She watched impassively as Ah Sum dropped to his knees, still facing the curtain. He grunted again and threw both hatchets, then fell facedown on the floor. Without realizing he had even moved, Pine found himself at the man's side. He rolled Ah Sum over and saw three bullet wounds in the man's chest.

"He's dead," Pine told China Mary. She stared at him, her dark eyes lacking any expression.

Pine got to his feet and went to the curtain. He saw the bullet holes in the cloth as he pushed it aside. In the butcher shop lay four men, three dressed as miners and one of the butchers. The intruders had used six-shooters. The butchers had flung their meat cleavers to deadly effect. Ah Sum's double hatchet throw had brought down one of the dead miners.

He walked out into the shop and rolled over a dead man. He looked up from the body to see China Mary in the doorway.

"This is one of Wakefield's men. I recognize him. I don't know why he's dressed as a miner unless Wakefield wanted everyone to think you're at war with the mine owners."

China Mary motioned to him. He left the bodies and returned to the bare room. This time China Mary did not sit.

"You will work as lawyer?"

"I will," Pine said.

"You are hired. Stop Wakefield. In court. Outside court. It does not matter. Stop him." She glanced at Ah Sum, then left without another word.

Pine heaved a deep sigh. He had a new client who would bring him a considerable amount of work. Getting rid of Colin Wakefield was something he would do on his own, but getting paid for the chore suited him just fine.

He stepped over Ah Sum's body and was taken aback by the butcher shop. The bodies were gone. All of them. Two butchers had been working when he came in. Although one had been killed—he had seen the body with his own eyes—two were still working.

And the bodies were gone as if they had never existed.

Jackson Pine worried about working for China Mary, but not that much. He left to find some way to stop Wakefield dead in his tracks.

24

The Apache knelt and studied what looked like undisturbed desert sand, running his finger over small ridges that seemed to be baked into the ground. He finally looked up and pointed toward the mountains.

"You're sure they went that way?" Slocum asked. He couldn't see any trace of Childress and Claire's passage, but Billy Wolf had shown himself to be a far better tracker than Slocum ever could be—and Slocum considered himself to be pretty damned good.

"Two riders. A day ago."

Slocum took off his hat and scratched his head, staring toward the mountains. He had ridden by this section of countryside a few times as he chased the Circle Bar K cattle but didn't know the area as well as Childress obviously did. The rustler had made a beeline from Tombstone to this spot, never deviating from his trail. That meant he had a hideout nearby and felt safe there.

In a way, it made sense. Childress and his gang had worked as rustlers for quite a while, moving the cattle they stole south of the border and then returning to steal even more. They had to have a secure spot to hide from cavalry and federal deputies and any other lawman hunting for them. Slocum snorted. Even if Conway had sent out trackers to find the rustlers, which might have been the greatest threat to the cattle thieves, Childress had to feel secure wherever he ran. He might be a low-down snake in the grass but he wasn't stupid when it came to cattle thieving.

"Thanks," Slocum said, thrusting out his hand. Billy Wolf looked at him for a moment, grinned, and then shook. "Now go find your family. Good luck reaching Mexico, though I don't think you'll have any trouble avoiding that shavetail and his squad."

"Caught me once. You saved."

"We were both tired. We're rested now." Slocum looked from the Indian toward the mountains again. He was anxious to get on Childress's trail. The quicker he got Claire away from the rustler, the better off she would be.

The Apache nodded once, then lightly jumped on horseback.

"Wait," Slocum said. He handed the reins of one horse to the Indian brave. "Yours." Again he got a single nod, then Billy Wolf let out a long, loud howl and galloped off. Slocum watched him disappear behind a rise on his way south. The thunder of his horses' hooves eventually faded so only the soft whisper of a desert wind remained. Like so many others, the Sonora Desert had swallowed the Indian whole.

Slocum mounted and led his other horse behind him. If the rescue went well, he would have both the horse Claire rode and Childress's to take back to Tombstone, but he counted having this one as a spare horse for the redhead as insurance against Childress doing something desperate. If lead started flying, horses presented big targets.

The trail might as well not have existed as far as Slocum could tell. He had to trust the Indian's uncanny ability to track a ghost through this desert. Less than an hour later he found a game trail. A smile came to his lips. For the first time he had found spoor he trusted. A pile of fresh horse flop still attracted flies. He rode less than an hour behind the horse that had dumped this marker on the trail.

Slocum stood in the stirrups and tried to get a better idea of the terrain ahead. He was in the foothills now, providing more opportunities for ambush and for lookouts to spot any rider trying to find Childress. Whether the rest of his gang had remained after Slocum and the riders from the Circle Bar K had recovered the cattle the rustlers had stolen mattered less to Slocum than finding them in the first place. He was good enough to approach without being sighted. After he determined how many men he faced, he could decide how best to get Claire back.

Even if he had to let Childress ride away, getting Claire Norton free from his clutches was the most important thing. Slocum could see her back to Tombstone and then come back for Childress. There wasn't anywhere far enough away that Childress could ride that Slocum wouldn't find him and even the score.

The foothills provided several potential hiding places for the rustler. A larger canyon branched off to his right, but Slocum preferred the winding path going deeper into the hills. The higher elevation gave a better spot for a sentry. Taking his field glasses from his saddlebags, he slowly studied the hilltops all around. Not seeing any trace of a lookout, Slocum rode deeper into the hills. The trail curved about and formed a meandering canyon with tall walls.

Several times Slocum stopped to use his binoculars. Still nothing.

He rode for another mile and then drew rein, something not right. The insects buzzed in the hot, dry air trapped between the canyon walls. Any sweat evaporated right away, keeping him cool enough to tolerate the heat, but it wasn't the terrain or the air sucking the water from his body that caused his uneasiness.

The bullet tore past him from behind. Slocum bent over,

put his heels to the gelding's sides, and rocketed forward. The sudden lurch almost unseated him, but he hung on. The other horse tried to rear and was pulled along because Slocum had fastened its reins to his saddle. When the horses had galloped a hundred yards, Slocum regained control and hunted for cover. Rocks to his left gave him some shelter.

Not much but enough.

He hit the ground and let the reins dangle. Drawing his Winchester, he waited to see if Childress showed himself. Others might be inclined to take a potshot at a stranger riding this canyon, but Slocum put his bet on the rustler. If Childress had rejoined the others in his gang, one of them might have taken the shot. It didn't matter. Slocum was going to find out where Childress was holed up in a thrice.

Rather than let the kidnapper come to him, Slocum left his horses and worked his way back down the canyon. Most ambushers thought their victims would try to run. Very few believed their targets would come after them.

Slocum rounded a bend and waited to see if he could spot where Childress had fired on him. A wry smile came to his lips when he saw the glint of light off a rifle barrel. Childress had gone less than twenty feet up to make his shot. Settling his Winchester down, sighting in, and waiting, Slocum knew Childress would show himself eventually. Men like him lacked the patience that Slocum had developed over the years. During the war he had been a sniper and a good one because he would wait hours for a single good shot.

He fired almost immediately. The bullet hit high and to the right above Childress's head. And it was Childress. The rustler jumped to his feet and threw up an arm to protect himself from a cascade of rock knocked loose by Slocum's bullet. The next shot caused Slocum to gloat. He had hit Childress. Over the years he had developed a sense of which shots were accurate and which went off target.

This one winged Childress, causing him to tumble back and roll over and over down the hillside.

Slocum swarmed over the rock he had used as a rest for his rifle and rushed forward to finish off the rustler.

"John, go back. It's a trap. He's going to—" Claire's outcry was suddenly stifled. Slocum imagined a hand going over her mouth to silence her.

He didn't stop advancing until he reached the man at the foot of the hill. The smile faded when he saw that the man he'd killed wasn't Childress. Slocum didn't recognize him, but it could have been another in the gang of cattle thieves. He wore the clothing Slocum had last seen Childress wearing. Childress had set him up—and was willing to sacrifice one of his partners to kill him.

Rather than lament how he hadn't killed Childress, Slocum kept moving. That was the way to correct his bad luck.

As he rounded a boulder, he saw Claire sitting in the middle of a sandy spit, her arms tied behind her back. A bandanna had been crammed into her mouth to silence her. She saw him and jerked her head around. Her eyes went wide with shock.

Slocum heard the burning fuse before he saw the bundle of dynamite. Childress had timed the fuse perfectly. If he had rushed to Claire's side, the two of them would have been caught in the open.

Standing, Slocum lifted the rifle and fired, once, twice, three times. The dynamite exploded. The explosion knocked him back and covered him with a shower of dust and rock splinters, but he recovered fast. He raced to the center of the spit. Claire had been knocked several feet across the sand by the explosion and lay moaning. A huge cloud of smoke and dust shrouded the spit, hiding him from Childress and his new ambush.

He yanked the bandanna from her mouth, scooped her up, and carried her over his shoulder.

"John, dynamite," she moaned out. "He tried to blow us up!"

"It wasn't intended to kill us, just to knock us out so Childress could capture us. I knew he wouldn't kill you since he wants to swap you for the Molly E Mine. By setting it off before he intended, I wasn't caught in the blast the way you were."

"You risked my life!"

Slocum grunted as he ran, the woman beginning to struggle as she dangled over his left shoulder. When he couldn't go any farther, he heaved and got her to her feet.

"You're going to have to walk on your own. Childress isn't going to let you slip out of his hands."

"What do you mean he wasn't going to kill me? That was enough dynamite to kill a dozen men!"

"He had it placed wrong for that. He's smarter than I reckoned. He wants to trade you for Tarkenton's mine when Pine finally weasels it out of the court."

"My head hurts. I don't know what you're going on about."

"Keep running," he said. Slocum took two quick shots when he saw Childress behind them. The bullets went high and forced the kidnapper back under cover. Slocum followed her more slowly, firing as he went. When he was sure Childress was going to keep his head down, he turned and ran after a struggling Claire. She stumbled and almost fell. He caught her around her waist and got her back on her feet.

"Get these ropes off my hands," she said, some of her spirit returning as the shock from the explosion wore off.

"When we get to the horses."

"My horse is back there," she said, trying to turn. He had to catch her again and keep her moving deeper into the canyon. She fought him for a moment, then stared into his face and quickly kissed him. "Thank you."

"We're not out of this pickle yet," he said, but Slocum was feeling more confident about escaping. He had to pick Claire up a couple more times to get her over large rocks since she couldn't use her hands to scramble over them, and then they reached the horses.

"I can't ride without a saddle," she said, staring uncertainly at the second horse. "Oh, that feels . . . awful. My hands are numb."

He had finally worked free the knot on her ropes.

"Ride my horse. I can get along just fine bareback."

"Oh, yes, I remember," she said, a glint in her eye again. "I owe you, John. I owe you a lot."

He helped her into the saddle, then vaulted onto the other horse.

"There's plenty of time for that later," he said. "We have to get away from Childress. I shot one of his henchmen. How many are with him?"

"Only the one. At least he's the only one I saw. I think the others hightailed it south to Mexico. He cursed you for scaring off the rest of his gang."

"Then it's just Childress after us," he said, considering his chances of turning the tables and laying an ambush for the rustler. Childress wouldn't give up Claire easily since he needed her to get Tarkenton's deed from Pine.

"Leave him, John. I want to get the hell away from here— and him."

Slocum understood. He pushed his horse to greater speed. The canyon walls lowered on either side as the distance between them widened. The desert had to lie not five miles away.

"We've gotten away from him. There's nothing between us and Tombstone but a whole lot of desert," he said.

"I . . . I don't know how long I can ride. He didn't feed me much."

Slocum started to ask what Childress had done to her but held back. If Claire wanted to talk about that part of her captivity, she would. He leaned to the side, using his knees to get his horse closer to hers so he could reach into his saddlebags.

"Here," he said, handing her a hunk of jerky. "It's not much, but it'll keep you going."

"Salty," she said, making a face.

"There's the canteen," Slocum said. He grabbed for it, and

as it came free, a bullet took his horse from under him. The horse fell into the gelding, causing it to rear and throw Claire hard to the ground. She lay on her back, momentarily stunned.

Slocum rolled to his belly and saw Childress galloping from the canyon. He had his rifle to his shoulder, ready to take another shot.

"Come on," Slocum said. "We've got to get under cover." He grabbed Claire's hand and pulled her to her feet. Childress fired, which put some speed into her step.

Slocum hung on to the canteen with one hand and Claire's hand with the other. He dragged her along, not bothering to zigzag to confuse Childress's steady fire. At this distance from horseback, Childress had to be luckier than skillful to hit them, but that didn't mean they could make a stand out in the open.

"There, a cave. Get in there," Slocum said, yanking Claire around and sending her reeling. She balked at going into the small opening. "Do it or you'll be in a grave alongside your pa," Slocum said harshly.

This motivated her enough to wiggle through the narrow entrance. The sides were as smooth as river rock and she popped in.

"There's a bigger room here, John."

He tossed the canteen in and drew his six-shooter, intending to take Childress out of the saddle if the shot was decent. Childress saw his danger and remained out of pistol range. He kept shooting, his rifle fire improving until he drove Slocum into the hole. For him it was a tighter fit than for Claire, but Slocum wiggled like a sidewinder and got through to find the larger chamber Claire mentioned.

"It's mighty dark in here, John," she said.

"Hush. Let Childress think we've gone exploring deeper in the cave." He looked around and couldn't see the roof high over their head. A humid breeze came from deeper in the cave, causing his clothing to plaster wetly against his body.

The heat out in the desert was extreme but he had felt cooler from his sweat evaporating. The air inside the cave was so wet he felt like swimming in it.

Claire moved closer to him. He held out his arm to keep her out of the line of fire. Childress could only send bullets in a narrow field of fire. Slocum intended to blast Childress's head off when he stuck it through.

His hand turned sweaty on the butt of his six-gun. After several minutes he knew Childress was willing to wait them out.

"I'm going to wait till dark and go out after him. It's the only—"

The explosion knocked Slocum back into Claire. They went down in a heap.

He wouldn't have to wait till sundown. The mouth of the cave had been sealed by an explosion. The complete darkness of the grave encircled them.

25

"He dynamited the opening! We're trapped!" Claire let out a shriek of pure anguish and bumped into Slocum. He caught her to prevent her from blundering around in the cave. Never had he been plunged into such complete darkness.

"We can get out. Stop it, stop it!" He struggled to hold her as she thrashed about. She finally settled down and began sobbing, her face against his chest. He felt her hot tears soaking into his shirt.

"He had a case of dynamite. I should have told you. We wouldn't be trapped in here to die if I'd told you."

"There wasn't any other way for us to get away from him. He had a rifle and all I had was a six-gun. Childress could take potshots at us from a distance until he managed to hit us, like he did my horse."

"What happened to my horse—your horse—the one I was riding?" Claire sniffled now. Slocum eased up on the bear hug he had held her in, and she backed off but remained close enough so she could rest the palm of her hand on his chest.

"Doesn't matter. We have to see if we can get out of here." Slocum had a good sense of direction and knew where the cave mouth had been. Holding Claire's hand, he edged back to the wall and began exploring using his free hand. The closer he got to the once-slick stone opening, the more he regretted trying to find safety in this cave. The explosion might have been from only a stick or two of dynamite, but it had effectively sealed the mouth.

Worse, just running his hand over the tumble of stone plugging the way out caused him to sweat like a pig. The temperature inside the cave couldn't be anywhere as high as the desert outside, but the high humidity made it feel worse. Every breath he took made him think he was sucking water into his lungs.

"What is this place?" Claire asked. "My clothes are sticking to my body like plaster. I can't remember sweating like this, even in a hot Boston summer."

"I don't know," Slocum said. He gave up his investigation of the opening. The way out of the cave was sealed as surely as if Childress had driven a huge cork into the hole. "I'm going to light a lucifer. Close your eyes or it'll blind you."

"Wait!"

"It's all right," he reassured her, taking his hand from hers. Their skin was drenched with sweat. She tried to grip down and hold on to him, but the slickness let him pull free. "Close your eyes."

"All right," she said dubiously.

Slocum found the tin with his lucifers and pulled one out. From his quick inventory by feel, he had a dozen matches. He wasn't sure how long he could make them last, but he had to light the first to get an idea of how big a jam they were in.

He took his own advice and screwed his eyes shut tightly. The match hissed, flared, and then settled down to a fitful flame. Only then did he slowly open his eyes. Even squinting, the light hurt. He held the match up high and opened his eyes all the way.

His heart skipped a beat when he saw that the light didn't

go very far into the cave. The faint glow from the sputtering lucifer wouldn't even show how high the cave ceiling was, much less illuminate anything deeper in the cave.

"There's nothing here, John. I mean, there's nothing I can see but more cave. It stretches to forever."

"Yeah," he said. "That's the way it looked to me, too." He snapped his fingers when the wood burned down and scorched his skin. The match tumbled to the floor and then hissed out in a small puddle of water.

"We're in a cave with more water than I've ever seen in the desert. Why hasn't someone found this place before?"

Slocum grunted. She blundered into him in the dark. It took a few seconds for them to get their bearings again. She pressed close to him, but this made them both even more uncomfortable. The moisture and stifling heat caused them to sweat even more.

"I can use some water. Where's the canteen?"

"I dropped it when you shoved me in," Claire said. She gripped his arm and began running her foot around until the toe of her shoe collided noisily with the canteen. Claire bent and retrieved it. "May I have a sip first? I hadn't realized how thirsty I was."

Slocum told her to go ahead and drink. He knew that, in spite of the sticky air inside this cave, if they didn't find something more than a puddle, they might die of thirst. Still, with such a thick atmosphere, there might be an underground river coming up inside the cave. The San Pedro between here and Tombstone ran underground and surfaced at odd places along its course.

"We need to find if there's a river," he said. "We can swim out."

"Oh, no," she said. "That's not possible. I can't swim."

"Let's find the river and worry about that later." She pressed the canteen into his hands. He lifted it and got two mouthfuls of water before the canteen ran dry.

"How do we explore, John? It's too dark to go by feel." Her hand slipped down his belly and worked lower to squeeze his crotch. "Though not too dark."

"Let's explore some before that," he said. "I've got an idea." He pulled out his fixings and found a rolling paper in the pack he carried in his vest pocket. He had built so many cigarettes in his day he could do it with his eyes closed. In the inky darkness of the cavern he had to. When he'd finished, he slipped one end into his mouth and lit another lucifer.

"Oh, the coal on the end of the cigarette seems so bright!"

He held the match high again and started walking. By the time it burned out, he had taken a couple dozen steps deeper into the cave. Then he puffed on the cigarette and got more light, albeit dim and brief, from the coal at the tip.

"Look sharp for water," he said.

"And a way out."

He burned three more matches and two cigarettes before they discovered a large pool of water. Sitting on the slime-slick edge, he dipped the canteen in and let it burble itself full. He took a deep drink. The water had a strong mineral taste, but it wasn't alkali.

"Here," he said, pressing the canteen into Claire's hands.

"Is it safe? Should we boil it or something?"

"If we had wood, we could make a torch. But I don't think there's a forest growing in here."

"Oh," she said. "It doesn't matter much if the water kills us, does it? We're going to die in this humid place anyway." She choked and then began to cry. "We're going to die in the dark and nobody will ever know what happened to us."

"I'm not letting Childress win," Slocum said. He put his arm around her quaking shoulders. He felt her lay her head against his shoulder. At the edge of the unseen pool, they sat in the dark, each lost in their own thoughts.

"John?"

He knew what she wanted. He had to admit their situation looked hopeless. He had only a few matches left and wandering aimlessly in what might be dozens of miles of underground passages would only tire them out. The heat and oppressive humidity wore him out faster than he would have thought possible.

He reached around her and found the buttons to her blouse.

"My clothes are soaked," she said. "They feel like a second skin."

"No, they don't." He peeled away the cloth and found sweat-slick naked flesh beneath. Using only his sense of touch, he explored her body. Bit by bit he stripped off her clothing until Claire was naked to the waist. Her breasts fit perfectly into the palms of his hands. The tiny nubbins at the crests hardened as he tweaked them, twisting and turning them from side to side until she moaned softly.

"My turn," she said. It took Claire longer to strip him of his coat, vest, and shirt, but they had nothing but time. Then their half-naked bodies pressed into each other. Their lips met in a deep kiss that stretched out forever.

"More," she whispered in his ear. "I want more." She moved her hand down to his crotch again so he would know exactly what she meant. As if there was any question.

It took even longer for them to get the rest of their clothing off, but they soon lay fully naked on the smooth rock, surrounded by the impossibly damp, hot air. Slocum scooted around until he felt her body along the entire length of his. Then his explorations became more intimate. His hand tangled in the fleecy thatch between her legs. When his middle finger slid into her, she gasped and ground herself down around his hand. Her hips bucked and moved slowly so he stirred about inside her like a spoon in a mixing bowl.

"I want something bigger inside, John," she said. She ran her hands down his sweaty body until she found what she wanted. She tugged insistently on his manhood, drawing it toward the spot where his finger continued to swirl about.

Slocum repositioned himself between her legs. He wished he could look down into her lovely face, but even when he kissed her, he couldn't see anything of her beauty. This had to be what it was like to be blind. It focused his attention on senses other than sight. His touch became more acute. Every light brush of his hand across her silky skin was a delight. The sound of her breathing told him about her arousal. Smell and taste and touch and hearing became paramount and he used them all in the absence of light.

His hips moved forward and he slipped easily into her moist interior. They both gasped at the deep intrusion. Then he began moving with great deliberation to get the most out of every gesture, every light touch, every movement.

Without light to mark the passage of time, their lovemaking might have lasted for hours or only minutes. He couldn't tell. All Slocum wanted was to make the sensations last as long as possible, and when they were both sated, he held Claire in his arms.

"This was so different, John," she said. "But I wanted to see you."

"The next time we'll do it under the noonday sun," he promised.

She giggled.

"You'd sunburn your ass."

"Not if I made it fast."

"I don't like it that way," she said. "And the sand. There'd be sand all over and in places where neither of us would like. No, let's do it the next time in a pool of water."

"That's the way it feels to me now," Slocum said. "I'm still sweating."

"Get me more water, will you?" she asked.

He sat up and fumbled around to find their canteen. He froze when he heard a noise deeper in the cave.

"What is it?" she asked, clutching him in the dark. "I've heard that before, but I don't recognize it. Not exactly."

"Wings," Slocum said. "Flapping wings."

"It doesn't sound like any bird."

"Bats!" He dropped the canteen and searched through his

vest until he found the tin box with his remaining lucifers. A quick movement lit one. He squinted and peered through slitted eyes to see a bat fluttering about high above them. As he watched, the bat flitted off to their right and disappeared out of the circle of wan light cast by the match.

"I don't like them. They get in your hair and—" Claire stopped talking, then gasped. "If they got in, that means they can also get out."

"Come on," Slocum said, gathering their clothing. He slipped and slid on the slick rock but the crushing humidity was forgotten as he began moving in the direction he had seen the bat fly.

26

"This is my last match," Slocum said. He tried to keep his voice neutral and not spook Claire. He wasn't sure he succeeded because the thought of dying in the utter darkness made his heart hammer like a blacksmith pounding on an anvil.

"Another cigarette. You need to roll another cigarette," Claire said, a hint of panic in her voice. "There's no sign of that bat or how it got out of the cave."

Slocum lit the lucifer and waited for the flare to die. He had used the last of his tobacco some time ago. He had considered setting fire to their clothing, but the humid air and their sweat had soaked them too thoroughly. The temperature never varied, forcing him to give up any hope of drying out even a small patch of cloth to use as a torch.

"Where do we go, John? There's only endless cave."

Slocum got a whiff of bat guano. He inhaled more deeply and almost gagged.

"We're getting closer," he said. "Hurry before the match goes out."

"You've got more, don't you?" When he didn't answer her, Claire panicked and ran, slipping on the slick rock and crying out in anguish.

"Stop, Claire. We're close. The bats are around here close. Smell them. Go on, smell them. They're our way out."

The match sputtered and died sooner than it ought to. He cursed and used the afterimage of the woman to guide him. He fell over her.

"We're not going to get out of here. I know it, John. There's nothing we can do."

"If we're going to die, we might as well keep going," he said. Her attitude irritated him. He wasn't the kind who would ever give up as long as he drew breath. Reaching down, he found her arm and pulled her to her feet. She trembled with emotion.

"You go on, John. I'll stay here."

"We're in this together. And the way out of the cave is ahead."

"How do we know the bats didn't go out the way we came in? The hole that Childress closed?"

"No bat guano near it. No bats at all. And the hole was too small."

"You make it sound logical, but—"

He heard a shrill sound high above and fluttering wings caused tiny air currents to caress his cheek. Without arguing further, he pushed her ahead in the direction of the receding wing noises. He wanted to laugh aloud when he saw the faint light high above them.

"John, am I hallucinating?"

"We're sharing it. Come on." He didn't have to urge her now. She preceded him into a chamber whose dimensions came into focus as the light from the hole brightened. High above dangled thousands of bats. A few flitted about, hunting for a spot to hang.

"How do we get there? It's so high," Claire said.

"I'll boost you up."

"I won't be able to pull you up after me. I'm not strong enough."

"You get out, then we'll worry about that."

Slocum grabbed her around the waist, then heaved. She let out a cry of surprise at the ease with which he lifted her. Her fingers fumbled against the slippery rock. Slocum got her knees on his shoulders, then she stood.

"There's a rock. It's dry. I can hang on it." Her weight suddenly vanished from Slocum's shoulders. He looked up and saw her feet vanish through the hole.

He wiped his hands on his clothing, but this did nothing to dry them. The moisture in the cave was too pervasive to ever do that. Instead, Slocum blew on his hands and got them a little drier. He studied the rocky wall and the hole high on it, then jumped. His fingers closed around an outcropping and began slipping.

He kicked, found a toehold, and boosted himself up. Reaching through the hole, he found the knob Claire had used. With a powerful tug, he scooted through the hole and hung half out to see Claire below him on a ledge looking out over the desert.

"I never thought I'd want to see such dry, desolate land. But I do. It's beautiful!"

Slocum grunted, kicked hard, and slid headfirst out of the hole. He landed hard on the ledge beside her, then swung his legs around so they dangled over the edge.

"Yeah, beautiful," he said. "But it's a long walk to Tombstone."

"We can go somewhere else. Closer."

"The Circle Bar K Ranch can't be too far. We might find cowboys out with the herd before we reach the ranch house."

"I need a bath," she said, looking at her disheveled clothing.

"I don't know if I want to dunk myself in water ever again." Slocum stood and shook like a wet dog. Droplets from his clothing went in all directions. It was good to hear Claire laugh again.

"I'll scrub your back."

"Then I reckon I've changed my mind about that bath." Slocum got to his feet, already looking for a way down the hillside. It wouldn't be too difficult.

An hour later they were at the mouth of a canyon Slocum recognized.

"A mile that way is where Childress sealed us up." When he mentioned Childress, he reached down and touched his six-shooter. It would be good having the rustler in his sights. Only a bullet through his foul heart would settle the score.

"Do you think he's still around?" Claire began turning, as if she expected Childress to pop up from behind every mesquite or clump of greasewood.

"Why stay? He wanted you to trade for the Molly E Mine. If he thought we were dead, he'd head back to Tombstone to work some other deal with Pine to get Tarkenton's claim."

"He was really swapping me for the mine? Jackson Pine was good with that?"

Slocum didn't answer. If Pine had figured out a way to get Claire back and keep the mine, he would have. Whether he would have worried more than a few minutes if Childress killed Claire was another matter. His anguish would have been eased with a mound of silver from Tarkenton's mine.

They started walking, the canteen ominously empty by the end of the second hour. Although they had been in the cave for only a short while—Slocum guessed only a day or so—they had gotten used to having water all around. He had complained about too much water, and now he wanted just a little more.

"The ranch house is still a lot of miles away. The Circle Bar K is a big spread."

"John, do you hear that?"

Slocum stopped and turned his head slowly until he caught

the faint sound of a horse neighing. He drew his six-gun and found himself face to face with Billy Wolf. The Apache grinned from ear to ear.

Claire moved behind Slocum and gripped his shoulder.

"An Apache," she said in a choked voice. "Shoot him, John. Shoot him before he kills us!"

"He wouldn't kill you," Slocum said, not sure why he was feeding her obvious fear. "Not right away. Do you think I could trade you to him for a horse?"

"John!"

"Your squaw?" The Apache brave reached out to touch her red hair. "Good."

"Mine," Slocum acknowledged, ignoring Claire's outrage. "I hadn't expected to see you again. Did you find your family?"

"You know each other?" Claire was doubly offended now. Slocum continued to ignore her. It wouldn't do to seem as if he were under her thumb when dealing with the Apaches.

"South. A few miles. Needed water."

Slocum nodded. Then he looked past the Apache and saw the brave had a small remuda.

"My horses," Slocum said, pointing. "How did you get them?"

Claire gasped when Billy Wolf reached behind and pulled a scalp from his belt.

"It looks like you robbed me," Slocum said. "Childress was mine."

"Tried to shoot me. I shoot better."

The negotiation went on, Slocum ignoring Claire until she fell silent and he finally began to enjoy the dickering with the Apache brave.

"You take one horse only," Billy Wolf said.

"You keep the scalp and give me one horse and my gear."

This set off another round of negotiation until the Indian thrust out his hand. Slocum shook hard, and then Billy Wolf lithely vaulted onto horseback and led off two horses, the one

Slocum had brought with him and Childress's, leaving behind Slocum's gelding and his saddle.

Claire watched the Apache ride away. "What just happened?"

"We just got a ride back to Tombstone," he said.

"He killed Childress? Took his scalp?" She shuddered.

"He saved me the time and fuss of tracking Childress."

"You wouldn't have taken his scalp. Would you?"

Slocum thought about it a moment and then said, "Probably not. I'd have been more inclined to cut his *cojones* off."

Claire sputtered but did not question him any further. Slocum stepped up, settled down comfortably in his saddle, then reached for Claire. She caught his hand and he pulled her up easily behind him.

"First we find some water, then we ride to Tombstone."

And they did.

27

"Things are changing in Tombstone," Dr. Gottschalk said. "After we buried your father, Wakefield began to foreclose on businesses that nobody knew he had an interest in. He must own a quarter of the town now."

"But not China Mary's part," Slocum said. "She'd never let him take any of the Hop Town property."

"There's almost open war between them. Her bodyguard was killed, and she is staying in Hop Town for the time being. She had an opium den not a hundred feet from one of Wakefield's saloons, but it burned down."

"Wakefield," Claire said. "All this is about Molly E Mine, isn't it?"

"More," Gottschalk said. "He wants more than any single silver mine. Wakefield got a taste of money and power and doesn't know when to stop eating. And he is one very hungry man."

Slocum started to ask about the new marshal when the door to the doctor's office flew open and slammed against the wall. Slocum had his six-gun out, cocked and aimed. Only quick reflexes kept him from sending a bullet straight through Jackson Pine's head.

"Claire, you're back!" The lawyer rushed in and stopped a few feet from the woman. The two stared at each other for a moment, then Claire looked past the lawyer at Slocum. He tried to read her expression but couldn't.

"If you try busting in like that again, you might not be so lucky," Slocum said. He lowered the hammer and slipped his pistol back into his holster.

"I just heard you were back in town and came right over. I had to see you!"

"Where'd you hear it?" Slocum asked.

"Why, a . . . a client." Pine licked his lips and then added, "China Mary. I'm representing her interests in Hop Town and elsewhere, now that your pa's dead, Claire."

"Then you and Wakefield are on opposing sides of the bar."

Pine laughed and said, "You pick up the lingo quick, Slocum. You can say that. I'm working to keep him from foreclosing on many of China Mary's properties. He's going after the legitimate ones first, like her whorehouses, then will try to shut down or take over the opium parlors."

"What about Tarkenton?"

"Nobody's seen him, not since Claire was . . . taken." He looked at the redhead as if he could tell more of her travails. Slocum wanted him to stay on the topic of Tarkenton.

"I'd told him to hide out south of town. It's really amazing that he's done it."

"He might not stay much longer," Pine said. "Rumors are popping up all over town about how Wakefield has gotten full title to the mine. It's a lie, of course. I'm still working on that—there's no need to ransom you with the deed, Claire. I was about ready to get it when—"

"Wakefield started the rumors to flush out Tarkenton?" Slocum had to admit the lawyer knew his opponent's weakness. Slander Tarkenton's name, say whatever else about him, and the miner would never budge from hiding. Hint that the mine was forfeit and Tarkenton would come running if he had to do it barefoot from the burning depths of hell.

"How long have the rumors been going around town?" Slocum asked.

"I haven't heard them," said Gottschalk, "so they must be recent."

"Only this morning."

"How many men does Wakefield have working for him. Gunmen?"

"I don't know, but he can hire an army if he wants it."

Slocum put his hand in his coat pocket and pulled out the scrap of cloth he had ripped from the lawyer's jacket just before Wakefield had ordered his men to take Slocum out and kill him. He put it back in without letting the others see it.

"I'll need supplies. Do you think China Mary would pay for whatever I need?"

"I think so. I can always charge it to her as my personal expense. If the job of removing Wakefield is done, she won't care. She's quite rich, you know, for a Celestial."

"She's filthy rich for anybody," Slocum said. "I need plenty of ammo for both my Colt Navy and the Winchester, plus food for a week. When Tarkenton hears that his mine is in jeopardy, he'll be out there in a flash. I want to be ready when he shows up."

"You think Wakefield's men are already there, John?" Claire's emerald eyes got big. She pushed past Pine and put her hand on Slocum's arm. "You don't have to go. We can talk to the marshal."

"Marshal Eakin seems amenable to actually enforcing the law," Gottschalk said. "It might be that nobody's decided he's worth bribing yet." He looked pointedly at Pine, who didn't notice. He had eyes only for Claire.

"I'll handle this since I was the one who convinced Tarkenton to hide out. The last I heard, Tarkenton is still wanted for a jailbreak."

"I can get that quashed," Pine said.

"Do it. If I have to get him back to town, I don't want him on the wrong side of the bars."

"Go on, John. I'll be all right," Claire said.

"I'll make sure of that." Jackson Pine looked straight at Slocum for the first time.

"I believe you," Slocum said. He had plenty of preparation to do before riding out to Tarkenton's silver mine.

Slocum approached the silver mine cautiously, aware that Wakefield's men were probably already there and had set a trap for Tarkenton. If he was clever and found them before they spotted him, he could even the odds and maybe be waiting when Tarkenton showed up. And Slocum knew he would. The rumors in Tombstone flew fast and furious, taking on a life of their own after a day or so. In spite of being hidden out in the desert, Tarkenton would hear that Wakefield had claimed the mine.

The miner would swarm back to his claim like ants to a picnic.

The sun was setting when Slocum crept up to the mouth of the mine, taking full advantage of the afternoon shadows to hide. Nowhere did he see or hear any of Wakefield's gunmen. The stench of the burned cabin still hung in the air, making it an unlikely spot for anyone to hide. There were only a few timbers left and no walls to hide behind.

Slipping into the mouth of the mine, Slocum stopped and closed his eyes. He shuddered at the notion of going into the mine, even with a tin full of lucifers and two bags of fixings. The memory of the utter darkness of the cave over in the Whitestone Mountains was too recent. A pair of miner's candles perched on a rocky shelf. He couldn't tell if there had been more and if Tarkenton was already in the mine.

He pressed his ear against the rock and listened. If Tarkenton had come back, he would be digging like a berserk prairie dog. A curious sound came to him he couldn't identify. It was a low rumble, distant, not made by any man or machine.

Before he could puzzle it out, he heard a sneeze. Slocum moved back to the mouth of the mine and looked out over the deepening shadows in front of the mine where Tarkenton had dumped the tailings. The sneeze came again, followed quickly by a whispered, "Cut that out. You'll give us away."

"Can't stop. Damned weeds make me sneeze. Besides, ain't nobody here."

The two argued in whispers, not realizing that pitch carried farther in the twilight air than if they'd both spoken aloud.

Slocum moved away from the mine, not wanting to get trapped there again, and went around the hillside, thinking he could climb the face and get a decent shot at Wakefield's henchmen as they came closer.

A new sound ahead caused him to freeze. Two shadows drifted across his line of sight and disappeared. He heard pebbles being dislodged as the men made their way up the hill to a point directly over the mine. They had the same idea as Slocum.

Another sneeze from behind warned him he faced four men, two above and two directly out from the mouth of the mine.

He followed the same path up the hill that the two climbers had used. He saw how they had settled down a few yards apart. One watched the approach from the direction of the arroyo and the other kept a view on the road leading to the mine. With their two partners below, they were in good position to spot and shoot anyone coming to the Molly E.

Slocum climbed higher on the hill until he was above the lookouts. Since one was in view of the other, he'd have to move cautiously. When he was immediately above the one watching the arroyo, he jumped and landed with both feet in the middle of the man's back. There was a snap, a gasp, and nothing more.

"That you, Dave? You just make that—son of a bitch!" The other lookout spotted Slocum and realized what had happened to his partner. He swung his six-shooter around and opened fire.

Slocum dropped flat and couldn't reach his own pistol. Instead, he pried Dave's six-gun free and began firing at the spot where the long tongues of orange flame leaped out of the dark. One slug hit the other man's gun and knocked it flying.

Slocum was on his feet and crossing the few yards between them. They grappled but Slocum had the edge, twisting and kicking out at the same time. The lookout let out a shriek and fell the fifteen feet to the ground. He hit with a thud. From the way he stirred, he had broken bones but nothing that would do him in. Slocum picked up the fallen man's pistol and opened fire at the two rushing toward the mine. He winged one and drove the other to cover some distance away.

"We gotta get out of here. There's a whole damn army up there. Pine musta sent 'em!"

Slocum rapidly emptied the guns he had taken from Wakefield's men and then added a couple rounds from his own pistol to get them running back to town. They thought they were up against an army.

Slocum smiled wryly. Pine's army.

He sat on the ledge just above the mine, legs dangling, as he waited for Tarkenton.

The miner never showed up.

28

"Tarkenton is in jail again?" Slocum stared at Jackson Pine, who looked like a cat with a bowl of cream.

"I turned him in," the lawyer said. "Wait!" Pine stepped away as Slocum came for him. "You don't understand. Marshal Eakin can take better care of him in jail than Tarkenton can of himself out in the desert. You said it yourself. Tarkenton was likely to head for his mine."

"I killed a man and shot others for nothing," Slocum said.

Pine swallowed hard, then said, "It wasn't in vain. It wasn't. Wakefield thought Tarkenton would go back there or he wouldn't have sent his gunmen to the mine. You were both right. Tarkenton would have gone back if I'd given him the chance."

"Wakefield can kill him in the jail cell since he knows where he'll be twenty-four hours a day."

"I'm not letting Tarkenton rot in jail. I've got a hearing set up in a couple hours. I trust the marshal to keep his prisoner alive that long."

"I wish I was back out in the desert," Slocum said glumly.

"This will work out, Slocum. Trust me."

"I trust Billy Wolf more." And he did. Slocum under-stood what made the Apache run, what made him fight. He had no idea what drove Jackson Pine other than the vague notion of winning a legal point. Plains Indians counting coup he understood. Savagery he understood, whether it was a red man or white man doing the killing, but Jackson Pine was a different breed, and Slocum didn't understand him at all. That made him more dangerous than Childress ever had been.

"There you two are," Claire Norton said, coming into the lawyer's office. She dropped a stack of parcels on a chair. See-ing Slocum's gaze, she smiled brightly and said, "New cloth-ing came in yesterday from Fairbank. I had to see what there was for my ensemble."

"You're singing?" Slocum asked. Both Pine and Claire laughed.

"No, silly. My wardrobe. My clothes. How funny you'd think of, what, a barbershop quartet?"

"More like a half-dozen dance hall girls warbling," Pine said. He shut up when he saw Slocum's dark look.

"Eliminate Wakefield and the trouble goes away," Slocum said, turning back to the most serious of their concerns.

"I can deal with him," Pine said confidently. "I've got a dozen precedents the judge cannot possibly overlook."

"Why? Have you bribed him to agree with you?" Slocum asked.

"Judge Rollins is possibly not an honest man," Pine said, "since he has been bought and paid for by Wakefield after he took *my* bribe, but he dare not overlook my argument."

"Why not?" Slocum didn't understand.

"He'd be overturned in appeal, that's why. He would look incompetent."

"He's a crook that's been bribed by every lawyer in town. What's he care if he looks like an idiot because he came to the wrong decision?"

"Slocum, Slocum, you don't understand. There's greed at

work, of course, but Rollins values his judicial integrity. You wouldn't understand."

"Reckon not," Slocum said. He saw how Claire hung on the lawyer's every word, but this might be nothing more than being familiar with the legal arguments. Her pa might have spewed nonsense like this, too, for all he knew. Slocum had known the man only enough to bring him opium for his pain and to see him with a knife shoved into his heart.

"You get Tarkenton out of the jail and over to the court where everyone can see him. If Wakefield tries to kill him in public, I want the lynch mob that went after Tarkenton to string up Wakefield."

Pine nodded, rubbed his clean-shaven chin, and finally said, "That's a good idea, even if I don't support the concept of a mob taking justice into their own hands." He looked up, his face bright with anticipation. "Meet me in the courthouse in an hour. I'll be sure to have Tarkenton there. We're going to settle this matter once and for all!"

"I'll help you with your packages," Slocum said to Claire. She started to say something, then graced him with a bright smile.

"That would be fine, John, since Mr. Pine is obviously busy with his defense arguments."

The lawyer was already lost in a welter of books and notes. He scratched out line after line as he copied from the books. Slocum grabbed an armful of the parcels for Claire and pushed open the door with his toe for her to leave. She preceded him out into the hot morning sun.

"This will all work out, won't it, John?"

"Ask Pine. He has a scheme to get Tarkenton his mine free and clear."

"No, I mean about my papa's death."

Slocum had no reason to believe anyone but Childress had killed Sam Norton. The Apache brave out west of town had brought as much justice to Childress as any court could have—

and then some. The reminder of the man's scalp dangling from a rawhide strip ought to be presented to Wakefield. That silent promise of retribution would do more to settle the mining claim than anything Pine could conjure up using his law books.

"What more do you want done?"

"Childress was working for Wakefield. He ought to be held accountable somehow."

Slocum didn't bother correcting her. Childress had been Pine's bully boy. While Childress had begun acting on his own when he caught the scent of silver, Pine had been responsible for getting him out of jail. After he had done even more to rile the law in Tombstone, Childress had separated himself from Pine. Slocum wasn't sure this suited Pine that much—or maybe it had. He couldn't figure out the lawyer's motives other than for personal gain.

And Claire Norton's attention.

"It is another hot day, isn't it?" Claire said, dabbing at her forehead with a handkerchief.

"It's even hotter carrying so many packages," Slocum said.

Claire started to speak, then a wicked smile crossed her lips.

"Perhaps you would like a private showing. I can model the clothes for you so you can see how they look on me."

"I'm more interested in seeing how you look without any clothes," he said.

"Why, Mr. Slocum, a young lady might take that as a downright forward suggestion."

Slocum climbed the steps to her porch. Claire opened the door. He spun behind her, herded her forward with the packages, and simply let them fall to the floor so he could take her into his arms and pull her close.

"It wasn't a suggestion." Before she could reply with some lighthearted banter, he kissed her. She pushed against him for a moment, trying to get away, then she melted into him. The kiss deepened. Claire threw her arms around his neck so he could bend a little and scoop her up into his arms. Still kissing, they went into the small bedroom.

"Take me, John. I want you so!"

He dropped her onto the bed and stepped back.

"Strip for me. Everything."

"My, it is getting hot in here, isn't it?" Claire stood and began unbuttoning her blouse, slowly revealing the swell of her breasts. She tossed her head and sent a coppery cascade of hair floating on the tepid breeze coming through the bedroom window.

As she slipped her blouse off and stood naked to the waist for Slocum's appreciation, he began matching her. He stood bare-chested in a flash.

"Keep going," he said. "If you want me to take off more, you have to also."

"Very well," Claire said. She fumbled at the hook and eye on her skirt, then stepped free of the small mountain of cloth around her ankles. She was clad only in bloomers. "Your turn. I want to see you. All of you."

Slocum kicked off his boots and dropped his gun belt. His jeans followed quickly. He was naked, but she was still half-dressed in her frilly undergarment.

She started to slide it over the flair of her ass, but Slocum reached out and stopped her.

"Let me."

"Oh!" Claire exclaimed as he spun her around. She gripped the rail at the foot of her bed and leaned forward a little as Slocum began sliding the bloomers down. He made sure to work slowly, carefully, giving every inch of intimate flesh revealed his full attention.

Some patches of lily-white flesh he touched. When he got her bloomers down around her knees, he bent forward and began kissing. She shivered with his every oral touch in spite of the heat in the room.

When he parted her legs and began kissing the insides of her thighs, she almost collapsed.

"I can't stand this any longer, John. Now. Do it now!"

He didn't pay any attention to her. She was turned on and he was horny. That made for a powerful combination. His hand slid between her legs and opened them a little more until the bloomers acted as restraints around her ankles. She started to kick free.

"No," he said. "Don't do that."

He moved behind her and reached around her trim waist. Her legs spread apart as she bent forward and left her in a vulnerable position. With a quick movement of his hips, his manhood parted her butt cheeks and ran along her nether lips. She gasped at the touch. Slocum grabbed the rail outside her hands and braced himself.

His hips moved back, found the right target, then slipped forward in a well-lubricated assault all the way into her heated core.

She shoved back with her rump and began grinding down hard, letting his steely length stir about inside her. Slocum released one hand and slid it along her heaving belly and then went lower so he could stroke over the tiny spire rising at the top of her hidden lips.

Claire went berserk when he touched the right spot. She began slamming backward into him in an effort to get even more hidden away inside her. He began to lose control. The urgency that had grown within him demanded release. He stroked faster and kept running his finger over her until it was slick with her inner juices. The heat mounted along his length and then he had to circle her waist with his arm and hold her tight against his groin.

They fit together perfectly, her roundness matching the curve of his body. Slocum lifted her off the floor and used her weight to ram even deeper into her center. This set them both off. Claire let out a loud cry of release. Slocum fought to keep back the fiery tide rising within him, wanting the sensation rampaging throughout his loins to last forever. But he shot his load and then lowered the panting woman to her feet.

Again, he leaned forward, gripping the foot rail of her bed. Droplets of sweat glistened on her back and dripped from her nipples. Slocum was covered in sweat himself, but seldom had he ever worked up this much of a sweat in such an agreeable fashion.

"That was spectacular," she said in a husky voice. Claire looked over her shoulder at him. He stepped forward and ran his hand up and down her back. When he came to her perky bottom, he gave it a quick swat.

"Show me some of those fancy duds. We're supposed to be in court pretty soon."

"Oh, you're right. I can't believe it's been an hour."

"Seemed shorter," he said.

"Time, maybe," she said, that wicked gleam in her eye again. She caught his limp organ and stroked over it a few times, then dropped to her knees and kissed it. Before he could say anything, Claire was on her feet and hurrying from the room.

Slocum heard the rustle of brown paper as she tore into the packages. He dressed, made sure his gun belt was settled, and went into the front room, where Claire was fastening the last button on a high-necked dress.

"You're hiding your assets," he told her.

"Really?" She laughed, turned, and hoisted her skirt, mooning him. "The bloomers were torn so I decided not to wear them."

"Good to know," Slocum said.

Claire looked at him, then averted her emerald eyes and reached for her purse.

"We have to hurry. Jackson will be in court already. We don't want to miss that."

"No, we wouldn't," Slocum said. He held out his arm for her. Claire hesitated, then took it. They walked at a quick clip back to the courthouse, talking of nothing important. If anything, Slocum thought she tried to avoid serious matters.

"It's begun," she said as they came into view of the courthouse. A crowd had lined up along the steps.

"Something has," Slocum agreed. There was a commotion coming from Judge Rollins's courtroom. The bailiff started to keep Slocum and Claire from the room, then saw he wasn't going to succeed. Even if Claire hadn't been insistent, he had no way to stop Slocum.

All the spectators were on their feet, shouting so loud Slocum couldn't hear the judge's gavel hammering hard on his desk.

He pushed through and Claire followed in his wake.

Pine stood at one table, mouth open but not spewing the usual legal objections he might have.

At the other table, Tarkenton gripped Wakefield by the lapels and was banging the lawyer's head against the railing separating the crowd from the lawyers.

As much as Slocum enjoyed the sight of the lawyer's blood being spilled, he knew no one else in the court was likely to stop Tarkenton from murdering Wakefield. The miner had enough legal trouble. Slocum pushed past a man, who simply had found a better spot to watch, and grabbed Tarkenton.

The miner was old but wiry and strong from all the hard work he had put in over the past months. Slocum had to wrench his hands free of Wakefield's fancy coat. This only allowed Tarkenton to go for the lawyer's throat. His powerful, gnarled fingers clamped down on the exposed windpipe.

Again Slocum had to struggle to get Tarkenton off his victim. Wakefield had turned red in the face. When the strangling fingers left his throat, Wakefield could only gasp for breath. Like Pine, he was speechless. For once.

Slocum interposed his body between Tarkenton and the lawyer.

"What the hell are you doing? They'll lock you up in jail and throw away the key."

"He shouldn't have said a thing like that. I won't let him!" Tarkenton surged again, and once more Slocum found he almost had more than he could handle.

"What'd he say? It was probably a lie. You know lawyers."

"He said he was gonna blow up the Molly E! Flood it!"

"I want the mine," Wakefield grated out, rubbing his throat. He stood, smoothed the wrinkles from his fancy coat, and said, "I will blow it up if that's what it takes. There's an underground river nearby that will eventually flood the mine."

"Nobody gets the silver then," Slocum said.

"I have the money to clear away debris and pump out the mine. It might take a month, but when the water's gone, the silver will belong to me."

"He knows all I got's still in the Molly E Mine!"

"I made a decent offer. He ought to take it, or he'll end up with nothing. I'll even drop the assault charges if he agrees right now. The offer won't last long. You tell him what's good for him, Slocum, since his stupid lawyer won't."

Slocum could hardly hear himself think. Tarkenton screamed, the judge swung his gavel repeatedly, and the crowd in the courtroom all yelled encouragement to continue the fight. If he was having trouble concentrating on what to do, he could imagine where that left Tarkenton.

"I'll kill you, you weasel!" Tarkenton screamed.

This set off a new round of shouting in the courtroom that ended with Marshal Eakin dragging Tarkenton back to the lockup.

Slocum faced Pine and asked, "You got your hearing. Now what do you do?"

Jackson Pine stuttered a moment, and then said, "I don't know."

Slocum did. It wouldn't be pretty, it certainly wasn't legal, but he knew what had to be done.

29

"There's no way to stop Wakefield from blowing up Tark-enton's mine," Slocum said. "You could post a guard around the clock and it wouldn't matter. All it would take would be a few sticks of dynamite tossed down into the mine."

"Is it true that the mine would flood?" Claire asked.

Slocum shrugged. He had heard what might be the rush of water through the rock the last time he had been at the Molly E Mine, but he was no mining engineer. Somehow, Wake-field's threat rang true. While the lawyer might make up any number of improbable things to do, only the ones that Tark-enton saw as being possible mattered. The miner had reacted strongly to the threat of filling the mine with water.

"He's right about Tarkenton being too broke to pump it out," Pine said. "Hell, he can't even pay me, and he's sitting on a mountain of silver. That's just not right."

Slocum wondered what part of the problems Tarkenton faced that the lawyer found "just not right." It probably had more to do with Pine not going after the deed rather than anything mattering to his client.

"What kind of a deal is Wakefield offering?" Slocum asked.

"It might be the only way Tarkenton will see a dime out of his mine." As galling as it was to give in to the extortion, Slocum saw no way for the miner to come out ahead. He was back in jail and would stay there until Wakefield decided whether to press charges. He likely would if Tarkenton didn't agree to selling his mine.

The added bitter pill to swallow came in Tarkenton being screwed out of the mine, even if he beat the assault charges resulting from his court appearance. Wakefield held all the aces.

"Pitiful, that's what. If Tarkenton took what's being offered, he would hardly be able to pay me for my services, much less come out with a fraction of what the mine is worth."

"You've done so much for him," Claire said, putting her hand on Pine's arm. The lawyer patted her hand. She withdrew it almost guiltily.

"Putting him back in jail was the wrong thing to do," Slocum said. "If anybody'd be willing to defend the Molly E from Wakefield's henchmen, it'd be the owner."

"I couldn't get the charges dropped. Wakefield had everything tied up in a nice package, with a bow on it. Worse, Tarkenton tried to choke Wakefield in front of the judge. It's hard to argue that it was all a misunderstanding on Wakefield's part when everyone saw what happened." Pine slapped his hand down on his desk so hard papers jumped into the air. "I should have offered more of a bribe to Rollins!"

Slocum settled back in a chair at the side of the room. Claire stood beside the lawyer, looking worried. Pine, for his part, took Tarkenton's predicament seriously. Even if he wasn't getting paid, he hadn't mentioned dropping the case. Slocum had to give him some credit for that, even if that fee might amount to becoming owner of the Molly E Mine.

His hand drifted to his shirt pocket, where he had a sizable wad of greenbacks. He could pay Tarkenton's legal fees, if necessary, and maybe even bribe the judge to let the miner go free. He still carried a considerable number of gold double eagles and some silver coins taken off the various robbers he had sent to the Promised Land. But why bother? With the miner out on the street again, somebody would die. After the scene in the courtroom, Slocum doubted Wakefield would be caught unawares. Tarkenton would get himself shot down the instant he showed his face around the lawyer's office—and there wasn't any doubt he would. The mine meant everything to him. The notion that Wakefield could swindle him out of it would infuriate Tarkenton all over again.

"Any good ideas?" Slocum asked.

"I think there might be a way of making Wakefield responsible for anything that happens at the mine," Pine said. "It'd be a complicated legal maneuver—you'd call it shenanigans, Slocum—but I might have the court put him in charge of maintaining it."

"So he blows it up, floods it, and claims it was a natural disaster."

"We can specify the problems and—"

"Never mind," Slocum said. "I need to poke around some and see what I can do."

"It'd better be legal, Slocum. I'm an officer of the court and am sworn to uphold the law."

Slocum thought Pine was making a joke, then saw he was serious. From the way Claire looked at him, she thought he was, too.

He left, his mind tumbling over and over. He had thought about just gunning down Wakefield and riding the hell out of Tombstone. Nobody would mourn the lawyer's passing and there might even be some celebrating. Wakefield continued to tighten his grip on the businesses in town, and stealing away the Molly E would be his crowning triumph. He would have enough money then to legally purchase the businesses he wanted rather than relying on intimidation and fear.

"You cannot," came a soft voice. Slocum swung around but did not go for his six-shooter. He recognized China Mary right away.

"I'm sorry to hear about Ah Sum," he said. "I didn't much like him, but he saved my life. He was a terror with those hatchets of his."

China Mary bowed slightly. Her hands were hidden in the folds of an ornate gown that might have been chased with real gold thread. Designs Slocum could barely identify crept around at the hem, just above the ground. They might be dragons or some other mythical Chinese creature. There was nothing mythical about China Mary. Something had flushed her from her safe harbor in Hop Town and brought her to the end of Rotten Row.

"You want to go somewhere to talk?"

"I have business with Pine," she said. Slocum frowned. "He offers to replace Mr. Norton as my lawyer."

"You're taking him up on that?"

"He is earnest. Do you find him an honest man?"

Slocum thought for a moment, then nodded reluctantly.

"He's more honest than any of the others I've come across, but I'm not sure how far that goes toward being completely honorable. I never knew Norton or how he conducted himself."

"Pine cowers in the shadow of Mr. Norton," China Mary said. Slocum wasn't sure what she meant by that, not exactly, but he had some inkling from the way Claire increasingly listened to every utterance Pine made and the way the lawyer tried to impress her. Slocum doubted Pine could ever live up to the reputation of Sam Norton, but that wasn't going to keep him from trying.

"You getting a steady supply of opium now? For the doctor, of course?"

"Dr. Gottschalk has all he requires," she said. "You would not work for me?"

"Replace Ah Sum? I couldn't do that."

"No?"

"I don't speak Chinese."

China Mary burst out laughing. It was the first true emotion Slocum had seen from her. The laughter was musical, and for a moment, he saw her true character. She was old, but her spirit was young. The laughter abated and she bowed slightly.

"You will find the answer to your problem if you do not allow morality to burden you."

"You've done mighty well by following that trail," Slocum said. She tensed slightly, then relaxed. He thought he might have offended her, then wondered if that were possible. She accepted whatever hand fate dealt her and played it to the end.

"So I have," China Mary said, bowing again. "So have you." With that she moved as if she floated rather than walked toward the door to Pine's office. Slocum looked around for her bodyguards but saw no one. Still, he had the feeling of being watched and knew she would not venture out to this part of town without someone to defend her, should it be necessary. Wakefield had ignited a shooting war.

He found himself walking in the direction of Dr. Gottschalk's office. He thrust his hand into his pocket and stroked the piece of cloth in his pocket. Slocum took it out and stared at it for a moment. He had ripped this off Wakefield's coat just before Wakefield's henchmen had dragged him out to kill him in the desert. The fabric was distinctive—and Slocum remembered how other parts of the coat had been tattered. This was an expensive piece of finery and Wakefield wanted to flaunt his wealth at every turn but probably didn't have enough extra cash to replace the worn coat.

Yet. When he took over Tombstone, he would be rolling in money.

It was too bad that his cuff had been worn away to a ragged edge. And then Slocum had ripped away another piece from the lapel of the coat.

His stride lengthened. As he walked, he worried at the edge of the cloth, thinning it and making it look more like a piece of cuff rather than lapel.

Slocum stopped outside the doctor's office as he considered if he wanted to continue. He did. He opened the door and looked around. Gottschalk was gone. His medical bag and hat weren't on the table by the door, telling Slocum that he was out on a call.

Sure of himself now, he went to the doctor's desk and tried to open the middle drawer, only to find it locked. Jiggling and tugging finally defeated the simple lock without destroying it. In the middle of the otherwise empty drawer lay the paper-wrapped knife Childress had used to murder Sam Norton.

Taking it from the drawer, Slocum carefully removed the paper and held up the knife, examining it as carefully as he had before when he had pulled it out of Norton's chest. The cloth caught in the guard matched what he remembered of Childress's shirt. The rustler had killed Norton, pinning the kidnap note to the dead man's chest. Norton might have struggled, causing the swatch to get tangled in the knife guard. Or maybe Childress had been careless or excited. However the crime happened, Childress had left behind evidence of his guilt.

It was time to wipe this murder off the slate of crimes Childress had committed.

Slocum went to the doctor's surgical table and found a sharp-tipped knife. He began working on the piece of Childress's shirt until it was entirely free of the knife. He started to pull the cloth from Wakefield's jacket onto the guard when he noticed how bloody the other cloth had been. It was impossible to stab a man through the heart the way Childress had and not spatter blood everywhere.

Including the bit of cloth ripped from Childress's shirt and trapped in the guard.

On the surgical table stood a bottle of grain alcohol. Slocum dampened his finger with some and rubbed it along the knife handle, getting a damp smear from the dried blood. He wiped it off using the bit of Wakefield's coat. Then he pulled, tugged, and twisted the fabric into the knife guard.

He studied his handiwork, nodded, wound the paper around the knife, and then returned it to the center desk drawer, placing it as close to the way he had found it. Slocum worked a bit more to close the drawer and see that it was secured. The lock didn't work well, but Gottschalk might have had trouble with it before Slocum had jimmied it open. If the doctor had trouble opening the lock, it wouldn't be a matter of concern.

It was time for Slocum to go to Marshal Eakin.

30

"Don't be absurd," Colin Wakefield said, barely containing his anger. "I wouldn't kill a colleague. Why, Sam Norton was respected by everyone along Rotten Row. I, for one, revered him and still honor his memory. Kill him? That's more the province of a hired gunman like John Slocum." Wakefield made a dramatic gesture and pointed at Slocum.

"It is a mighty serious charge, Slocum," the marshal said. He looked uneasy but stood his ground. Wakefield's office was intimidating, with no chairs except for the lawyer behind the vast desk. Slocum saw the spot where he had put his hand as he reached across to grab the lawyer's lapel. It was a faint outline of his palm. Seconds after he had made the hand print, Wakefield's gunmen had pistol-whipped him and taken him out into the desert to kill him. They had gotten what they deserved. It was time for Wakefield to share his shootists' fate.

"The knife used to stab Norton is evidence," Slocum said. "Doc Gottschalk's got it."

"What possible evidence could that knife be?"

"It's the murder weapon," Marshal Eakin said. "Leastways, that's what Gottschalk told me."

"He's an honest man," Wakefield said. "However, we have no idea how he might have been duped by a known liar like Slocum."

"Whatever else he might be, I ain't seen how Slocum's a liar." Eakin cleared his throat. Slocum heard him add under his breath, "Not like most lawyers."

"I did not kill Norton. There's no way that knife could ever tie me to the crime. It was done by someone else, that rustler Childress, for example."

"Did he work for you? Childress?" Slocum saw the contempt on Wakefield's face as he asked the question. He could almost read what was going through the man's mind. Such simple traps would never be sprung, not when the one being interrogated was a lawyer of Wakefield's stature. Slocum was willing to wait this out.

"If I remember correctly, you and Childress rode into town together," Wakefield said.

"I was bringing him to jail for cattle thieving," Slocum said.

"A likely story, considering all the mayhem and mopery that's gone on since you and Childress arrived."

"What's mopery?" Marshal Eakin asked. "Never mind. It don't matter a hill of beans. I sent Dr. Gottschalk and a deputy to fetch the knife. We'll see what kind of evidence it is against you, Wakefield."

"*Mister* Wakefield," the lawyer said, drawing out each syllable until it almost screamed.

"There they are," Slocum said, distracting Eakin from the verbal battle Wakefield intended to start. Any advantage the lawyer could gain, he would. Arguing with the marshal was only a prelude to what was to come.

"I got it right here, Marshal," the deputy said, holding up the paper-wrapped package. "The doc, he tole me to leave the paper around it so I wouldn't disturb none of the evidence. Said that was your job."

"Put it on the table," the marshal ordered. He licked his lips and looked a mite nervous about opening the package.

"You want me to do it, Marshal? I wrapped it so I can unwrap it," Gottschalk said.

"I kin do it. I don't want a lot of folks pawin' at it 'til I get a good look." The marshal peeled back the paper and left the bloody knife resting in the center. "Well, it surely does have blood on it."

"Norton's," the doctor said.

"You, uh, stipulate that, Wakefield? That it's Norton's blood and that this was the knife that killed him?" Eakin looked at the lawyer, who openly sneered now.

"You've learned the lingo, Marshal. I have no idea if this is the knife that killed my friend and colleague, but if you are satisfied that it is, then, yes, I so stipulate. So what? There's no way you can put that knife in my hand to even accuse me of the murder."

Eakin bent low and caught light coming in from the open office door so it reflected off the knife blade. He reached out and poked a bit at the guard. Slocum caught his breath. He didn't want to point out the cloth unless the marshal missed it. Eakin ran his finger across the bloodied swatch Slocum had so carefully jammed into the guard.

"Mind comin' a bit closer to the desk, Wakefield?"

"Why?"

"Do it." Eakin's cold order caused Wakefield to take an involuntary, obedient step. Before he could refuse, he was pressed close behind his desk.

The marshal lifted the knife and squinted, letting the sun fall on both the knife guard and the lawyer's coat.

"I ain't an expert in things of a sartorial nature," Eakin said, letting the words roll around his tongue before spitting them out, "but I think I got evidence here. What do you think, Doc?"

"What are you looking at?" Gottschalk came closer and moved reading glasses down his nose. "Ah, yes, I see. Fabric in the knife's guard and . . . Wakefield's coat."

"What are you going on about, man? Don't talk rubbish."

The marshal signaled for his deputies to pin the lawyer's arms to his side.

"Get him on over to the jail. Me and the doc here have to talk to a judge about the speediest trial we can arrange."

"That's not my coat caught in the knife. It can't be. I didn't kill Norton. I didn't do anything!"

Marshal Eakin scratched his head and settled his hat back before saying to Slocum, "You done Tombstone a favor. Wakefield ain't much liked. He will certainly be hated when it comes out he killed Sam Norton."

"Just doing my civic duty," Slocum said.

Pine and Claire had crowded into the office. Pine was agitated and demanding to know if Wakefield would receive proper legal representation, but Claire looked hard at him. Her bright green eyes blazed. It wasn't anger directed toward him or even accusation. Slocum couldn't figure what it was.

He decided it didn't much matter.

"Your Honor, this entire hearing is a farce," Colin Wakefield said. Although he sounded confident, sweat beaded his forehead and his hands shook as he picked up a sheaf of papers. "There's no evidence to hold me. I demand that all charges be dropped."

The murmur passing through the crowd assembled in the courtroom told the story. The townspeople wanted a trial and didn't much care whose it was.

"There's plenty of evidence, Your Honor," the prosecutor said. "The knife with a hunk of this varmint's coat caught on it is proof he done the crime."

"That's so," Pine said to Claire. Slocum sat behind them and eavesdropped on their whispered conversation. "How he could have been that careless is beyond me."

"But Childress kidnapped me. From the way he bragged, I thought he'd killed my papa and then waited for me to come to the doctor's office."

"He and Childress worked together. That's the only thing

that makes sense. Wakefield killed your father and Childress kidnapped you to force me to turn over the Molly E Mine as ransom."

Slocum saw how uncomfortable Pine was with that lie. Childress still worked for him when he killed Claire's father and spirited her away. He doubted Pine would ever tell her the details swirling around her kidnapping because he still angled to win the deed to Tarkenton's silver mine. To get it now, he had to screw his own client. Slocum doubted Claire would look favorably on such a tactic.

The arguments raged in front of Judge Rollins, but Slocum saw how the wind blew. The judge couldn't turn Wakefield loose without causing a riot in his courtroom. For all he knew, the judge might think it was time to remove Wakefield and cultivate new sources for the bribes that flowed quicker than spring runoff in Tombstone.

Slocum stood and pushed through the crowd. Before he reached the door, someone had claimed his seat, leaned forward, and added his voice to the jeers whenever Wakefield spoke.

The afternoon was hot, but Slocum hardly noticed as he walked to the jailhouse. Two deputies stood guard outside, sitting in the shade and passing a pint bottle back and forth to pass the time.

"You wantin' to talk to the prisoner, Slocum?" The deputy closest to him took a pull on the bottle before passing it to his partner.

"The marshal's busy at the trial, so I didn't think there'd be much of a crowd here."

"Just don't go tryin' to bust him out. Ike done that before and got away. This time we'd have to shoot him—and you—down."

"You won't catch me setting him free," Slocum promised. The two almost drunk deputies would present no barrier to busting Tarkenton from the jail, but Slocum wasn't inclined to do that a second time. He went inside and found immediately why the deputies stood guard outside. Heat threatened to boil the skin off his bones.

"You push me that bucket o' water, Slocum?" Tarkenton strained against the bars to reach a bucket of water left for him. Slocum pushed it over with the toe of his boot.

"They treating you all right?" he asked.

"I want out. I want to stop that son of a bitch from blowing up my mine. He promised to do it, he did. He said it would flood. I ain't makin' that up!"

"Settle down," Slocum said. "Wakefield is in court right now, and it looks like he'll be convicted of killing Sam Norton."

"All them lawyers deserve to have their throats slit." Tarkenton dropped to the cot. He looked up and looked sheepish. "Maybe not Sam. He was a nice fella—for a lawyer." Then he grinned. "That daughter of his sure is a good-lookin' filly, too."

"I've made a deal for you to keep the Molly E from getting blown up."

"You gonna gun down Wakefield?"

"He's probably paid men to do it if he gets convicted, so I went down a different trail. You willing to give up a quarter of the mine for protection?"

"A quarter? You mean fer every dollar I take out, I gotta give some sidewinder two bits?"

"That's what I mean. Along with that will come some money for new equipment and a guarantee of miners to help you."

"All that and I'd still get six bits outta every dollar?"

"Protection, less work, you still own the Molly E Mine, and can work it as you see fit."

"What jackass'd agree to that?"

"You're not the only one in Tombstone who has it in for Wakefield."

"I ain't throwin' in with no lawyer!"

"China Mary would be your silent partner." Slocum worried that Tarkenton might rebel at having a Celestial as a partner and have her men not only guarding the mine but working it.

"That's all right by me," Tarkenton said after a little consideration. He smiled crookedly. "If she's part owner, that mean I kin claim some free time at her whorehouse?"

"That's between the two of you. You agree?"

"I'll shake on it."

Slocum said, "She'll be by to get you out of jail. You can agree on the terms then."

He left the jail before loud, angry shouts from a growing crowd filled the street. Slocum pressed against an adobe wall as the mob made its way to the jail. From what he could tell, Wakefield had been convicted and was on his way back to jail. The mob wanted blood. This time it was Wakefield's.

31

"That settles it, then," Jackson Pine said, blowing on ink to dry Tarkenton's signature. He held it up and frowned, then looked at China Mary. "That *is* your signature?"

China Mary bowed slightly and said, "That is my chop."

"I'll make sure it's witnessed properly, just to be sure."

Slocum sat at the corner of the office and looked around. Tarkenton and China Mary made unlikely partners, but having the Celestial as Tarkenton's partner kept Pine from trying to steal the silver mine away, at least the way Wakefield had. Slocum also saw the way Claire stood at the lawyer's side, hand on his shoulder. She would keep his more larcenous impulses in check. If she didn't, then they deserved each other.

"Have any of Wakefield's men shown up at the mine, trying to blow it up?" Slocum asked.

China Mary turned and bowed more deeply in his direction.

"No one attempts such destruction."

"Your men are good. Nobody's willing to risk a hatchet parting their hair all the way down to their chins."

"Their attention is directed elsewhere." China Mary spoke in a tone so low only Slocum heard. The others were too busy congratulating themselves on the deal to make the Molly E Mine a profitable venture for all concerned.

"What do you mean?" Slocum asked. He stood and stepped closer to her.

She lowered her voice even more as she said, "Three are all that remain in his employ. The others have left."

"And?" Slocum knew there was more to the story than she said. He heard it in her voice and saw it in the way her lips curled upward in a slight smile.

"Is midnight near?"

Slocum took out his pocket watch and popped open the case. He nodded. Then he heard distant gunfire. He clocked shut the case and tucked it away in his vest pocket.

"They just busted Wakefield out of jail, didn't they?"

China Mary smiled a little more.

Slocum didn't know what he thought of Wakefield escaping. The man had ordered him killed. Slocum couldn't forget that, but he preferred to settle his score with a blazing sixshooter, not the way he had framed the lawyer for Norton's death. While he wouldn't lose any sleep if Wakefield went to the gallows, he wished he could have watched him die after taking a few rounds from the Colt Navy.

"Will Marshal Eakin go after him?"

"How would this one know such a thing?" China Mary asked.

"I get the feeling there's not much about Tombstone you don't know—or run."

"I am only a poor Hop Town store owner." She stared hard at Slocum, then asked, "Will you work for me?"

"I'm not replacing Ah Sum," he said. "You've got plenty of talent for that."

"Opium is most valuable. Losing even one shipment can be a great loss to me."

"You've got your share of the Molly E. You've got your

whorehouses. How many are there? Three?" He saw his guess was right. "Wakefield was trying to take over most of the businesses in Tombstone. I suspect you already own them—or have a cut of the profits. You don't need me."

"Your skill is great and appreciated." China Mary reached into the folds of her robe and drew out a small parcel wrapped in brown paper. Bowing deeply, she held it out to him. "For your work."

Slocum took the package and pulled back a corner of the brown paper wrapper. She had given him a stack of greenbacks that could be a thousand dollars or more.

"I don't reckon I'll get paid anywhere else in this town for my trouble," Slocum said. Returning to work the Circle Bar K herd didn't appeal to him anymore, in spite of Kennard's promised steer for saving the ten beeves from Childress's partners. Even without China Mary's money, he had plenty to keep him on the trail to anywhere he wanted. "Thanks."

China Mary bowed even more deeply, then turned and joined the conversation. Slocum caught snippets of it. Claire was telling Pine how her father had represented the downtrodden of Tombstone. Pine and China Mary began a discussion how to best give her people a fair shake in the face of the Anti-Chinese League and the possibility of Exclusion Laws such as in San Francisco getting passed in Arizona Territory. This social conscience caused Claire to smile.

Slocum basked in that smile for a moment, even if it wasn't aimed at him for anything he had done.

He left the office, no one noticing. It was best that way. He went to the livery to get his horse and asked the stable hand about the jailbreak. He listened in silence while the young man rattled off all he had heard. Word was that Wakefield and three henchmen had ridden south, heading for Bisbee or more likely the Mexican border.

Wakefield had ridden south. That made his decision an easy one. John Slocum rode east. It had been a spell since he'd been to San Antonio. Texas could be as hot as Tombstone in the summer, but he had plenty of money riding in his pocket to buy a cool beer.

He was sure he could find plenty of shade to drink that beer in, too.

GIANT-SIZED ADVENTURE FROM
AVENGING ANGEL LONGARM.

BY TABOR EVANS

2006 Giant Edition:

**LONGARM AND THE
OUTLAW EMPRESS**

2007 Giant Edition:

**LONGARM AND
THE GOLDEN EAGLE
SHOOT-OUT**

2008 Giant Edition:

**LONGARM AND THE
VALLEY OF SKULLS**

2009 Giant Edition:

**LONGARM AND THE
LONE STAR TRACKDOWN**

2010 Giant Edition:

**LONGARM AND THE
RAILROAD WAR**

penguin.com/actionwesterns